THE GHOST OF VILLA WINTER

CANARY ISLAND MYSTERIES BOOK 4

ISOBEL BLACKTHORN

Copyright (C) 2020 Isobel Blackthorn

Layout design and Copyright (C) 2020 by Next Chapter

Published 2020 by Gumshoe – A Next Chapter Imprint

Cover art by CoverMint

This book is a work of fiction. Names, characters, places, and incidents are the product of the author's imagination or are used fictitiously. Any resemblance to actual events, locales, or persons, living or dead, is purely coincidental.

All rights reserved. No part of this book may be reproduced or transmitted in any form or by any means, electronic or mechanical, including photocopying, recording, or by any information storage and retrieval system, without the author's permission.

For Philip Wallis

ACKNOWLEDGMENTS

I am hugely grateful to Jill and Ian Terry for driving me down to Jandía in February 2020 while I was on holiday on the island. And to Gaynor Harris and Juan Olivares for showing me around the island. The apartment Casa Berta where I stayed is featured in this story with permission from the owner. This book could not have been written without the support of my mother Margaret Rodgers, whose appetite for good mystery and crime fiction is boundless. Every writer benefits from having a sharp-minded, critical reader go over their manuscripts. I am fortunate to have the friendship of film-critic Philip Wallis who gives up his time freely and in the most dedicated fashion. And where would I be without Miika Hannila and the team at Next Chapter! Thank you!

Note: The details given about Villa Winter and the island are to the best of my knowledge true. Other than that, this is a work of pure fiction.

1

A TUESDAY IN MARCH

Mid-March, and the day had turned out a little hotter than she cared for but at least the horizon wasn't hazy. As the sun made a languorous approach to its zenith in a clear sky, she stopped to admire the ocean, a deep turquoise, lapping at the harbour wall. A cool sea breeze shooed away the worst of the heat rising from rock and concrete. The wooden seats, evenly spaced along the short stretch of paving and painted a vivid shade of blue, were empty. No one sat on them, not at this time of day at this time year and even with her sore hip, Clarissa wasn't tempted.

A quick dart of pain and she altered her stance. Something was not right with that joint. Despite the physio she'd received here, she would need to book an appointment with her doctor as soon as she arrived home from this trip.

Trip? Holiday? Vacation? The last few weeks had been nothing of the sort.

The seats faced the small bay. Behind her, to the north, was a low, rocky headland. To the south, and poking up behind tiers of cuboid dwellings, the mountains. A spray of bougainvillea cascaded down the side of one of the houses built into the rocky cliff over near the restaurant. Palm trees were everywhere, some newly planted, others towering. It was the pretty coastal village of Las Playitas and Clarissa had arranged to meet Claire for lunch. One of those villages too out of the way for the bulk of the tourists, those seeking the safety of the eateries run by the Brits. Here, the fare was authentic, the produce locally sourced, and the prices matched the luxury of the location. Also, there was no beach, not at this end of the village, and the beach at the far end sported black sand. The Brits, of course, wanted white. As did the Germans. Still, just like everywhere else on the holiday island of Fuerteventura, the local authorities had gone to a great deal of trouble, building a promenade at the foreshore that extended all the way along the beach, where an array of outdoor facilities catered for a smattering of small resort hotels.

Having caught the public bus from the larger town of Gran Tarajal, Clarissa had arrived early. She'd spent the spare half hour ambling along the promenade, reflecting on whether to raise with her niece Claire the recent developments concerning Trevor. Probably best to leave it. Claire had fixed in her mind that Trevor was no good and deserved all he got, but that was where Clarissa differed. Whenever she brought up the topic – usually after one of her prison visits – the same conversation took place.

'He had the stash of cash on him when he was arrested at the airport.'

'That means nothing.'

'It means he was planning on leaving the island with money that didn't belong to him. He should have handed it in.'

'That doesn't make him a murderer. He found that rucksack in the pink cave at Puertito del los Molinos. You were there. You know that part's true.'

'I just don't understand why you have to make a pet project out of that flaky author.'

'Because if I don't, no one will.'

And it was true. Clarissa had started up a campaign for an appeal and Trevor's release after hearing the story from Claire and her husband Paco on one of her regular holidays. She couldn't help feeling sorry for the man. The evidence he had been convicted on was circumstantial. He was in the wrong place at the wrong time, twice. He was a literary thief, yes, having used a transcript he found to inspire his own story, and he was a thief in the finders-keepers sense as well, which did warrant punishment, but he did not kill that priest or the young man washed up on a secluded beach. To her, it was an open and shut case. From the moment she heard about Trevor's predicament, she decided it was that young man washed up on the beach who had taken the cash from the priest, cash destined for a dog's home in Venezuela. For a long time, she thought either he had got caught by the vicious ocean or he, too, was murdered by someone for reasons unknown, and the mystery would never be solved until Trevor was absolved of all involvement.

Claire was adamant her aunt shouldn't be wasting her time on a person of ill-repute. They'd been over it and over it. There was no point trying to persuade the intractable. Besides, Clarissa thought, as she stopped in a parcel of shade to gaze out at the brilliance of the ocean, she wasn't preoccupied with the appeal. She was much more interested to hear from Trevor, the only Brit in the Tahiche prison in Lanzarote – Fuerteventura didn't have one – his opinion of an inmate who was released only last week. And then there was Trevor's view of one of his visitors, a prison counsellor assigned to help him mend his evil ways. Clarissa looked forward to hearing that as well.

She was convinced she had discovered a way of freeing Trevor. She had the evidence in her handbag. She had an appointment with her lawyer that very afternoon at three, and she would call in to see Inspector García at the police station after that. She just needed to sort out the facts of the last weekend in her mind. Come to terms with what had happened on the so-called Villa Winter guided tour.

Would there be in an inquest? Or just a funeral.

Part of her wished Claire had forgotten about their lunch date and she could enjoy a plate of grilled fish from the morning's catch in solitude, but she caught sight of that unmistakable shower of copper hair falling on slender shoulders and she stepped out into the sun to greet her niece.

2

THE JOURNEY SOUTH

Four days earlier, and a current of intrigue pulsed through her as the tour bus swung into the bus station's service road, coming to a sudden stop in the drop-off area. She was standing on the concourse, about ten paces back. Nearby, a small group comprising the tour party were gathered. It was eight o'clock and the sun already had a bit of a sting to it. There was no shade. A trickle of people wandered past and headed through the entrance of the rather grand bus station building to her rear. All of the public buses that entered the service road went around to the parking bays at the back. The tour bus didn't belong in the station, that much was clear. Clarissa shot a look behind her. Judging by the puzzled and annoyed looks the officials inside the building were giving the invading vehicle, she anticipated a fracas at any moment and wondered why the tour operator hadn't arranged an alternative pick-up location.

Leaving the engine running, the driver stepped out of the vehicle which, on reflection, could scarcely be called a regular bus. It was a minibus painted to look like a zebra and set high off the ground on large wheels, and appeared to seat about sixteen passengers. No wonder the leaflet had mentioned the need to book early. In the absence of a photo of the bus, when she'd first read the leaflet, Clarissa had imagined a standard sized, luxury coach, not a van. Taking in the dusty, beat-up vehicle, she began to wonder what she'd paid for, indeed what sort of adventure altogether lay in store.

Misgivings crowded around her. She should have paid attention to the planetary alignment taking place that weekend. No good would come of that particular arrangement of Saturn, Pluto and Mars, not when a Scorpio Moon was involved. Back in her apartment she'd taken another look at the stars, this time at the positions of all the heavenly spheres. She'd noted Venus and Mercury were favourably placed near Neptune. Astrology was all about balance and the weight of possibilities. She'd ignored the heavyweights and gone with Venus. Get out of Puerto del Rosario, Claire had said. What's the point of coming here on holiday and corralling yourself in that dusty port town when there's the whole island to enjoy? Claire, as usual, had a point. It was an ironically Venusian point.

Clarissa had arrived on the island three weeks before, escaping a dreary, wet winter after the slew of Christmas and New Year social obligations was over, obligations that encroached on much of January due to her friends' birthdays and a number of funerals. She'd already taken advantage of the public bus service and had lunch in half a dozen villages, inland and coastal, and was rather tiring of playing tourist when her sole reason for the trip, other than her niece, was to visit that poor man Trevor in prison in Lanzarote and see what could be done about his release. So far, not much. With her trip coming to an end, frustration and impatience had put her in ill humour, ill humour reinforced by a dull cramp in her hip, the result of misplacing her foot in a dip in the sand when she was walking along the beach at El Cotillo the other day. She should have taken a couple of anti-inflammatories before setting off this morning but she'd forgotten. A quick rummage in her canvas bag and she found she'd also forgotten to bring any with her.

She hung back as she waited to board the bus, assessing the other passengers, hopeful of decent company. Perhaps it was her jaundiced mood, but not one of them held any appeal, not the dreadlocked and evenly tanned young man in his sleeveless t-shirt or his equally tanned companion – they'd evidently left behind their surfboards – not the pigeon pair of plump, nondescript women of middle age and Anglo-Saxon appearance, not the pale and frail, sparrow of a woman with legs so spindly they appeared like sticks beneath her loose capris, and especially not the rather tall and undeniably handsome man with come-hither eyes who would have been a real a charmer, no doubt, in his day. He looked about a decade younger than herself and seemed to exude the kind of unjustified self-assurance of the overly pampered. He, she decided, was trouble. Always trouble, those who stand out in a crowd, and she was not disposed to accommodate his sort of company. She determined to sit well away from him, preferably at the opposite end of the so-called tour bus which, she thought, would likely have a series of single seats along one side and if that were the case, she would choose one of those.

The wind picked up a little, parting the bottom edge of her blouse below the last button, a disconcerting tendency of loose blouses designed to hang over trousers, especially when the designer skimped on length. Manufacturers ought to include an additional button nearer the hem for women like her, women of a certain age, women who didn't want the world to see any portion of their midriff. She'd have worn a spencer had she realised, but then again, it was too darn warm for that. The lack of a button was just another minor irritation adding to an already irritable humour.

She was in half a mind to march off, forfeiting her ticket in favour of a quiet day in her apartment. As if in agreement, the sky to the east had turned milky. She knew what that meant. The island was in for another dust storm, or calima, as it was known locally. Not ideal, but you couldn't arrange your activities around the dust. You'd never do anything. Hopefully, it wouldn't be too bad.

In the three weeks of her stay, the dust had come and gone and come and gone and she had been untroubled by it. Only, this particular day would be somewhat ruined if that easterly air flow strengthened. Still, she reminded herself she would happily put up with a bit of dust in preference to the British cold and damp that seeped into her bones and made her joints ache. She was not getting any younger. And in a sudden revolt against her jaundice, she determined to make the most of the day, regardless of the dust, regardless of the van-cum-bus and the motley passengers, regardless of the stars, regardless. This was Fuerteventura, and she was going to do her absolute best to enjoy what remained of her time here even if it killed her.

She'd come to favour Fuerteventura as her holiday destination ever since Claire tempted her here with talk of her haunted house. After three visits to Claire's mansion in Tiscamanita, she'd taken to booking a city apartment eager for a different sort of experience to the almost cloistered existence Claire seemed bent on leading with her photographer husband Paco. They'd become stay-at-homes and Clarissa suspected it was the influence of that ruin she'd restored with most of its rooms looking inwards on the patio. An ancient house with some ancient ghosts rattling around inside. She'd stopped telling Claire the place still had some unearthly visitors after Paco told her in a private moment to drop the subject. They'd done all they could to expunge the supernatural elements and whatever vestiges remained were best left unacknowledged. Clarissa took no offence. Instead, she switched focus and booked an apartment in Puerto del Rosario, the better to pursue her own interests away from judgemental eyes. The close proximity of the various offices of government and law were also beneficial when it came to Trevor and her campaign for his freedom. Besides, since they'd started hosting a writing group and a book group and running short courses in photography, there were evenings when Claire and Paco's historic house lost its monastic air and transformed into a drop-in centre for friends and neighbours. In the evenings, Clarissa favoured her privacy.

The apartment was situated above a bakery opposite a much-used plaza and there was every amenity close to hand. The owners had decked the rooms out with antique looking furniture which appealed to her. The place was spotless too, something she had come to expect from the Spanish. She also enjoyed the cosmopolitan atmosphere of the tiny city, the presence of Moroccans and Venezuelans, and the absence of tourists except when a cruise ship docked at the port. Yes, the city had been a wise choice. After all, she would never have come across the leaflet advertising a fascinating tour of Villa Winter otherwise.

It had been an odd moment of happenstance that she was departing her table in a busy café the other week as a woman came in hoping to sit down. It was as Clarissa was standing up and the woman was sitting down that the leaflet tumbled from the woman's hand and fell to the floor and Clarissa picked it up. The woman thanked her and insisted she keep it. A spare, and the tour was really very good, she'd said. Lunch at a restaurant in the small village of Cofete was included in the price, making the outing rather a bargain.

She was jolted out of her reflections when one of the officials in the bus station called out. Eager to avoid a confrontation with the two uniformed men staring him down from inside the bus station and another who looked to be heading his way, the driver – a tall, suave man decked in an oversized safari-suit – flung open the van's side door and began hurrying the passengers aboard.

Clarissa edged closer and noted his small, penetrating eyes, the flaring nostrils of his meaty nose, a nose dominating his face, and his thick-lipped mouth that was stretched into a most disagreeably insincere smile. There was something askew in his visage, the result of a distorted bone structure – congenital or accidental Clarissa couldn't decide – with his left cheek a fraction smaller than his right and a touch sunken, rendering a subtle lop-sidedness to his lips. In all, he had an unpleasant face, no doubt an indication of an unpleasant character, the type of shifty individual that would be cast in the role of antagonist in every film ever made. It didn't help that he spoke with a French accent. Perhaps he hailed from Senegal or from one of the other West African nations that were former French colonies. It seemed impolite to pry. He sure was capitalising on the mystique with Zebra Tours plastered across his zebra-striped bus.

Perhaps she was being unfair, viewing him through the lens of her shrewish mood which refused to abate. She had to wrestle with herself again. Her cynical attitude really was unbecoming. If anyone were to read her mind, they would accuse her of being a racist. But skin colour had nothing to do with the matter. The man just looked plain mean.

As she took a step forward a sharp pain darted through her hip, and she put her negative attitude down to that, since the twinges always seemed to make her critical of others and she reminded herself to be more accommodating.

The bronzed duo dived into the van first and went straight to the back. The matronly pair heaved themselves inside and took the front seats behind the driver. The birdwoman was next, requiring the driver's assistance to make it up the two steps. She sat in the first single seat to the left of the door. That left Mr Suave and herself. Sensing he was about to turn and do the gentlemanly thing, she lowered her gaze and fumbled with her bag. When she looked up, she had a full view of his backside as he got inside the van. She was disappointed to see him sit down behind the sparrow. There were three double seats remaining. Shooing away the driver's hand, she climbed into the van and went straight to the middle of the three empty double seats, a safe distance from the surfers and the matrons, but, annoyingly, alongside Mr Suave. She took the window seat, hoping he was not about to use the opportunity of their proximity to strike up a conversation.

The two women talked quietly. Behind her, the lads were laughing and chatting in what she now heard was German. Miss Sparrow – a miss, surely – stared out the window, her face turned away from Clarissa's view.

In her side vision she caught Mr Suave fiddling with his fanny pack. Not an American phrase she was inclined to favour under normal circumstances – she found it crude in British translation – but there was an occasion for everything and this, she decided, was it. Fanny pack. One with multiple zippers. At his feet lay a red backpack, bulging full. Seemed to be bringing with him enough paraphernalia for an entire weekend. They'd be back in Puerto del Rosario by five. Not so suave, after all. The suave don't wear fanny packs and carry around red backpacks. The suave would have only a slim leather wallet in the breast pocket. She was stereotyping, she knew, and you could never properly judge a book by its cover; she'd made enough errors over the years to know that. But overall, she had a high success rate when it came to first impressions. What she was sure of was no one on this tour appeared the least bit interesting, to her at any rate, and now she couldn't decide if she was disappointed or relieved. The absence of a congenial companion meant she could give the trip her full attention, particularly when it came to sensing the atmosphere of the mysterious Villa Winter, but it might have been fun to share her insights with a favourable soul. Perhaps someone of that sort would join the tour down the coast. When she'd booked, she was told she had purchased the penultimate ticket. She shifted in her seat, making sure the base of her spine was hard up against the seat back for the sake of her sore hip, forcing herself yet again to adopt an attitude of optimistic anticipation. There was no point going on a guided tour if you were determined not to enjoy it. Misgivings be damned!

The driver closed the side door and hurried to his seat behind the wheel as the irate official drew near. A rev of the engine and they were away.

They had not journeyed as far as the main-road roundabout when a violent screech ripped through the tour bus, succeeded by a loud apology from the driver who appeared to be adjusting his headset.

'Bonjour. My name is Francois,' he said in heavily accented English. 'Welcome to Winter Tours.'

The party waited for him to say more but he fell silent, concentrating on the road.

What he lacked in the vocal department, he made up for with his feet, choosing to be heavy on the brake and causing the tour party to lurch forwards at every intersection. Mr Not-so-suave gripped the backrest of the seat in front, his fingers catching some of Miss Sparrow's hair. At the next intersection, as her head lurched forwards, she gave a little start and reached a hand behind her. Clarissa suppressed a laugh. Mr Not-at-all-suave caught Clarissa's eye and gave her an apologetic smile. She thought the gesture misplaced. It was the bird-woman he should have apologised to.

'It's my back,' he said.

'Bad, is it?'

'Had I known...'

'Had any of us known, I daresay.'

A cultured accent, Home Counties, Sussex probably.

She drew her near-empty canvas bag to her side and turned to look out her window.

She had chosen the coastal side of the bus, the sunny side but for the thickening haze. Her single-seated companions enjoyed the views of the mountains. With their chalky rocky scree, their interesting shapes, their grandiosity, the way they emerged discretely out of the plain, those mountains made Fuerteventura a natural sculpture park. Paco told her they were the remnants of three ancient shield volcanoes, the ferocious wind having eroded the softer rock over many millennia, leaving a series of ridges. The ranges on the western coast formed a massif, all sensual undulations, moulded, like the curves of a pregnant woman. There were very few trees about to detract from the nudity.

As appealing as the mountains were, she had no strong need to gaze at what she had been introduced to already.

Better the others enjoyed the privilege. Claire and Paco had made a point of taking her down every road on the island, save for the road to Cofete. Odd, they'd never taken her down there.

The leaflet advertising the tour afforded an opportunity to test an idea. Ever since she heard about the strange theories surrounding the old farmhouse, of German U-boats and secret bunkers, she'd felt drawn to the place. Ghosts spoke a language of their own and if a member of the spirit world inhabited the abandoned abode, she was sure to pick up on it. She was never wrong in these matters. Only three of the thirty or more premises she'd investigated on so-called ghost tours had contained a legitimate ghost. She prided herself on her mediumistic prowess. She was apt to pick up on preternatural inhabitants of places said not to be haunted. Sometimes she thought she could singlehandedly re-write history based on the information she had gleaned, but that was being arrogant. She followed her dreams and her visions and her intuition, that was all. A natural psychic and a cynic to boot. At her age, it was a healthy mix. Would she encounter the spirits of the dead in Villa Winter? There seemed little doubt.

Once past the airport and the tourist enclave of Caleta de Fuste, the road curved inland, rounding a mountainous ridge before cutting across the lava scree of the more recent eruptions near Pozo Negro. The landscape here was always mesmerising, the hazy sunlight picking out the clefts and ridges of the mountains all around. Many a time Clarissa complained to Claire there were not enough places to pull over and admire the scenery. The island benefited from being traversed on foot. Not that she was fit or agile enough for that.

The Ghost of Villa Winter

The others on the bus seemed equally taken by what they saw. Even the boys in the back had gone quiet.

The bus bypassed Gran Tarajal and Costa Calma and was making straight for Morro Jable, the last town before they entered the wild land of the island's southern tip. Having come this far, she thought perhaps there were to be no further passengers.

She was wrong. When the bus pulled up at the public bus stop in the centre of Morro Jable – once an isolated fishing village, now what amounted in its entirety to a tourist resort – one plump, squat and eager-looking couple who stood out from the locals in their figure hugging I Love Fuerteventura T-shirts stopped craning their necks and scurried to the kerb. A deeply tanned, bulldozer of a man sporting a Caesar-cut hair style and a stubble beard stood a few paces behind them, looking like he'd materialised from an advert selling sports cars or jewellery in a glossy magazine, too cool to lift his eyes from his phone.

Francois went and opened the side door, and the man pushed past the couple and entered the bus in a single stride, choosing the double seat behind Clarissa. His perfume followed him – designer patchouli and no doubt expensive – and she noted the embroidered rainbow on his muscle shirt. She sensed him behind her, exuding cool indifference. The couple were still fussing with what appeared to be their tickets.

'I told you the bus would be late, Margaret,' the tourist, a balding, red-headed man, said in a thick Birmingham accent as he entered the bus. 'There was no need to fret.'

The woman, Margaret – a female version of her husband, although her hair was thick and curly and more sandy than red – did not look in the least fretful. He did. But his manner changed in an instant when he mounted the two steps and beheld Mr Non-suave who, Clarissa saw, was cowering in his seat.

'Richard Parry! Well, I never!' The man piled into the seat in front Clarissa and swivelled round to face the man she now knew as Richard. As Margaret squeezed by her husband to take up the window seat beside him, the man twisted round even further, the better to observe his friend. Friend? Clarissa thought not. Not by the way Richard transparently wanted the floor to swallow him up. A rather extreme reaction and one she thought he'd do well to hide. Whatever must the poor red-headed chap think.

He appeared oblivious. A wide grin lit his round, freckled face.

'Fancy meeting you on a tour bus. I can't believe it. I really can't. What on earth are you doing in Fuerteventura anyway? I never expected you to travel beyond Lanzarote. I always thought of you tucked away in that house of yours – up there in Haría, isn't it? – churning out your next book. How is the writing? Good? I have to say I haven't bought your latest yet. I must apologise for that. But to my credit, if you can permit me such an indulgence, I've gone back to reading *Killer's Heels*. Third time I've read that book and I think it might be my favourite. Mind you, *Haversack Harvest* is a corker, too. What stopped you writing books set in Bunton? I expect you've been influenced by the islands. They do have a powerful effect on people. Margaret, look who we've got for company.'

'I've seen. Hello, Mr Parry.'

'Don't call him that. He's Richard to us. We're practically old friends.'

'Fred, Margaret, it's good to see you both,' Richard managed with a strained grin.

Francois threw the gears into reverse and everyone other

than the newcomers braced for the inevitable lurch forwards. It came as Margaret was buckling herself into her seat and she raised a hand to the double seat in front and let out a soft cry. Her husband, Fred, found himself thrown, shoulder first, into its backrest, causing one of the matrons to half-turn her head. The motion ended the conversation, and Fred reached for his seat belt and attended to his wife.

Richard breathed a sigh as he turned his attention to the view. An author? Perhaps this Richard fellow might prove a touch more interesting than she'd surmised. She immediately thought of Trevor, her Jean Genet. How the genius must suffer for their art.

Francois, who'd remained silent during the entire drive down the coast, took the opportunity of the sweeping bends as he drove up into the deep valley above Morro Jable to launch into a short speech, peering into the rear vision mirror, the better to see the lads at the back. The tour party looked attentive.

'Ladies and gentlemen, welcome to Winter Tours.' He pronounced Winter with a V. 'We are now driving into the wild south of Fuerteventura, known as Jandía.' He pronounced the J as an aitch in the usual Spanish way, but with particular emphasis, which came across as a touch Germanic. Clarissa noted he hadn't pronounced the J in Morro Jable with quite the same vim. 'First, we head down to the end of the island, then back and over the mountain to Cofete, where we have lunch. After, we visit Villa Winter. Any questions?' He paused, but no one spoke. 'The road is rough,' he said, scanning the group in the mirror as a supercilious grin spread across his face. The bus was making straight for a hairpin bend.

'Steady on,' Fred yelled, voicing the concern no doubt felt by the rest of the tour bus.

Francois braked and laughed.

'Don't worry. I drive this road many times and I go slow and safe.'

He was doing nothing of the sort. Fred opened his mouth, but before he could form a word, Francois threw the bus into the bend, causing Fred to lean into Margaret and Richard to almost slide out of his seat. Clarissa caught his gaze and gave him a sympathetic smile before turning her face to the window. A plastic drink bottle rolled across the floor, hitting Clarissa's foot as they rounded the curve. She wanted to pick it up but the centrifugal force was too great. She had no idea who it belonged to.

A few more bends, none as sharp as the hairpin, and she was pleased when they were in open country, the road a wriggling snake following the rough terrain of the mountain range.

Another kilometre and the road turned to dirt. The mountains towered up to one side and the land – mostly coated in scree – fell away at a reasonable gradient at the other, but the road snaked around every curve in a seemingly endless series of blind hairpins. There'd been no rain on the island for almost a year, evident in the potholes and corrugations. Clarissa thought Francois might have slowed, but no, he maintained a steady speed, even over the corrugations. It was enough to make your teeth rattle. The plastic bottle rolled every which way, no one attempting to retrieve it. Perhaps it belonged to a passenger of a previous tour. And on each bend, the nerves in Clarissa's hip made themselves known in short sharp daggers of pain.

Presumably Francois was keeping to a schedule, but he might have given some thought to his passengers. And the oncoming vehicles. Not that there were many. Whorls of road dust trailing behind an approaching car blended into the already dust-laden air.

Despite the ordeal that was Francois' driving and the intermittent pain in her hip, she managed to enjoy the coastline slipping in and out of view in the mid-distance, even though the water had lost its usual sapphire sheen and a haze obscured the horizon. In open country, she could see that the dust was growing thicker by the minute. She hoped no one on the bus was asthmatic.

The road seemed to go on forever, the tour party hurled first to one side of the bus and then the other as Francois navigated the bends. Clarissa held onto her seatbelt and braced in anticipation. Every now and then, she glanced across at Richard whose face wore a look of apprehension. Fred and Margaret didn't turn their heads and Miss Sparrow sat with her head bowed. She appeared to be reading a book. The two matrons in the front seat behind the driver chatted amiably, their gazes turned to each other as though this was a bus trip they made every day. Behind her, she caught the occasional German phrase followed by a guffaw.

As the bus hurtled on, Clarissa succumbed to a disturbing and powerful flash which exited her mind as quickly as it came, and she was left feeling disconcerted. Something was not quite right about this tour but she couldn't put her finger on it. Whatever it was had nothing to do with her ill temper. It was the sort of flash that, had it occurred before the journey began, might have tipped the scales and seen her forego the tour and head back to her apartment.

To distract herself from her unease, she tried to find a way to describe the landscape to her friends back home. The island was shaped like a lower leg and Morro Jable sat at the heel of the foot, the land of Jandía beginning at the ankle and extending to the toe. Next, she imagined a row of dolls wearing ball gowns or brides in meringues. The mountain tops formed the torsos, and from the waist, the lower half were the full bridal skirts with all of those ripples and curves of fabric cascading all around. The road was located about halfway up the skirt and, far below, the ocean, gunmetal blue beneath the calima sky, met the mountain at a hem of low cliff.

In places there were dwellings, some abandoned, others perhaps inhabited, and off into the deep mountain gorges where the land pleated could be seen signs of a compound of small huts and barns. Clarissa could not fathom why anyone would bother with the land out here. Was it desperation that drove the poor farmers to cultivate every cranny? Or were these locales favoured by the reclusive, those of dubious repute, those with something to hide?

She couldn't decide.

She did decide there was only one advantage to Francois' driving: Richard was too apprehensive to speak. Two advantages, if travel time was a consideration.

Eventually, they reached the end of the ranges and traversed a stretch of flatter land. Before long, the island's toe came into view. Although it wasn't shaped like a toe as the land fanned out to the north and south, leaving a short stretch of rugged coastline to the west.

They passed a tiny village and headed up a narrow isthmus, Francois pulling up in a car park beside a lighthouse. Faro de Punta Jandía and the structure was impressive, although not that tall. It was more the formal way the stout brown-stone lighthouse had been incorporated into the flat-roofed keeper's dwelling, the whole making a strong statement on the narrow outcrop of land, just as the surroundings made an equally strong statement, with the jagged coastline, the low cliffs and the ocean pounding the rocks not far below. And then, looking back there were the Jandía ranges they had driven past.

'Ten minutes,' Francois announced as he alighted to open the side door.

The party decanted, the two lads wandering off following the cliffs westward, away from the lighthouse. What were they up to? Mr Cool headed back through the car park. Again, a peculiar direction to head. The matrons hung back, and the frail woman didn't venture far beyond the leeward side of the lighthouse. She seemed in a poor state and Clarissa wondered if the dust was affecting her.

Clarissa felt bolder. Despite the insistent wind, she went over to the edge of the railings and then out onto the gravel concourse, the better to see the rocky ledge below. She had to hold on to the seam of her blouse to stop the easterly from exposing her midriff but she soon forgot she was doing it as her awareness was taken by the setting.

Before long, she sensed someone beside her. It was Richard. He seemed to want to pair up with her. She knew it was only to avoid Fred and Margaret who had disappeared from view but would likely reappear any minute. She introduced herself to the curiously uptight author and they exchanged pleasantries. Then she returned her gaze to the view, this time conscious of her hand gripping the edge of her blouse. She was prepared to endure the man's company, but she allowed her gaze to drift further away from where he stood, hoping to indicate politely that she was on the tour to observe, not socialise.

He seemed content with the silence and used the opportunity to take some photos.

After standing mesmerised by the ocean pushing against itself as the waters to the island's east met the waters to the west, she turned back to admire the lighthouse and, beyond, the two coastlines of the isthmus. He turned too. She met his eyes and smiled.

'Feels like the end of the earth,' he said.

'A good setting for a novel, do you think?'

'Probably.'

He didn't sound convinced. It was a lacklustre reply to a genuine question, one she thought might have resulted in an interesting exchange. Instead, she stared down a potential rabbit hole. No follow up advised. She decided she'd had enough of getting blasted by the dry and dusty easterly wind that seemed determined to give the island a thorough whipping, and she headed back, pleased when the last of the tour party had bundled into the van and Francois closed the side door.

He then hurried around the front of the bus and jumped in the driver's seat. When he turned the ignition key, instead of the usual firing up of the engine, the tour party were treated to a protracted whine. Glances met with worried glances. Francois made five attempts before popping the bonnet. There was an anxious wait. When he got back in and tried again, the engine started and they were away. Clarissa glanced at Richard but said nothing.

Francois took them north to the second tip of the island's toe, traversing about five kilometres of corrugations that sent juddering vibrations through the passengers and caused the plastic bottle to bounce about on the aisle floor. Clarissa wondered where he was taking them until they arrived at another lighthouse and she overheard Fred telling Margaret it was known as Faro de Punta Pesebre. From what she could see, the lighthouse amounted to a door set in a solid concrete frame, mounted on a stone platform. A curious structure, and well worth the bone-jarring trip. This time, Clarissa was first off the bus.

Before anyone could join her, she headed past the curious lighthouse and carried on as far as she dared, the little promontory narrowing the further she went. Then, she turned to view the land behind her, gripping her blouse for the sake of modesty. Despite the dust haze the setting was phenomenal, with the high cliffs of Jandía rising in the middle distance, the low cliffs nearby, the rocks gnarly, volcanic, uncompromising. The ocean, treacherous here, churned, smashing into the basalt shelf, sending spume high into the air. She turned her back on the land and faced that expanse of water, feeling the strong easterly wind as it threatened to push her over the edge and onto the rocks below. Here was a place to lose a life to the elements. It was like being on the prow of a ship in a violent storm. Despite the wind, she would have liked to have lingered, although here was no place for a picnic. She glanced behind her at the bus and saw Francois waving and the others walking back. She joined them, noticing the women already sitting in the bus. She doubted they'd got off.

As she resumed her seat, she caught the gaze of the stubble-bearded man seated behind her, and he quickly looked away without so much as a smile. Rude, then. Probably viewed her as a boring old woman, nondescript and utterly dull with her short grey hair and her wrinkles. She considered herself anything but.

The engine started first time, and they headed back the way they had come, first the five kilometres of corrugations and then the road back to the mountains, taking the turn-off to Cofete after about a dozen hairpins. Francois drove the whole way to the western cliff as though he had a ten-ton lorry on his tail, throwing the minibus into the first few bends of the initial rise and fishtailing out. Even Clarissa felt rising alarm. Richard's knuckles on the hand that gripped his seat had turned white. One of the lads in the back said, 'Hey, ho,' and laughed without humour. It was Fred who did everyone a favour when he insisted Francois slow down.

'Margaret will have a heart attack if you keep this up,' he shouted.

There was some laughter from the back, humorous, this time.

'Vale, vale. I go slow for you.' Francois lifted his hands off the steering wheel and laughed. The van veered to the left, the direction of the precipitous fall. What was his game?

The larger of the matrons cried out, 'For pity's sake, Francois, pack it in!'

There was an air of familiarity in her choice of phrase. Did they know each other?

Francois braked and braked again, causing everyone to lurch forwards. If he wanted to instil terror in his passengers, he was doing a good job, especially in those with window seats overlooking the plummet. For a reason known only to himself, he took things steady from then on. Even so, Richard gripped his seat. Yet Clarissa thought she had more right to feel terrified since she was on the side of the bus facing the sharp fall and had she been Catholic, she'd have crossed herself and sought the lord's intervention.

As they crested the mountain range, a lookout appeared on the left, and beyond it there was a walk to an even higher peak to the south. There were cars in the small parking area and people standing around, gazing, one or two close to the edge, defying their own ability to remain on their feet with the blustery easterly wind pressing against their backs. It appeared too dangerous even for Clarissa and besides, what was the point of taking in the panorama when this wretched calima grew stronger by the minute, reducing visibility and making even things close up appear hazy.

Francois cornered the next bend and announced, 'We are now late for the restaurant and cannot stop at the lookout. Sorry. Maybe on the way back.'

He was clearly a man who did not take kindly to being told what to do.

The descent was more confronting than the ascent and anyone without a head for heights would have been absolutely petrified, especially with Francois behind the wheel, there being nothing to avert catastrophe should the minivan veer off the edge of the road, a road that was little more than a wide goat track, a scratch in the mountainside. Despite being flung from side to side as the bus cornered tight bend after tight bend in endless succession, Clarissa managed to ignore her fear and her discomfort and admire the vastness of the landscape, what she could see of it, taking in the coastline below the cliff, and the cliff itself that rose up beside them to between five and seven hundred metres or thereabouts, and stretched on ahead and disappeared into the haze to the north, a cliff of vertiginous falls, the declivity lessening towards the base and levelling somewhat near the long beach of creamy sand. Nowhere could appear more secluded, more remote, more bereft of life in any form. There was just the rock, the sand and the ocean.

Yet this was where some intrepid locals had established the tiny farming village of Cofete, a place with no running water, no electricity and no mainline telephone. On an island where everywhere beyond the main towns was isolated, remote, and in varying degrees inaccessible, locating a farm or even a village at the bottom of a cliff on the windward side of the island seemed relatively understandable. They were locals, after all. But this was also where in the 1930s, General Gustav Winter of the German military chose to build a farmhouse. Why, in heaven's name, did he decide to build a house here? It was a question that bounced around inside Clarissa's mind as the minibus traversed the sloping plain to the village.

3

LUNCH IN COFETE

When the minibus pulled up in the car park outside the restaurant, the lads in the back cheered. Francois killed the engine and exited the driver's seat, rounding the front of the vehicle to open the side door. Keen to be the first off, the matrons swung round in their seats. Richard was still gripping his. Clarissa took in the look of terror in his eyes and began to wonder why he bothered coming if he was that scared of heights. Maybe he hadn't known about the road to Cofete.

Fred said, 'There you go, Margaret. It wasn't too bad.'

Clarissa wasn't sure Margaret agreed with him, judging by the pale expression on her face.

The tour party decanted, the matrons leading the way, followed by Fred and Margaret and then Simon, his perfume trailing behind him like a wraith. Clarissa blocked the aisle and let Richard go in front of her. The lads followed close behind. The moment they were off the bus they hurried into the village, presumably to explore. The frail-looking woman was the last off and Francois had to almost carry her down the two steps. She appeared to be shaking and looked unhealthily pale. Wisps of mousy hair appeared stuck to her forehead. A fever? Her eyes were dull and her thin lips pinched. Perhaps it wasn't the dust after all. Perhaps she had a virus. Clarissa didn't like to ask and no one else looked bothered or had even noticed.

Awaiting instructions, they congregated in the car park between the bus and three cars parked closer to the restaurant. A few other cars were parked haphazardly further off. Meaty garlicky smells greeted her nostrils. Chattering voices and bursts of laughter carried on the wind. Not far away, diners, seated behind a low wall containing the al fresco area of the restaurant's frontage, were having a merry time. She looked forward to joining them.

Ignoring his charges or indeed his duty, Francois locked the minibus and disappeared into the restaurant. As if that were a cue, the matrons followed on behind. Unsure whether to do the same, Clarissa hung back with the others, pushing away locks of her hair that the wind had whipped into her face as she surveyed the surroundings. She'd carried no preconceptions, although she was not surprised to discover the locale had an atmosphere she didn't take to, made all the more desolate by the fast-gathering calima. She could appreciate the appeal of the remoteness and the back-to-earth lifestyle, harsh as it was, but there was something else, an undertow, something temporary perhaps, an energy that shouldn't be here, danger. That was as far as her clairvoyance would take her.

Cofete itself comprised a staggered cluster of about twenty ramshackle stone huts that blended in with the cliff towering a touch menacingly at this point with its jagged crest. The appearance of the village was best described as rough and ready. No one out here gave a damn about being tidy or giving order to anything. If you wanted to escape the modern world, here was the place to do it, although the tourists came, braving the road, as did some of the locals. And there were solar panels and satellite dishes and television aerials and Clarissa assumed the dwellings had every convenience, in their way.

In front of the village and somewhat obscuring the ocean view was a hill sporting a small steel windmill. The hill, more a mound protruding out of the steady decline to the beach, did not look as though it belonged in the landscape. Clarissa was pondering that thought when a woman appeared in the car park with two donkeys. She wore grubby dungarees over a loose and faded T-shirt, her voluminous hair gathered up and held in place with a large comb. Ignoring the tour party, she strolled across to the restaurant and greeted a scruffy-looking man in a long white apron who emerged through a side door. They chatted for a while. He seemed agitated. The woman fiddled with one of the pack saddles and handed him a small parcel. He scanned the car park and quickly disappeared. Steadfastly avoiding contact with the tour party, the woman gave the zebra bus a wide berth as she steered her donkeys back through the car park, disappearing into the enclosed compound of the farmhouse nearby. But for the curious behaviour of the man – who had the shifty demeanour of a drug dealer receiving his latest stash – it was a moment belonging to a century past.

Francois reappeared, marching to a spot halfway between the restaurant and the bus, where he came to a halt and hailed the tour party to follow him. Like sheep, they obeyed. Francois then stood at the entrance to the al fresco area, ushering the tour group to where two tables had been positioned end-to-end in a corner away from the other diners. Clarissa made her way past those seated in twos and fours and sixes – the restaurant was packed – as she struggled to rationalise the fact that people would want to come all the way out here to eat on any day, let alone on this dusty day. As for those who'd decided to open an eatery here in the first place, with all that that would entail, it was unfathomable, especially if they didn't live here. What a commute!

The matrons were already seated at the table in the middle seats on the far side, with all the appearance and manner of officials on a commission panel. Fred and Margaret sat opposite, their inquisitees. The frail woman took up a chair beside Fred. Richard, obviously seeing he could not avoid his fans, sat next to the matrons, leaving the bearded man to take up the chair at the end beside him. Clarissa was about to give Richard no easy ride when the lads bounded in from nowhere and plonked themselves opposite each other down at the other end, leaving Francois to take the head and Clarissa the last remaining chair beside Helen. No place had been laid at the table's foot.

A quick glance around and she saw she was the eldest member of the party by at least a decade, Richard taking second place. She'd put Fred and Margaret in their late-fifties. Everyone else looked younger. She had two options: assume a matriarchal role and command the table, or remain silent and observe. She chose the latter approach, knowing she would disappear as all old women do if they choose not to assert themselves. People were in the habit of assuming an old woman was done with life and had nothing interesting to offer. How wrong the world was, but there were times the assumption could be played to her advantage and this, Clarissa sensed, was one of them.

Francois, too, seemed disinclined to play host. There was a long silence peppered with exchanges of cautious looks, the strained atmosphere broken by Fred. 'Some introduc-

The Ghost of Villa Winter

tions, don't you think? I'm Fred. Fred Spice.' As if his surname mattered. It didn't.

He stood and proffered his hand to the woman opposite him. Rosy-cheeked and square-jawed, her robust face was framed by hair shaped like a combat helmet, and if it wasn't for her doe eyes, she would have come across too severe for comfort. As she shook Fred's hand her face lit a little and everyone seemed to relax.

'Vera,' she said. 'And this is Carol.' She pointed to the woman beside her and there was an exchange of handshakes.

'And this is my wife Margaret.' Fred looked to his right. 'And you are?'

'Helen.'

Fred ignored Clarissa and turned to the lads with an outstretched hand.

'Dave and Steve,' the blonder of the two said, pointing at his dreadlocked friend.

Uncertainty passed across Richard's face and before Fred had a chance, he introduced himself. Fred then sat down. Realising she had been thoroughly ignored, Clarissa stood and reached out her hand and announced her name and exchanged handshakes and greetings with the others. The group then all turned to the bearded man still buried in his phone.

'Er, Simon,' he said, lifting his gaze momentarily before returning to whatever was so compelling on his screen. It was almost as if he didn't recall his own name. As if he had made it up on the spot. Clarissa found his disengagement puzzling. His behaviour was not that of a typical tourist. Indeed, he didn't seem to want to be there.

Menus arrived and were passed around. Francois spoke

to the waiter, who hovered expectantly for a moment then walked away.

'So, you're a writer,' Vera said to Richard. 'What do you write?'

Everyone at the table glanced up. Fred lowered his menu and listened, smiling proudly. Clarissa felt Richard's discomfort. He kept his gaze on Vera's face and said, 'Mysteries mostly.'

'Nothing like a good mystery. I'll have to look you up. What's your full name?'

Richard recoiled slightly. Clarissa hoped no one else noticed. The poor man was overly self-conscious. An introvert perhaps. Certainly not given to holding court.

'Richard H. Parry,' he said, adding, 'You need to remember the aitch or you may end up with a different Richard Parry.'

'What does the aitch stand for?'

Richard hesitated.

'Harry,' said Fred.

'Richard Harry Parry.'

An amused look appeared in Vera's face. She managed to disguise her mirth by turning to Carol and talking about the last book she'd read. Finding himself no longer the object of her attention, Richard began to regain his equanimity. He might just as well have left the bit about his middle name out and done himself a favour. A short while later, he stood and excused himself. Simon left the table as well, presumably to visit the same destination. Vera then whispered something to Carol who laughed and they both returned to study their menus.

Clarissa presumed both women to be around fifty. Carol was the more buxom of the pair. Laughter notwithstanding, her disposition appeared anything but jolly. She carried a forthright, no-nonsense demeanour of the sort crafted through decades in positions of administrative authority. And she wanted the world to know it, the severity in her face accented by her cropped black hair, greying about the temples. Attired in a conservative outfit, she gave the impression of a career in the civil service. Health, perhaps, or education. Like her counterpart, she was not in the business of flattering men.

Neither was Helen, who sat a little hunched in her seat. On closer scrutiny in her side vision, Clarissa couldn't help noticing the drab, poorly cut attire the woman had chosen to put on for the outing. Perhaps she was a woman of limited means.

Clarissa had been raised to cultivate her assets, not in order to endear herself to the opposite sex but to present to the world the most appealing version of herself possible, whether that be through style of hair or dress, the use of scarves and jewellery, whatever it took to make a good and lasting impression. Which was why she sat in her smart new blouse and matching capris and leather sandals, all purchased from Mrs Fortescue-Blair's boutique in her local High Street back in England. She outdid everyone at the table, although she was certain she was the only one who spotted the fact. She also spotted that Helen's pallor had not recovered.

'Are you quite well?' Clarissa asked softly, head bowed and tilted in Helen's direction, hoping she was being discreet.

'I'm fine, yes, thank you. Just recovering from minor surgery.'

Clarissa had lost count of the times she'd heard that. In her friendship networks it was a euphemism for all manner of ailments, including the most serious. Anything, apparently, could be deemed minor. But she was reluctant to pry, especially at the table.

She glanced around at the others still perusing their menus and decided to do the same. The café specialised in fish and goat meat. She thought she'd try the goat.

The waiter returned and hovered expectantly over by Francois. With a quick glance around the group, he placed his order and the others did the same. The waiter had reached Carol when Richard returned, sat down and picked up his menu. Simon's seat remained empty.

'I'm trying the goat,' Clarissa said to Richard, hoping to help him make up his mind. The sooner they ate, the sooner they would be away from this awkward lunch party.

'I hear it's greasy.'

'A little grease won't hurt.'

'I think I prefer the fish.'

'Then have the fish.'

The waiter had started taking down Fred and Margaret's orders. He was moving through the group with speed. Helen was next, then Clarissa. Once he had taken down Richard's fish order, the waiter hurried away and in no time a carafe of wine and bottles of beer appeared, along with crusty bread and aioli and an array of tapas. Drinks were poured and the food was passed around. Everyone dived in, clearly as famished as she. Although, Clarissa was surprised to see Helen load her plate, given her pallor. Richard was a touch cautious, taking one of everything, fastidiously arranging the food items on his plate. Heaven help him when his fish came. She couldn't help noticing him aligning his plate with the edge of the table. Anxiety. Typical in an author.

Conversation began as the tapas and bread had all but disappeared into greedy bellies when Fred said to no one in particular, 'Pity about the calima.' He raised his gaze skyward to press home his observation. He was ignored. Although Clarissa did note the sun had turned red and the sky was no longer blue except out over the ocean. She thought it reckless the restaurant encouraged outdoor dining on a day such as this, but then they probably needed the business.

No one could have anticipated a remark about a weather event would trigger the intense conversation that followed. Clarissa had been expecting the usual shallow and light repartee one would expect among strangers thrown together on a tour.

Things started off mildly enough when Fred responded to his own remark with, 'You can blame Chad.'

'Chad?' said Helen doubtfully as she nibbled on the last of her bread soaked in aioli.

'The dust comes from dried up Lake Mega-Chad and the Tibesti mountain area in the north.'

'You are a fount of knowledge, Fred.' Margaret looked at her husband with fond appreciation. It was not a manner shared by the others.

'Comes a fair way, then,' said Steve blandly.

'Where's Chad?' murmured Richard. No one answered.

Then Helen said, 'Well, they say it's going to be a bad one.'

Fred came back with, 'Oh, I don't know. I've seen worse.'

'It's still rolling in,' Helen replied, raising herself up a little as she turned to him.

He scrutinised her face. 'Were you here in 2007?'

And that sparked a chain reaction when Vera said, cutting in, 'I've got a long-standing connection to these islands after visiting in 1988. And I've never known a calima as bad as this.'

'Me neither. And I came in 1986,' said Carol, stabbing a little meat ball with her fork.

'For holidays?' Helen asked with genuine interest.

'I never wanted to leave.'

'Why did you?'

'Long story.'

'Aren't they always,' Fred said.

Carol's face reddened. There were times least said was best. Clarissa braced herself, watching as Carol formed her reply. 'My relationship with this place is complex,' she said. 'A lot has happened to me here.'

All eyes were on her, even Francois'. Clarissa wondered if she was about to spill. Instead, Vera saved the day by addressing one of the lads – Steve, possibly; Clarissa wasn't sure – with, 'And you. Where are you from?'

'Australia.'

'I thought so.'

'It's fairly obvious from the accent.'

'I try not to make assumptions, Steve.'

'Whereabouts?' Margaret said, taking an interest.

'North of Perth. I live on the same latitude as here, only in the south.'

There was a brief pause as the table contemplated that geographical titbit and Clarissa wondered at the German she'd heard the lads speaking in the back of the bus. Exchange students?

'What brings you all the way here?'

'Just travelling. A chick we met in Bonn mentioned the beaches.'

'Even so, it's a long way to come,' said Margaret.

'Australians are known to be good travellers,' Fred said, patting her arm.

There was an awkward pause as the other women

absorbed his gesture with looks of disapproval, and the lads lost interest in the conversation and started chatting to each other. Simon re-appeared, resuming his seat without making eye contact with anyone at the table.

'The waiter has already taken our order,' Clarissa said with a forward lean, hoping to gain his attention.

'I ordered at the bar,' he said without looking up.

Her gaze lingered momentarily on his pectorals and the flat of his belly, his muscle shirt leaving none of his torso to the imagination.

Richard said, addressing Helen, 'What draws you here?'

Her reply was instant and heartfelt. 'I love the old farming ways. In the valleys. The way they bank up the edges of the fields to make little dams. That's pretty cool. They had huge underground water tanks too. Enough to last four years, apparently.'

'No one is doing much of any of that here anymore,' Fred said, ever the authority. 'And the terraces, you don't see them farmed either.'

'They were for the poor farmers,' Helen said. She had pushed her plate to one side and had taken to fiddling with her napkin. 'I've been reading up about it. The rich landowners had the fertile, tillable land in the valleys. The peasant farmers were hardly paid anything. They took their donkeys up the mountainsides and farmed the terraces.'

'That's practically feudal,' Carol said with genuine interest. Clarissa warmed to her. She always warmed to no-nonsense women harbouring concerns for social justice.

'Nice to see some solar out here,' Steve said, cutting in with a cheeky grin and gesturing at the village.

Cheeky, but also rather rude, stealing the conversation from Helen. Clarissa was not the only one to be annoyed by it.

'You'd need them out here,' Carol said, eyeing him coolly.

'You won't see many panels here, mate. They rely on oil for power on the island,' said Fred, missing the point. 'It's the flat roofs, you see. No one wants their roof terrace cluttered with solar panels.'

One man besting another. Typical.

'There's wind,' Steve said.

'There's always the wind.'

A titter of laughter ensued. It was unconvincing.

'It would be nice to see things become more sustainable, though. Don't you think?' Steve mused.

'On Fuerteventura?' Helen said. 'You have got to be joking. You've seen all the electricity poles and pylons. They could have put those wires underground. But they didn't.'

'No political will,' said Vera.

Fred leaned forward. 'I don't know about that.'

Vera didn't respond. Fred filled the gap with, 'What do you think, Richard?'

Richard looked up with alarm.

'I'm sorry, I wasn't paying attention.'

Fred laughed. He was forming a reply when Steve said, 'It's the same in Australia.' His tone became droll as he warmed to the theme. 'We have a love affair with coal.'

The other one, Dave, piped up with, 'My mum installed solar on her roof. Five-kilowatt system, and she produces more than she uses. Says she needs it to run the air con day and night.' He paused for effect. 'It's her age.'

The lads eyed the women of the group with cautious but pointed amusement. Simon smiled. So, he had been paying attention after all. Even though, ever since he returned to the table, he had scarcely lifted his gaze.

The main dishes arrived, forestalling any further

The Ghost of Villa Winter

awkward remarks. But not for long. Clarissa had only just deboned a hunk of her goat when Fred piped up again.

'And what do you make of Fuerteventura, then, lads?'

'Great. You can't get away from the tourists here though, hey. Not like back home.'

'You mean us,' Helen said.

Vera and Carol both laughed, but no one seemed all that comfortable.

Fred went on, plainly keen to display his knowledge. 'You can't expect much, here. Fuerteventura is only six hundred and forty-two miles square with a population of about a hundred and thirty thousand, according to the stats. And the island gets about two million tourists a year. That makes twenty tourists for every resident. I worked it out.'

'You sure did,' Helen mouthed with her head bowed. Clarissa thought she might have been the only witness to the remark.

Steve issued an apparently sincere, 'Wow!'

Vera leaned forward, fork in hand. 'And a fair portion of those hundred and thirty thousand residents are European and British migrants.' She stabbed a hunk of goat and raised her fork to her mouth before pausing to add, 'Half, maybe. Or even more.'

'You mean expats,' Fred said, munching on a potato.

Vera pursed her lips as she chewed. She swallowed before she spoke.

'Some are expats, some are migrants. And then there are the swallows. Depends if they still have a home in their country of origin that they go back to, in my humble opinion.'

'Bali has a tourist for every resident,' Steve said. 'I thought that was full on.'

'I think Fuerteventura is overburdened,' said Carol in

support of her friend. 'Think about it. All that food, all that bottled water, all those goods, they all have to come from Spain by boat. That's a distance of over a thousand miles.'

'Or from South America.'

'Even further.'

'So?' said Steve, grinning. 'In Australia, food is trucked at least that distance. Probably more like double.'

'Treble, even.'

'It's all relative,' Fred said sagely.

'*And* they have to rely on desal, here,' said Carol, attempting to reclaim lost ground.

Clarissa caught an eye roll from Steve.

'Heaps of places have desal.'

'Yeah, Australia has heaps of desal,' Dave chimed.

'As does the Middle East.'

Carol put down her fork and stabbed the table with her finger. 'Look. This island is so overrun by tourists and migrants, for the locals, the place is not their own. That's the point Vera's making and I'm making.'

'Then why come here and add to it?'

It was a cutting remark. Steve waited for a reply which was not forthcoming. Vera and Carol turned their attention to their plates. Clarissa noticed Richard painstakingly separating little flakes from the bones of his fish.

Indifferent to the mounting tension, Fred eyed Carol appraisingly. 'You talk about the locals, but this island hasn't belonged to them for hundreds of years.'

Carol ignored him.

'Since the Spanish came, you mean,' said Margaret in support of her husband.

'And then, the Germans,' said Steve.

Fred said, 'That was a lot, lot later, my friend.' Which was something Steve clearly was not. But the conversation

The Ghost of Villa Winter

was diverted as the three men began talking amongst themselves about Villa Winter.

Cupping her mouth, Carol leaned across and whispered to Helen, 'Expert's disease.'

'Bad case of it, I'd say,' Vera added, leaning across as well.

'Fatal.'

The three women exchanged a snigger.

'Less talk, more eating.'

It was said with conviction. Everyone turned to Francois who had folded his arms across his chest before his empty plate. Even Simon, who looked up from his grilled chicken and gave a small shrug.

The rest of the meal was eaten in relative silence, broken only by side conversations held in low voices. Having made her assessment of each member of the group, Clarissa had no interest in conversing with any of them. She was trying to preserve her inner perception. She could only do that if she maintained an interior focus. If she chatted with Vera or Carol or Helen, as interesting as they appeared, she would quickly become over-stimulated. If she spoke to Fred or Steve or Dave, her poise would be lost in an instant. Margaret seemed to be little more than a Fred sidekick. Pity. Clarissa hated to see women lose themselves to their men in that way. And Simon was not a contender for conversation. As for Richard, he seemed lost in his own world, focused as he was on picking the flesh off his fish bones.

She had to admit, if begrudgingly, that Richard was proving the most pleasant of the group. Perhaps that was because unlike the others he held back on his opinions. Perhaps he, like her, was observing, taking mental notes, grist for the literary mill. She'd begun to warm to him, a little. Trevor would likely have made much of the situation,

Fred Spice no doubt taking a lead role in a future work. She looked forward to telling him all about it when she saw him in two days' time. It would give them a fresh topic to natter about, perhaps even stimulating in Trevor a creative spark.

In all, she could happily say she'd spent her time in the restaurant intrigued by the tensions while enjoying the food, which so far had almost made up for the arduous journey on the bus. Although she didn't care for the tour party's dissections one bit, which seemed to her mostly superficial judgements in a dance of one-up-man-ship. She preferred to accept Fuerteventura as it was, an island full of contrasts, holding much diversity for its size. The east, west, north and south were distinct, each village a little different from the last. The capital was compact and charming. The island was filled with small pockets and secrets held together by good roads. A dual carriageway was being built to connect north to south on the eastern seaboard. Fuerteventura was an island of strength, in the wind, in the ocean and in the panoramas, which were always bold and striking. She could never tire of the landscape and was pleased Claire – her only living relative, a niece she had half-reared after the sudden death of her sister and Claire's mother Ingrid – had decided to live here. She felt at times she'd entered *Travels with my Aunt*, one of her favourite Graham Greene novels, although she had no secret past, no old passions in need of fulfilment. She had always sought independence and found great pleasure in that.

The dessert was a pleasingly tangy fruit compote topped with mock cream. No choice. Francois polished his off in three gulps and stood and hovered behind his chair, looking at his phone as though it was a watch. He seemed more agitated with every passing moment, as well as being in a foul mood.

The Ghost of Villa Winter

It was Fred who refused to be rushed. As a table behind them emptied of a party of six, everyone sat waiting for him to spoon the last bits of fruit from his bowl. 'I cannot be doing with indigestion,' he said at last. Lifting his gaze, he added, all innocent as you please, 'Am I holding us up?'

They filed out of the al fresco seating area now only a quarter full, headed through the near-empty car park and piled into the minibus like dutiful soldiers anticipating the last leg of the journey. There was a moment of tension when Francois's first attempt at starting the minibus failed. The second attempt went on for much too long, the whine of the starting motor little short of winsome. Clarissa was steeling herself for a long walk. Then, on the third attempt, the minibus sprang to life and the tour party applauded and cheered. As they set off, Clarissa took in the Atlantic rollers crashing on the shore and then the looming cliff. It was an inhospitable locale, an end of earth kind of place, and beyond the confines of the village and the luxury of the pristine beach, here was nowhere to spend too much time, especially in a calima.

4

A GUIDED TOUR

They headed up a dirt track about halfway between the coast and the cliff, and a few minutes later, the minibus came to a halt in a small parking area below the house. Once the passengers had decanted, Fred sidled up to Richard and said, 'You were very quiet during lunch. Are you alright? You seem a bit off, if you don't mind my saying. Man-to-man, as it were.'

The entire group was in earshot. Clarissa saw a look of exasperation appear in Richard's face. The poor man. What an irritation it would be to have a reader turn up with nothing on his mind but to annoy and harangue.

She was about to remark, but a disturbance distracted her. Before Francois could intervene, Simon had marched off up the steep path to the house with the lads trailing behind. Francois called after them, but his voice was lost on the wind. He marched on up behind them, no doubt hoping to stop them before they went too far.

The others followed, Vera and Carol maintaining a steady stride and clearly fit for their size and age. Fred and Margaret kept pace. Richard appeared determined to keep up. Helen struggled, pausing now and then to lean against the stone wall for support. Clarissa hung well back, taking her time. She knew better than to power uphill with a sore hip, panting in a calima.

She passed wide terraced fields edged with neat drystone walls, fields that might have been farmed but were fallow. She took in the imposing house up ahead, more a fortress tucked beneath the cliff as it made its final and steep ascent to the crest, a fortress overlooking the long stretch of beach in the mid-distance below. In the thickening dust haze, Cofete could scarcely be seen.

About halfway up the drive she began to wish Francois had taken them right up to the house. She thought he'd decided to make them all walk as some sort of punishment. She'd never encountered a more bad-tempered and indifferent guide.

The so-called farmhouse sat proud on the final strip of terraced land, but instead of a normal façade with doors and windows, Villa Winter presented its visitors with a very high and imposing stone wall that appeared to serve as the dwelling's foundations. The two corners of the wall were finished off with square turrets, each sporting a small casement window set about two-thirds of the way up the front wall – too high for anyone outside to peer in – and topped with a stone parapet.

The house itself sat above the stone wall and sported a somewhat austere veranda contained within a series of stone arches. A low-pitched roof of terracotta tiles completed the look. Attached to the front of the house on the far side was a large round tower. The whole edifice was more imposing close up than she'd imagined viewing photos on the internet.

She stopped to catch her breath, the tower capturing her

gaze. She was about to carry on when a figure appeared in one of the uppermost tower windows. Appeared, and then was gone. At least, what she thought to be a figure. Could have been a ghost. Her skin broke out in goose bumps as though in agreement. Although the apparition might just as well have been Simon or one of the lads.

When she at last reached the back entrance to the courtyard where the others had congregated, she found Vera and Carol still a little breathless, Helen seated on a large boulder, flushed and looking done in, and Richard, panting and mopping his brow with a handkerchief. Fred and Margaret stood like stanchions, scarcely out of breath. The lads hung back, chastened, and Francois and Simon were nowhere to be seen.

The door to the courtyard was open. Clarissa caught site of a man in dusty overalls making repairs to a low concrete wall inside. He stood as she watched, wiped his hands on a rag and disappeared from view. Not long after, an engine fired up. Then a car emerged from the far side of the villa, roared past the tour party drenching everyone in dust and headed off down the long drive.

A few moments passed before Francois and Simon exited the courtyard. Francois was furious, his face, never pleasant, worsened by a deep frown and a downturn to the lips, expressions enhancing the lopsided quality of his face. He was impossible to look at.

'We are about to enter Villa Winter,' he said with a snarl. 'You must stay together in one group. No one is to walk off. Do you understand? Also, parts of the house are not open to visitors. Doors are locked. You must not try to access the areas that are sealed. Before we look around, I will now tell you about Villa Winter. Come.'

He ushered the group into the courtyard with an impatient wave of his hand. As the tour party arranged themselves around him, Clarissa drank in the setting. A series of rounded arches along three walls flanked a loggia that provided access to various rooms. The loggia was edged with concrete planters. Entry to the loggia had been provided at each end of the courtyard's rear. Someone had decided to do something with the outdoor space. A pair of straggly fig trees clinging to life occupied one corner and succulents grew in the planters. A curious model village of Cofete had been created in the soil in the centre of the courtyard, fenced off with rope. Farm tools hung decoratively on whitewashed walls. From this purview, the terracotta roof tiles leant a welcoming Mediterranean feel to the building. Standing in this courtyard, it was possible to forget about the strange bunkers below and the imposing tower. Although an upward glance and there it was, rising above the roofline at the northwest corner where a recess in the roof provided for small walled balconies, one in each wall.

Richard came and stood beside her and fumbled in his pocket. He extracted a voice recorder and managed to hold it out of Francois's view by making to step behind Margaret, requiring Clarissa to take a step to one side. She observed the doors of the house, as many as she could see. She felt watched.

Francois read off a script, beginning his introduction with, 'General Gustav Winter was born in Germany in 1893 and moved to the Canary Islands in 1925. He was an engineer with a long association with these islands. He'd been working on projects in Fuerteventura and Gran Canaria since 1915. He was also one of over a hundred German residents in Spain accused of being a Nazi agent. His behaviour, some say, was highly suspicious.'

'There were calls for his repatriation to Germany,' Fred said to Margaret, loud enough for the others to hear.

Francois glared at him.

'Don't interrupt me, please.'

'I wasn't interrupting, thank you. I was talking to my wife.'

'Be quiet.'

Fred sucked in his breath. He was about to make a retort when Margaret prodded him.

Francois went on. 'There were calls for Winter to be put on trial, but Spain did not hand him over and he died in Las Palmas in 1971.' He paused, waiting until he had everyone's attention. 'Ladies and gentlemen, many believe you are standing in a secret Nazi base.'

The reaction was mixed. Without waiting for comment, he turned and led the group across to the loggia entrance on the north side of the villa and along to where a door stood open.

'The villa was used as a hideaway,' said Vera as the party followed Francois into the house.

Steve glanced at her. 'It was used to repair U-boats, I heard.'

'That theory has been debunked.'

'You think?'

Francois stood with his back to an impressive fireplace, one arm raised to gain attention. There was some resistance as the group were keen to take in the space they were in – a sparsely furnished living room – but Francois was insistent. Once the tour party were all gathered in front of him, he said, 'Pedro Fumero would have shown you around but he cannot be here today.'

'And he is?'

'His grandfather helped build this house, and Pedro's

The Ghost of Villa Winter

aunt and two uncle lived in the house until recently. So, Pedro knows more than anyone about Villa Winter. His family lived in very bad conditions, let me tell you.'

Vera looked around. 'I can well imagine. I wouldn't like to spend one night out here. This place has a real vibe to it.'

Clarissa agreed. She'd been on countless ghost tours and this was one of the few occasions she felt a sense of unease.

'I thought a Spanish building company had bought the property from Winter's descendants and evicted the Fumero family,' Fred said.

'That's correct,' said Francois in an effort to hold on to narrative control.

He lost it in the next instant when Helen said, 'That's an outrage.'

'It's just business,' Fred said, using his patronising tone. 'They own the place; they have every right.'

'What will they do with it?' Steve said.

'Open a hotel probably.'

'I read Winter was a radio operator and military operative,' Carol said, clearly eager not to let Fred trumpet solo. 'That the OSS had evidence on him from 1947.'

'The OSS?'

'The old CIA.'

'And I heard the house was built in 1946,' said Richard.

Heads turned. It was the first sentence he'd uttered since the tour began and he was instantly contradicted, not by Fred but by Francois, who seized the chance to regain the upper hand.

'Señor Fumero is certain the building was built much earlier,' he said coolly. 'Winter bought the land off the previous Spanish owner and took control of the whole of the Jandía peninsula when Franco took power.'

'That was 1936, then,' said Fred.

'I heard the house was built in '37,' said Carol.

'Two years before the start of the war.'

'Right in the middle of the war.'

'I meant the Second World War.'

Francois puffed out his cheeks. He might have been irascible by nature but given the behaviour of the tour party, any guide would have felt consumed with frustration at this juncture. The only other time Clarissa had been in a similar situation was a tour of Beaumanor Hall in Leicestershire, the entire experience ruined by one self-appointed authority and one upstart with attitude determined to bring him down. The tension in the tour party had grown intolerable, and, after suffering an hour of endless interruptions and contradictions, Clarissa managed to break off on her own. She planned on doing the same this time if only to rid herself of the insufferable Fred Spice.

There were whispered side conversations as the group fell into disarray. Richard appeared to have given up with his voice recorder and Simon inched further from the huddle.

'In 1937,' Francois said, raising his voice almost to a shout, 'Winter signed a lease for the whole of the Jandía peninsula from the Conde de Santa Coloma, based in Lanzarote. He then left for Germany to seek funding. In 1939, Jandía was declared a military zone and the local people were barred entry. It appears Franco and Hitler had come to an agreement.'

'If this is true, then it compromises Spain's status in the war,' Helen said, stealing the conversation but then not taking it any further.

Seeing the others considering her remark and no doubt realising he hadn't a hope with this lot, Francois left them to it and went over to Simon who seemed determined to head off. The two men talked in low whispers.

Meanwhile, Vera was nodding slowly. 'They were neutral, weren't they? Spain, I mean.'

'Supposed to be,' said Fred. 'But Spain supplied Hitler with volunteer soldiers and minerals. And here in the Canary Islands, Franco gave Hitler logistical support.'

'Payback for Guernica,' said Helen.

'You could put it like that. One of the biggest threats to Britain in the early part of the war were the U-boats. They sunk an awful lot of ships.'

'What's this got to do with Spain?' asked Margaret.

'Spanish ports were refuelling the U-boats.'

'It's rumoured Hitler and Eva Braun escaped here in a U-boat and then fled to Argentina,' Carol said. 'Just thought I'd throw that in.'

Helen said, 'You're right. Alberto Vazquez-Figueroa wrote about it in his book *Fuerteventura*. He painted the villa as a kind of Nazi pleasure palace.'

'This house was never meant for pleasure,' Vera said grimly.

'True,' Carol said with a backward glance at her friend.

Carol's gaze then met Clarissa's and she quickly turned away without so much as a smile. Flashing into Clarissa's mind was the sudden observation that all through lunch, while she had been happy not to engage with the others, none of them had bothered to engage with her, least of all Carol and Vera, two women whom she might have thought would have made a point of including her.

The history lesson continued, each of the contenders for most knowledgeable person in the room vying for supremacy.

'The locals were kept out of Jandía until the 1950s,' Helen said. 'That was when Franco removed the fence that spanned the sand dunes near Costa Calma.'

'The Germans even had their own airstrip,' Steve said. 'Isn't that right?'

'Didn't we drive by an airstrip on the road between the two lighthouses?' chimed Dave.

'We did. But Winter had an airstrip down towards Cofete. You can see the lines of stones on Google Maps.'

Realising he now had a chance to steal the audience, Fred puffed himself up to his full height, which wasn't much, and, in an authoritative voice, said, 'What you have to remember is there are many, many lies. Winter even had his own sons either believing or telling lies. One has it the airstrip was needed in case his wife required urgent medical care, after having a difficult childbirth, apparently.'

'As if,' said Steve.

'That's what I thought.'

'I think we can safely say Winter had strong Nazi connections and was able to use those to gain investment to build the harbour in Morro Jable,' said Helen. 'He had a plan to electrify the whole island and build a cement factory.'

'What a guy.'

Helen shot Steve a cool look.

'I'm sure he was popular among the locals. Some of them, anyway.'

'There were rumours Winter was supplying fuel to the U-boats,' he said in response, keen to press home his U-boat theory.

'As Helen says, his economic plans for the island gained German subsidies, that much is proven,' said Fred, seizing dominance once more. 'As is the fact that U-boats were present in the Canaries. U-boats docked in Las Palmas six times in about two months in 1941, which triggered an official complaint by the British consul. And it is understood local island ports were used by tanker ships that would then meet up with U-boats out at sea.'

'How do you know so much?' said Steve.

'Has he swallowed an encyclopaedia or something?' Vera said mockingly.

'He's seen the documentary,' Carol muttered.

'I heard that,' said Margaret.

'I don't mean to be offensive, but your husband doesn't know when to shut up.'

'I beg your pardon.'

Margaret clenched her fists. Clarissa stood poised to intervene when Francois came over and said, 'There's no doubt in my mind Gustav Winter was supplying provisions to U-boats. Señor Fumero even found an old U-boat battery here.'

'He did?' Steve said with keen interest.

'I heard they built a couple of tunnels under the mountains,' said Dave.

'They were said to have extended the original lava tunnels, yes,' Steve said.

'Rubbish,' said Vera.

'Not rubbish.'

'Big enough for a U-boat? Come on.'

'Of course, they were big enough for a U-boat. There are still two submarines stuck in those tubes.'

'Stuck?'

'Didn't some team investigate that back in the '70s?'

'Yeah, until their boat exploded.'

'I wonder why that happened, hey,' Dave said sarcastically.

'Someone didn't want the truth to come out, obviously.'

'Lads,' said Fred, 'I'm sorry to say that local historians mostly conclude that Cofete's beach would have been unsuitable for naval use due to its shallow approach, but they also point out that the natural harbour of Ajuy, about twenty miles up the coast, could possibly have been used by submarines or other large craft.'

'Thanks for that, Fred.'

'Yeah, cheers, mate.'

Carol and Vera again exchanged glances. Helen looked like she needed a chair. Francois used that moment to take the party back out to the courtyard and on through an arched entrance immediately to the left of the living-room door, where a flight of brick and concrete stairs hugging the wall led up to the attic and the tower's first floor. There was no banister and no hand rail attached to the wall, and the stair treads lacked depth and looked precarious. Clarissa wasn't sure they were safe.

'Careful on the stairs,' Francois said in a perfunctory tone, leading the way.

The lads were right on his tail, taking the stairs in twos, followed by Simon. Fred and Margaret went next. Helen accepted Richard's ushering gesture. He climbed the stairs behind her.

'Isn't it funny how the boys go bonkers over the U-boat conspiracy theory,' Vera said to Carol as they waited their turn.

'I'd rather go bonkers in the bunkers, to be honest.'

Clarissa supressed a laugh. Neither woman looked around. She had a strong sense she was being pointedly ignored. Why? She'd done nothing whatsoever to upset them. Perhaps they found her silence disconcerting. Who felt that? Only those with something to hide or those who felt judged. It would have to be the latter. Once long ago a friend had told her she was apt to come across as authoritative and judgemental especially when she didn't speak.

Something about her watchful eyes. She'd looked in the mirror afterwards for proof and decided that yes, her eyes, in fact her facial features altogether did convey those qualities. It was only by reaching out and conversing that others were put at ease in her company.

She'd made up her mind to go last up the stairs. Her hip was playing up and she didn't want anyone to notice her struggle. She gave the two women a good head start as she braced herself for the ascent.

As anticipated, the treads were uneven and each footfall needed to be chosen with care, at least, for someone a touch incapacitated. She reminded herself to ask if anyone had any painkillers.

She made it to the top without mishap and followed a narrow landing that hugged the attic wall, a landing, like the stairs, minus a banister. At the end, on the left, was the entrance to the tower. The landing continued round, providing access to the space under the eaves of the west wing. She stood with her back to the wall and looked around. The attic room was bare, the floorboards dusty. To the west a pair of small dormer windows looked out over the roof. They were set too far back from the edge to see much below and were more for looking out at the coastline. Facing the courtyard were two large windows and a door opening out onto a small balcony cut into the roofline. The suite had the makings of a living area for whoever was charged with being the tower lookout.

She joined the others, first entering a vestibule and then on to the front of the tower where pairs of square windows were arranged around the wall facing westward. Access was denied to the tower's upper level, visible through a circular hole in the ceiling and featuring the arched windows Clarissa had seen on the walk up to the house. Arched windows, where she had also glimpsed a figure. Confirmation, then, that she had borne witness to an apparition. A living human would have needed a ladder.

Francois stood beside an old fuse box mounted on the wall and waited for the group to settle. (The fuse box was enormous.) This time, he put his fingers in his mouth and let out a shrill whistle. The group fell silent in an instant. He took a breath and rattled off a little speech, not pausing to allow space for interruptions. Could the tower have been used for communications, alerting counterparts in Las Palmas or even the U-boats themselves of passing British ships? Had it been used as a beacon to send messages out to sea? The fuse box alone suggested the tower was used for much more than would be required for a farmhouse.

Clarissa hung back as the others followed Francois through the vestibule and down the stairs in single file.

As the vestibule emptied, she found herself facing a door leading into the northern section of the farmhouse roof. She turned the handle. Finding the door unlocked, she pushed it open and went in.

Beneath the eaves was an arrangement similar to that of the west-wing attic, although less well-lit with only a windowed door beside a small window in the near corner of the room leading out to a balcony overlooking the courtyard, and without the dormer windows looking out over the roof on the other side.

Clarissa was about to join the others when she noticed at the far end of the balcony a narrow door, no more than a metre high. She went out for a closer inspection. It was a remarkably small door, and she wasn't sure she could fit through it, but she tried the handle and found it open as well. From what she could see it was a storeroom. There was her escape from the others if she needed one.

She caught up with the group as they were making their way down to the basement via a narrow set of stairs tucked behind those leading up to the tower. Many were using their phone torches. These stairs were in good repair and although there was no handrail, it was possible to use the wall to either side for balance which Clarissa found useful when the stairs turned a corner, twice.

Immediately ahead of the base of the stairs was a doorway leading into a long and narrow room. The moment her feet touched the tiled floor, misgivings sparked through her, and she felt suddenly, preternaturally cold. With the group filling the space, she didn't have an opportunity to look around to ascertain the cause or the source. The sharp light of multiple phones shining this way and that added a surreal quality to the atmosphere. Her psychic sensitivity was further dampened by the friction in the group, friction which looked set to worsen as an altercation broke out amongst those standing closest to Francois. Clarissa shifted location the better to see and hear the fracas.

'There's no hard evidence that anything you people are saying is true,' said Simon dismissively.

'Then tell me why anyone would build a tower like that?' snapped Vera, shining her phone's light into his face.

'More's the point, why would anyone build a kitchen that looks like an autopsy room?' Steve said in an elevated voice, squinting and shielding his eyes. 'Jeez, must you?'

The smile on Vera's face was not pleasant. Finding the light show a bit much, Clarissa pinned her gaze to the floor. Autopsy room? That would account for her reaction on entry. She wished the others would leave so she could assess the claim for herself.

Steve's remark triggered a heated debate. Clarissa knew there were many stories about Villa Winter, but one common theme was that it functioned as a safe house for the Nazis. Steve insisted that at the end of the war, a number of Nazi leaders, including Adolf Hitler, arrived on the island and plastic surgery was undertaken to change their identities before they escaped to South America, Argentina being the favoured destination since Peron was a friend and ally of Hitler.

'As if cosmetic surgery took place here. It's hardly equipped,' Carol said.

'It was a long time ago. Things were different then,' said Steve, who seemed prepared to believe any conspiracy theory that came his way.

'Nah. This place looks more like an abattoir than an operating room,' said Fred.

Clarissa thought he had a point.

Steve was having none of it. His face filled with fury. This time it was his turn to use his phone's light like a weapon, spotlighting Fred, Vera and Carol in turn.

'And I'm telling you Hitler escaped and is living the high life with his cronies,' he said.

Carol laughed loudly. 'So, you're saying Hitler is still alive?'

'Could be.'

'Don't be ridiculous. He'd be a hundred and thirty-one by now.'

Jeering laughter rippled around the room. Steve looked ready to explode. 'Wer sind diese Idioten?'

Carol shot him a look cold as ice and whispered something inaudible to Vera. Clarissa wondered if either of them had understood what he'd said. Who were these idiots? She admitted to herself she was inclined to agree, although she would have included him in the sentiment.

'Has anyone searched for his grave in Argentina?' Dave said.

Fred, Vera and Helen all started talking at once. Any continuation of the guided tour was fast becoming hopeless. Francois, who'd been listening without interest, glanced at his watch, then stood taller with eyebrows raised in a half-hearted effort to gain control of the group. He gave up and said instead, 'You are now free to wander around by yourselves. You can stay down here and explore the basement rooms and you can wander around the open rooms of the house. Some rooms you cannot enter. They will be obvious. Meet me in the courtyard in exactly one hour.'

He forced his way through the group and disappeared up the stairs. Simon followed.

Vera and Carol left the kitchen and headed down a long dark passage with Helen taking up the rear. Clarissa felt no compunction to follow suit. The bunker reminded her too much of Trevor stuck in prison in Lanzarote.

The lads congregated in the kitchen with Fred and Margaret, leaving Richard at a loose end.

Clarissa caught his eye and mouthed, 'Come with me.'

He hesitated, glanced back at Fred, and then took a step in Clarissa's direction. She led him back up to the tower. She was prepared to brave the steps one more time if it meant some peace and quiet. Besides, there was a certain entity worth investigating, if the group hadn't seen him off.

'I thought you needed rescuing,' she said as they took in the panoramic coastline out of the westernmost windows, impressive, even in the dust haze.

'Thank you.' He sounded genuinely relieved.

They were silent for a while. She went to the centre of the tower and looked up at the arched windows above. Then she turned her gaze inwards, feeling the room. Nothing. No ghost. Hardly surprising. The energy of the room was still disturbed by the others. She joined Richard whose eyes hadn't left the view. She found him an amusing sight, standing there with his fanny pack pressed against the wall and his bulging backpack on his back.

'They're an astonishing bunch,' she said reflectively, hoping to strike up a conversation. 'All that bickering.'

'It's Fred. He's a pest.'

'He sure is,' she said. 'But the others are not any better.'

There was a long moment of silence. They were both still gazing at the ocean when she said, 'I couldn't help overhearing you're a writer.'

'A novelist,' he said, talking to the window pane. 'Although these days it does feel rather in the past tense.'

His frankness was a little unsettling. He sounded despondent. She pulled back from the window to observe him. He didn't appear to register her gaze.

'I'm sorry to hear things are not going well for you,' she said gently. 'Lost your inspiration?'

No doubt realising the inappropriateness of his divulgence to a stranger, he became vague. 'Sales. The market. I'm surviving on my backlist.'

'Let's hope today provides you with a bestseller, then,' she said, endeavouring to sound upbeat. She made to walk away and, seeing he showed no sign of doing the same, she tapped him on the arm. 'Come and look at this.'

She led him through to the attic space in the north wing and out onto the balcony where she went over to the little door.

'I spotted this earlier. It's why I brought you up here.'

'Is it open?' he said as she crouched down and turned the handle. She had to kneel and duck her head to enter.

He followed, crouching down on his knees and crawling

as he eased his way through the door with his backpack on his back.

'I feel like Alice.'

'Where's the Cheshire cat.'

He laughed. She laughed with him, thankful he had at last displayed a sense of humour.

She sat down and brushed the grit off her hands. The room smelled of old dust. No natural light entered the space. She pulled her phone out of her trouser pocket and switched on the torch.

The eaves tapered down to the floor uninterrupted. Unlike the rest of the attic space, the floor was concrete. In the far corner of the room was another door. They went over and discovered it was a bathroom.

'What is this place?' Richard said, standing stooped at the apex of the ceiling and looking around.

'Somewhere for small people, I would say. Given the height of the door.'

'Children?'

'Of a young age.'

It was a disturbing thought.

'It's a weird set up,' he said.

'My thoughts exactly.'

'This was for Winter's family?'

'I doubt any mother would be happy having her children ferreted all the way up here. An attic play space, maybe, but why the concrete floor? It makes no sense, unless...'

'Unless you were wanting to hide those children.'

A look of strange fascination appeared in Richard's face. Clarissa shivered. Mengele flashed into her mind. Surely not. Why come all the way out here when he had enough to deal with back in Europe? Unless the Nazis had another heinous experiment going on, something so top secret it needed to occur far away from the centre of operations. No. Clarissa dismissed the idea straight away, not willing to give credence to conspiracy theories, even as her skin prickled and she felt a compulsion to run out of the attic and get right away from Villa Winter.

Instead, she suggested they decamp to the other room. At least it had a window. Richard didn't hesitate, although he had the grace to let her exit through the tiny doorway first. Once there, he eased his backpack off his shoulders and set it down on the floor with a sigh of relief. The weight was no doubt hurting his shoulders. She wondered why he hadn't left it on the bus.

They went and stood together by the balcony window, observing what they could see of the courtyard, which wasn't much. Clarissa thought it likely no one was down in the bunker rooms anymore and toyed with the idea of heading down there when she heard voices echoing in the stairwell.

'Sounds like Fred,' Richard said grimly.

'You really don't like him, do you.'

'Do you honestly believe there is anything much to like?'

'If you want to avoid him, you'd better close it,' she said, pointing at the door to the tower.

He followed her suggestion.

'There's a key in the lock,' he said.

'Then use it. Keep the others out.'

A little thrill went through her as he turned the key. It was one of those moments from childhood, hide and seek in a big old house, every girl and boy's favourite spooky game.

They waited for a while in silence, taking in the bare surroundings. There was nowhere to sit and Clarissa's hip dearly wanted a chair. The voices in the stairwell soon faded, but then others grew louder and before long they heard Carol's enthusiastic cackle and Vera's throaty laugh. The door handle turned and the door shuddered in its frame.

'I could have sworn this door was open earlier.'

'That bloody Francois. I bet he's been up here and locked it.'

'What would he do that for?'

There was a brief pause. Then, 'Come on, let's get back downstairs.'

Their voices faded. Clarissa realised she'd been holding her breath and exhaled.

'Not exactly the Ritz,' Richard whispered, looking around.

'Not exactly guest accommodation either. I imagine this was another bedroom or office and the other attic space served as the sitting room and adult bedroom. Whoever was charged with operations in the tower remained separate from the rest of the house.'

'They could come and go through the courtyard. That is the main access.'

'Officially, yes, I'm sure they did. But unofficially, no. Didn't you see?'

'See what?'

'There's access to the bunkers in the southern wall below the terrace. I spotted an entrance on the walk up from the minibus. There could have been all sorts of activity going on down there and up here unbeknownst to the occupants of the house.'

Richard thought about what she'd said. 'The design puts a different complexion on this place. It has a definite subversive feel.'

'You've noticed. Mind you, the way this place has been

set up, with the balconies overlooking the courtyard, suggests a degree of comradeship.'

'You mean, Gustav Winter would have been complicit in all the goings on here.'

'I don't doubt it. But his family might have been shielded. From down in the courtyard, you can't see who might be out on either balcony unless they stood right at the edge. If they kept the door to the stairwell closed, even locked, then it would be as though there were two separate dwellings.'

'The bunkers with direct access to the tower and the attics. And the main house and courtyard. I have to say that feels plain creepy.'

Their conversation was interrupted by a commotion downstairs. There were muffled shouts and the sound of heavy footsteps crunching on gravel, then more shouts. All went quiet for a short while and then they heard the revving of an engine in the distance. Richard went out onto the balcony and leaned over the solid concrete balustrade. There were more shouts and footsteps.

Clarissa went out and stood beside him. She wasn't game enough to bend over the edge of the walled balcony.

'What's happening?'

'No idea. Hard to see what's going on under here,' he said, pointing at the balcony floor.

'Except that Francois seems to be bringing the minibus up to the house.'

They waited. The voices faded. Richard turned to Clarissa, his face filled with concern.

'There must have been an accident.'

He was right. Or a medical emergency.

'I think it's Helen.'

'How do you know?'

The Ghost of Villa Winter

'Never mind.'

She caught the sound of Francois yelling in a room down below. Then Fred yelling too.

'Where is everyone!'

'Come on!'

Their voices faded again. Clarissa glimpsed the lads running across the courtyard and disappearing through the door at the rear.

'We'd better get down there. I think they're leaving.'

They made for the door. Richard got there first. He turned the key and then the handle. Nothing happened. He turned the key and tried the handle again and pulled hard. Nothing. He pulled again, jiggled the key in the lock, but the door wouldn't budge.

'Try re-inserting the key.'

'I have.'

'Try again.'

He did. Again, the door refused to unlock.

'Let me try,' she said, nudging her way past him and reaching for the key.

Richard stood aside, stooped, his head pressed against the ceiling. They both paused, listening. The voices below were barely audible. There was the clunk of a door closing. Then they heard the revving engine of the minibus. Richard rushed back to the window. Clarissa waited, clutching the key.

'Well?'

'The bus is leaving,' he said hopelessly. He turned and picked up his backpack, slinging it over one shoulder like a schoolboy doomed to walk the long way to school and face detention for being late. 'We're trapped.'

As he said that, Clarissa inserted the key and turned it once. She heard a click and the door opened.

'Unbelievable,' she said, pocketing the key.

'What is it?'

Four beeps of a horn interrupted her reply.

'Hurry. If we run, we might attract their attention before they disappear.'

Richard bolted down the tower stairs as fast as he dared. Clarissa took her time, not risking her hip. Once she reached ground level she hurried, careful not to stumble as she raced to the back of the house. She'd made it to the courtyard's rear entrance as Richard cornered the lane. He started waving frantically. By the time she had joined him at the top of the drive, the minibus was cornering the bend at the bottom of the slope and was gone.

Richard dropped his red backpack at his feet.

'What on earth are we to do now?'

It was a good question. The sky had all but disappeared in the thick haze of dust. Visibility was reduced to about a hundred metres. She didn't fancy trudging back to Cofete, a distance of about two kilometres. Although there really was no choice. She was about to tell Richard they'd better leave when he covered his mouth with his hand and coughed. He coughed again and again and then he started wheezing and reaching for his throat, alarm fixed in his gaze.

5

A LONELY NIGHT

SHE HURRIED HIM BACK INSIDE THE HOUSE, CHOOSING THE first open door she could find and closing it behind them. Richard's breath was rasping. She steered him to a chair and guided him down and told him to breathe through his hands. She cast her eye around the room, spied an old newspaper by the fireplace and went and fetched a couple of internal pages. Then she made a makeshift bag and told Richard to breathe through the paper.

'Try to slow your breathing. That's it. Now don't pant. Take bigger breaths. That's the way.'

She watched on, placing a comforting hand on his back. Slowly, his breath returned to normal.

When he coughed again, she said, 'Try to repress it.'

She rummaged through her canvas bag and extracted a water bottle.

'Take a few sips.'

When he handed back the bottle, calm had returned to his face and she breathed an inward sigh of relief. The last thing she wanted was to find herself alone in Villa Winter with a corpse.

She left Richard's side and took a wander. They were in the large living room where Francois had delivered part of his tour. Two armchairs were angled away from the fireplace which was deep and constructed of stone. On the other side of the entrance door, a large wooden table took up the centre of the room with a single chair at each end. Richard was seated on one of them. Dinner, indeed the whole arrangement of the room suggested it was only ever meant for two. She wondered what had happened to the other chairs. A jumble of memorabilia – framed photos, a pair of animal skins, cloth bags, an array of tools, whatever had been left at Villa Winter – hung on display on all of the walls. The room opened onto another and then, to the right, another. Examining the windows of the furthest room, she saw she was at the southwest corner of the house. There were trunks, large and small, two dressers with a student desk sandwiched between, a workbench, an old wooden stepladder, and an animal cage, large enough for a big dog. It looked as though every stick of salvageable furniture had been arranged in this space. The result was both unappealing and intriguing.

She re-joined Richard who had not moved from his seat.

'Are you asthmatic?' she said.

'I didn't think I was,' he said, at last getting up, only to sit down again, this time in one of the armchairs.

'No inhaler then.'

She wondered if the day could get any worse. A dash to Cofete was off the agenda until the dust storm eased, which meant they could be stuck in Villa Winter for the rest of the weekend. She dearly hoped not. She had an appointment to see Trevor in prison Monday morning. He received no other visitors and she knew his mental stability hinged on her taking the trouble to see him as often as she could. Last time they spoke he had even suggested she move to the island. It would be good for her health, he'd said. No, it would be good for *his* health. She didn't object to his desperate manipulations. No one had ever needed her quite like he did. Not even Claire.

She reached in her trouser pocket and checked her phone. She told Richard to do the same. They exchanged expectant glances. No reception.

'I've got almost a full battery. You?'

'About the same.'

'Well, that's something. What's in that backpack of yours?' It was leaning against a table leg.

'Provisions,' he said. 'I didn't want to get caught short.'

'May I?'

She hefted the backpack onto the table and unzipped the compartments. Richard watched as she extracted the contents and arranged them on the table. She left his toiletries bag and made a point of only removing the foodstuff and his giant water bottle. Then she fished out her own supplies, along with the lightweight jacket she had brought along, just in case. It was unlined with three-quarter length sleeves and there was little warmth in it, but she put it on. There was already a bit of a nip in the air.

Between them they had two large blocks of chocolate and a family pack of jelly babies, two rounds of cheese and salami sandwiches, four apples, a large packet of potato crisps – his – and another of peanuts – hers – two protein bars, a litre carton of fruit juice and about two litres of water. If they were careful, they would get by until Sunday morning. Sunday evening at a pinch. And if by then the dust showed signs of clearing, they'd make a dash for it. Richard could always wrap something around his face. Or she supposed she could always leave him here and fetch help.

She considered doing just that when a muscle in her hip that had been poised to spasm all day finally followed through on its threat. The pain was deep and clenching. She winced. There was no way she was about to trudge back to Cofete in her condition, and she rued not asking Francois if he carried a First Aid kit.

She was about to leave the foodstuffs on the table and join Richard by the fireplace but thought better of it. The villa was unlocked. There was no telling who might turn up here. She looked around for a good place to leave a stash and chose the deeper of the hessian baskets hanging up beside the door they'd entered. She shoved in her canvas bag and Richard's backpack and then covered the stash with the sheets of newspaper Richard had used to breathe through. Not wanting to leave any evidence of their presence, she tidied the rest of the newspaper and positioned it in its original spot beside the fire. Richard remained where he was watching her movements with unmasked fascination. She eyed him critically for a moment, trying to decide if he was an asset or a liability.

'I suppose we might as well explore this place while it's still light,' she said, thinking she needed to keep mobile. 'See what we can find.'

He offered no response.

'I fancy heading down to the bunkers.'

'I was planning on staying up here.'

Was he chicken?

'Suit yourself.'

He hesitated.

'I think we should stick together though, don't you?' he said.

Yep, chicken.

'What for?'

'In case of another sticky lock?'

Neither of them laughed. Besides, he had a point.

He heaved himself out of the armchair. She eyed him with concern.

'You ready for this?'

'I expect so.'

'Try not to inhale too much dusty air.'

They headed out to the courtyard. Through the archway on the left were the tower stairs and the stairs down to the bunker. 'Come on.' Clarissa led the way, using her phone torch as she approached the narrow and boxed-in stairs.

At their base, running in the opposite direction to the kitchen, was an arched-roofed passage spanning the length of the house. A branch in the passage nearby led to a high square window. On the left-hand side of that branch a door led to a windowless room containing an iron bedframe. No Mattress. Pity. Although Clarissa couldn't imagine getting a wink of sleep down here. It was cold and had an air of sterility that felt ominous. Nothing good happened in a place like this.

They found four more windowless rooms – two with steel-framed bunk beds – on the left side of the main passage, and then a windowed bathroom. The passage itself ended in a door leading outside. That was the door Clarissa had seen on her way up to the house. She was certain of it.

A second branch of the passage, identical to the first, led to another high square window. Clarissa pictured the front of the outside of the house, the stonework walls supporting the terrace, and the two windows positioned in the buttresses at each end. Another passage, accessed via the second branch, ran parallel to the main passage and ended abruptly. It was narrow and apparently purposeless. It wasn't until Richard reached halfway down its length and extended his arms which touched the passage's sides that she pictured the manacles. What other reason could there be for such a space? The bunker in its entirety could have had only three purposes – to hide people, to torture people and to conduct medical experiments on people. Who? She doubted the truth would ever be known.

'Let's get out of here,' she said, lighting Richard's path as he exited the strange passage.

She led the way back to the stairs. Before returning to the living room, she went to inspect the kitchen. Although the room lacked the feel of a kitchen. There was nothing in it save for a sink unit, an oven that appeared on closer inspection to be an incinerator and, tucked in a corner, a second sink built into one end of a long and wide draining area. There was a window above the sink and another, more a ventilation slit positioned high in the wall on the other side of the room. Adding to the clinical austerity, the whole of the kitchen was tiled in white up to shoulder height. There was a drainage hole centred in the floor. The room had the feel of a mortuary and Clarissa could not imagine it was used as the main kitchen, which, she decided, would be found in one of the rooms upstairs. Here was a place for goodness knew what.

The room could of course be accessed from the tower, the bunkers, and outside.

Convenient.

She caught Richard's gaze. He shook his head in disbelief. Neither spoke. They headed back up the stairs. As she turned the final corner, Clarissa stopped in her tracks. Those low-ceilinged rooms in the attic also had direct access to that strange kitchen. No one in the main house would have known or needed to have known anything about the comings and goings of any children corralled up there. Chil-

The Ghost of Villa Winter

dren of parents sleeping in the bunkers? Or? It did not bear thinking about. But her mind kept returning to the possibility.

'What is it?' Richard whispered, his tone laced with fear.

'I'm not sure I want to spend any more time down there,' she said, her voice echoing around the stairwell walls.

'Me neither.'

Back in the living room, Richard strolled around, taking an interest in the artefacts. There was plenty to look at. He seemed to relax a little and his breathing was fine. She joined him, opening all the drawers and cupboard doors they passed.

'What are you looking for?'

'Nothing.'

Which was precisely what she found.

After surveying just about everything in the room, Richard sat down on the lid of a long wooden chest situated just inside the entrance to the second of the rooms. The chest looked as though it had been built in as an original feature. The lid creaked and he leaped to his feet like a startled cat.

To mask his reaction, he went to the far side of the main room and hovered near the fireplace. Curiosity overrode the discomfort in her hip, and Clarissa knelt down beside the box and tried to lift the lid a fraction. It was free at that end but appeared stuck at the other.

'Give me a hand, would you, Richard.'

'Shouldn't you leave it be?'

'Aren't you curious?'

'Not really.'

He came over anyway and made a half-hearted attempt to prise open his end.

'It won't budge.'

'Try harder.'

'I think not. We really should leave it as it is.'

'There might be a blanket inside, something we can use.'

Richard looked thoughtful for a moment.

'Very well.'

He scanned the walls for a useful tool and came back with a hammer. He used the craw. A long slow squeak and a nail came free. And another. Five more nails and they slid the lid off the chest.

A waft of fishy air hit her first. Then the realisation that what they stared down at was not the pile of neatly folded blankets she'd anticipated, but rather one large, olive-green blanket wrapping a bulk of something and secured with rope in two places. Clarissa knew instantly what they were staring at.

'Richard, you better look away.'

'Why?'

She wasn't sure she had ever heard a stupider question in her life.

She used the handle end of the hammer Richard had left on the floor and lifted her end of the blanket a little and folded it back. The hair was enough to confirm her suspicions, but she leaned down, pushed the blanket back further until the forehead was revealed, then the eyebrows and the nose, not satisfied until she had revealed the full face.

She looked up at Richard who met her gaze with a weak, 'Is it?'

'Richard, I'm afraid we have a body.'

He inched closer, peering down tentatively, eager to see and plainly repulsed all at once.

'Who is it?' he said.

What a question!

The Ghost of Villa Winter

She decided to humour him.

'No idea. Female, that seems clear.'

'I can see that. For heaven's sake close the eyes on the thing. I can't stand to look at her gazing at us like that.'

'Then look away.'

'Just do it, please.'

He was sounding hysterical. Clarissa obliged, even though she didn't like interfering with the evidence.

'What do we do now?' he said.

She felt her impatience rise.

'I thought a crime writer would know all about this.'

'Writing crime is not the same.' He sounded defensive. Then he said, 'We should contact the police.'

Which might have been a sensible response in another context. She was beginning to wonder if he had two brain cells to rub together.

'And how are we to do that, Richard?' she snapped.

He didn't answer.

In that moment, she decided she preferred to look at the corpse.

She took in the face which was young and pretty. She touched the skin of a cheek with a fingertip. As expected, warm. She reached in and pulled the blanket further back. Then, she made to turn the head.

'What on earth are you doing?' he shrieked. 'Leave the body alone!'

'For heaven's sake, Richard. Calm down. Many moons ago I was a mortuary attendant. Dead bodies don't faze me.'

The head wouldn't turn.

'Rigor mortis,' she said as she heaved herself to her feet. 'Which means the body has been dead between two and twelve hours.'

'How long have we been here?'

'I was about to ask the same.'

Richard examined his watch. She waited.

'A bit over two hours, I believe.'

'You believe? Not good enough. Let's think this through. What time did we leave the restaurant?'

'We arrived at midday.'

'Yes, but when did we leave?'

'One-thirty, wasn't it?'

'I'm asking you.'

'Call it one-thirty.'

'I'm not prepared to call it anything. What time is it now?'

'Four-thirty.'

'We had that walk up to the house which took, what, ten minutes. And then the courtyard talk. Another ten. Then we went up to the tower for a bit, and down to the bunkers. Say, twenty minutes, tops. Francois gave up on being tour guide at that point. We'd only been up in the attic, what, five or ten minutes before we heard the commotion and the others left. After that you had your ordeal with the dust, which seemed to last an age but was probably only ten minutes. We assessed our supplies, explored the bunkers and then came back in here. Allowing time for hovering about and moving between the various spaces, I would say, Richard, that you are probably right.'

'You mean we did leave the restaurant at one-thirty?'

'No, we left at about two o'clock. We've been here two, possibly two and a half hours.'

'Why is all this so important?'

She eyed him grimly.

'Because, Richard, it is possible the murderer was on our bus.'

His jaw fell open.

The Ghost of Villa Winter

'Murderer?'

'You don't think someone stored that body in this chest for the fun of it?'

'Of course not. It's taking a while to sink in, that's all. I mean, who?'

'That, Richard, is what I aim to find out.'

She cast her mind back. If the murderer was on the bus, whoever had committed the crime had only half an hour to act. Was that why the lads took off up the hill so fast when they arrived at the villa? What about Simon? He had been in a hurry too and he was awfully listless throughout the tour. There was another window of opportunity when the tour party was at the restaurant. Only four passengers had absented themselves. The lads had disappeared, apparently eager to wander off when they decanted the bus in Cofete. Long enough to commit a murder? Simon had disappeared for a while at lunch, as had Richard. She dismissed Richard right away. He was no more capable of murder than she. And surely Simon scarcely had time to whip over to Villa Winter, commit the murder, bundle the corpse into the chest and whip back. She thought over the day, wishing she had taken note of the time that had lapsed between his departure and return. He'd been quite a while. She imagined it would have been about twenty minutes. If he'd had transport, he could have done it.

'Are you going to tell me what you're thinking?'

'Better replace the lid,' she said. 'Don't want flies getting in, or the cadaver will stink the place out in no time.'

'You mean, leave it in there?' He sounded incredulous.

'Where would you have us move it to?'

'It's just that so far, this is the only habitable space in the villa. I'd rather relocate it to one of the bunker rooms.'

'An awful lot of effort for no good reason.'

'You're happy spending the night in a room with a corpse, then?'

'Not really seeing an alternative, Richard.'

She took one last look at the body. There was evidence of bruising around the neck. Looked like fingerprints. She'd been choked to death. The base of the neck sported a fresh-looking tattoo consisting of a row of numbers that looked remarkably similar to the identification numbers the Nazis used on the Jews. Only, the location was wrong. Why put a number on your collarbone? She reached into her pocket and extracted her phone.

'Will you come away from that thing!'

She lined up a shot.

'Don't be afraid. A dead body cannot harm you.'

Click. Click. Click.

'It's macabre.'

She slipped the phone back in her pocket and lifted her end of the lid. Richard took his end and when the lid was back on the chest, she passed him the hammer. He knelt down and she watched as he hammered in the nails one by one. They were new nails, cheap she thought, and on the third blow of the hammer the last nail bent as it sank into the wood.

'Damn,' he said, making to prise out the nail.

'Leave it.'

'Won't it look obvious someone's opened the lid?'

'It will look a whole lot more obvious if you muck about trying to get the nail out. We'll have to risk it.'

They both got to their feet. She removed her jacket then reached out for the hammer.

'I'll go hang it back up,' Richard said.

'Give it to me, please.'

He obeyed, and she rubbed the handle with a corner of

her jacket then used the fabric to transport the hammer back to its spot on the wall. Job done, she put her jacket back on.

'It isn't macabre to take photos of a body, Richard,' she said, keen to make him see things her way. 'I'm puzzled, that's all. We have a mystery on our hands.'

'Does that make us amateur sleuths?' he said, not buying into her perspective one bit. 'I think not.'

She couldn't curb her irritation.

'Stop behaving so appalled, Richard. It isn't becoming, especially in a crime writer.'

'I am appalled, as it happens. Appalled that I followed you up to the attic. If I'd stayed with the others, I wouldn't be in this pickle.'

'*We* wouldn't be in this pickle. You were the one who locked us in.'

'Oh, so this is all my fault, is it?'

'Hardly. It's just happenstance. Time won't be undone and we just have to get on and make the best of things.'

A look of incredulity appeared in his face.

'How do you propose we do that?'

'We can start by exploring the rest of the house. There might be another room like this, a kitchen, a bedroom even, somewhere else to be.'

She set off, then turned.

'You'd better wrap something around your face if you're following me outside.'

She waited while he delved into his fanny pack and fished out a spare shirt – ultra thin and neatly folded – and attempted to wrap it around his face.

'Come here,' she said.

She folded the body of the shirt in half and half again, then took the sleeves, wrapping the fabric around his face, covering mouth and nose, and tying the sleeves off at the back.

'Don't let that slip down from your face.'

'Thank you,' he said, his voice muffled.

Outside was unpleasant. The dust managed to coat the inside of Clarissa's mouth in just a few breaths. They hurried down one side of the covered walkway, trying all the doors they passed. None were open. They crossed the courtyard and tried the doors on the other side. All were locked.

'That's it then,' Clarissa said, heading back to the living room.

Once the door was shut, Clarissa watched Richard removing the shirt from his face.

'We could use that as a door sausage, if you don't mind. Keep the dust out.'

'Um.' He paused, reluctant to relinquish his shirt. 'Unless there's something else to hand.'

They both went on a tour of the space, surveying the various items hanging on the walls. Richard came back with a yellow wet-weather jacket.

Clarissa took it and rolled it up into a long sausage. As she was shoving it hard against the door, Richard said, 'Wait.'

'What is it?'

'Why don't we leave this place and head down to Cofete?'

She faced him squarely, hands on hips.

'You think you can make it with your asthma?' she said doubtfully.

'I don't have asthma.'

'You have asthma.'

This time, he didn't argue. She eyed him for a moment. It wasn't a bad idea, except...

'What if you collapse halfway? That'll be the end of you and then I'd be stuck with two bodies instead of one.'

'Thanks for the encouragement.'

'It's up to you. But you better make up your mind fast because daylight is fading. Take into account we'll get as far as Cofete but no further, and if no one is hospitable, assuming there is somebody there, the chances are we'll have to walk back here. In the dark.'

'You don't make it sound like much of an option.'

'Don't think I haven't thought about it.' Her hip had thought about it too, with an emphatic veto. She wasn't about to tell him. It would weaken her case, make it appear she was the one being obstructive, give him the advantage. When it came to micro-managing, you needed to have the upper hand. And Richard, she knew already, was a liability. 'I suggest we camp here for the night and head to Cofete tomorrow,' she said in a tone indicating she would brook no dissent.

'There's nowhere to sleep.'

'These armchairs look comfortable enough.' She went over and sat down in one. The webbing wasn't firm and she found the seat rather low. The foam had seen better days.

Richard looked askance. 'For you, maybe. But I have a bad back.'

Clarissa raised her gaze to the ceiling. How was she ever to suffer this human companion who was little short of pathetic?

'What's wrong with your back, Richard?'

He was going to tell her anyway, that much she did know.

'I injured it lifting a wardrobe. Slipped a disc.'

'Sciatica, then.'

'It can be crippling.'

'You just need some lumbar support. And make sure you keep your legs at a suitable angle. You'll be fine.'

'So reassuring.'

'No need for the sarcasm. You need to sit up straight, all the way back in your chair so your back and buttocks are supported. Keep your feet flat on the floor. Don't cross your legs and don't lean to one side. It's also a good idea to keep your knees even with your hips, or even slightly elevated.' She paused and smiled. 'I get sciatica too.'

They were both aware that the room had begun to darken. Richard went over to the door and examined the wall to either side. Then he looked up at the chandelier centred in the ceiling before wandering around the entire space examining every bench, shelf and drawer. He came back to the table.

'No sign of any sort of light?'

'Not even a candle.'

'I didn't expect there would be.'

'And no moonlight either.'

'Not with the dust storm.'

There was a long pause as they both considered the night ahead.

'What are we to do?'

'Let's be practical. We need to eat and drink and we need some sort of toilet.'

'I'm not going up to the attic or down to the bunker rooms for that, I can assure you.'

Clarissa laughed. 'Me neither. Walking up and down stairs will be too dangerous in the dark. Fetch me something to use as a chamber pot. I daresay you can water the plants in the courtyard.'

Richard dutifully went and scanned the artefacts. He returned with a small metal pail.

The Ghost of Villa Winter

'This do?'

'Marvellous.'

'Where shall I put it?'

'By the door. I'll pop it outside later.'

He did as instructed and then paced about with his hands in his trouser pockets. He was the most anxious man she had come across in a long time. Anxious, unsure of himself and preoccupied. Far too self-conscious. The way he'd aligned his plate at lunch. That was obsessive-compulsive. And he certainly couldn't handle Fred Spice. She was sure he could be charming with pretty young ladies, patronising even, but around her he was awkward. It was clear, too, that he was broken. It wouldn't be easy being an author knowing as you aged that all of your success was behind you and your future held nothing but diminishment. Writing was one of those activities you could pursue until you dropped and many successful authors did just that. As irritating as he could be, she felt sorry for him. She wanted to mend him somehow, if that was at all possible, and perhaps this lonely night would provide for that.

Hunger interrupted her reverie.

'Richard, stop pacing for a second, will you. We need to decide how much of our food supply we're going to eat tonight, keeping in mind we have tomorrow to get through.'

He obeyed her command with surprising grace.

'The sandwiches will be better eaten tonight,' he said. 'And the fruit.'

'The fruit will keep.'

'We can save the juice for tomorrow.'

'Sounds sensible. A sandwich and an apple each, then. If you don't mind sharing.'

'Not at all. We'll have a picnic.'

She emitted a grim laugh as she hefted herself out of the

armchair and went over to the hessian basket. After removing the newspaper, Richard's backpack and her canvas bag, she reached in and extracted the two water bottles, handing them to Richard who came and stood beside her. He went and put them on the table. Groping about at the bottom of the basket, her fingers came into contact with paper, smooth, glossy paper, the sort that belonged to a magazine. She used her body as a shield as she tucked the magazine inside her jacket before grabbing the sandwiches and apples.

'Need help?'

'Here you go.'

Richard took the sandwich and apple she proffered and sat down at the head of the table. She managed to put the magazine in her canvas bag which she'd deposited by the front door before taking up the chair at the far end of the table. She was aware that behind her back lay a corpse.

They ate in companionable silence. As she chewed, she tried not to think about the meagre meal. As though reinforcing her thoughts, about halfway through his sandwich Richard said, 'I'm beginning to wish I'd had the goat.'

'Much more sustaining than the fish.'

As sandwiches went, hers wasn't bad, and she was pleased to discover Richard had been generous with the fillings. She savoured every mouthful. She did the same with the apple. By the time their apples were reduced to cores, it was almost completely dark. The silence closed in. If Clarissa paid attention, she could hear the white noise of the breakers in the distance.

'You seem preoccupied,' Richard said.

'I just keep thinking that a chest is not a good place to hide a body. At least, not for long. In a week that cadaver

The Ghost of Villa Winter

will stink to high heaven. There's no smell quite like rotting flesh.'

'Please. We've just eaten.'

'My apologies.'

It was not her most sincere remark and she should probably have apologised again. And meant it. In deference to his sensibilities, she refrained from telling him she knew the murderer would be back to dispose of the body properly. She would have to carry that burden alone. And it was a troubling one. Either the murderer was one of the tour party, in which case there was no telling when he, or they, would return, or the murderer was someone else, in which case it was possible the arrival of the tour bus disturbed the killer in the act and they had to hide the body fast. She pictured that shady-looking workman who had left Villa Winter in a hurry shortly after their arrival. Given the circumstances, he now seemed the most likely candidate for the crime.

She took a swig of water. Richard did the same. Neither of them drank much. Using what little light there was, she cleared away the paper packaging and apple cores, and brushed the crumbs off the table. Then, she pushed in her chair.

'Push your chair in, Richard. It's a trip hazard.'

It was unlikely either of them would collide with the chair since it was not in the path of the door, but she was not about to tell her nervous friend the real motive behind the tidy up.

She put his backpack and her canvas bag back in with the food supply. As she deposited the rubbish in a corner of the hessian basket, in her side vision she saw Richard shiver. In response, she pulled out the thin pullover she'd found buried at the bottom of his backpack and tossed it in his direction hoping he'd catch it. He did. She was about to return the backpack to the hessian bag when she felt movement inside. She reached in a hand and felt a smooth rectangular box.

Painkillers!

She helped herself to two tablets without asking, before pocketing the pack and returning the backpack to the hessian basket and replacing the newspaper. It was rude not to ask, she knew, but she was desperate. Besides, he could hardly refuse. If only she'd found them sooner, she would have had them both rescued by now. Then again, if she had, she would never have discovered that corpse. That, too, might have been a blessing, were it not for Clarissa's perspicacious and inquisitive nature. She'd always fancied herself a sleuth.

Once they were both seated in the armchairs, Richard said, 'What will we do, now? Just sit here?'

'I suggest we make ourselves comfortable.'

Richard fished about in his trouser pocket.

'And refrain from using our phones.'

He pulled out his hand and folded his arms across his chest in something resembling a huff.

There was a long period of silence. Richard coughed.

'Are you alright?'

'Just a tickle.'

Even so, it was better he didn't think about the dust that was no doubt coating his mouth as it was coating hers, despite the jacket serving as a draught excluder. Every time they'd opened the door they'd let in a little more, and the dust was so fine it hung, suspended in the air. Sleep would be a long time coming, if it came at all. She stared into the gloom, trying to make out the shapes of furniture at the other end of the room. The moon was waning crescent,

The Ghost of Villa Winter

which meant late rising and little light. She felt the temperature dropping. The only blanket they'd found was wrapped around the cadaver. For all they knew, the body could be resting on a pile of other blankets. What of that fishy smell? Blankets or no blankets, whatever was usually stored inside that chest had something to do with fishing. Wrapping herself in a blanket reeking of fish was not an appealing thought. As chilly as the night might get, she was not about to suggest re-opening the chest.

'What's your opinion of Villa Winter?' she asked, hoping to strike up an interesting conversation.

'I don't really have one.'

That was not the response she'd been hoping for. Surely, he could muster a little bit of positivity, or even mild engagement.

It was with supressed impatience that she said, 'Then why come on the tour?'

She observed him collecting his thoughts. His eyes met hers in the gloom and she sensed in his manner the quiet desperation, and the hesitation.

'Tell me,' she said encouragingly.

He let out a long sigh.

'My publisher Angela said I needed to dig deeper into the Canary Islands' recent history, find something meaty to build a story around. Some friends in Haría suggested this place. I should have known.'

'Whatever do you mean?'

'Celestino and Paula enjoy winding me up.'

'I can't imagine why,' she said, struggling to suppress a wry smile she hoped he couldn't see.

'Neither can I.'

'Well, they've done you a favour.'

'They have?'

'You have to be kidding me?'

'Right now, all I know is we are sitting here in the dark in this hell hole of a place with a dead body in a chest for company. I am not given to writing horror novels. I'm also not given to writing true crime.'

'Don't limit yourself. This story could be the making of you.'

'I doubt it. I was doing perfectly well back in Bunton. It was only when I started setting stories on these blasted islands that things started to go downhill.'

'I'm sorry to hear that. Then why not write more books set in Bunton?'

'Because the setting is hackneyed these days. Mostly thanks to *Midsomer Murders*.'

'Rubbish. The Brits never tire of the same settings. You just have to come up with a captivating storyline. A ripping plot.'

'Perhaps I don't have any more left in me.'

Were there no bounds to his self-pity? She could have given up, changed the subject, daydreamed even and left him sitting there, but she had the impression all roads in Richard's mind led back to this one bugbear, his writer's block. She decided to persist.

'I don't believe you have no more stories in you. Creativity is boundless. It's only inhibitions that thwart it. What's blocking you, Richard?'

'My wife,' he said flatly.

She wasn't prepared for that comment. Typical of the self-centred and the vain to apportion culpability on their nearest and dearest for their own shortcomings. It took her a few moments to form a response.

'Oh, come now. That does seem a trifle unfair.'

'You don't know her.'

'That's right. I don't. But you cannot blame someone else for your own failings.'

She wished she could properly see his face, read the thoughts behind his eyes, gauge his sincerity. She waited while he prepared his next remark.

'Trish has her virtues,' he said, 'but she's very demanding. And bossy. I bought the house in Haría to get some peace.'

'You could just as well have converted the garden shed.'

'She would have kept interrupting.'

'You just need to be firm with her.'

'I've tried.'

Clarissa considered his comment. She had known some intractable women in her time. Still, there was the bottom line.

'Do you love her?' she said softly.

'I don't know.'

It was an honest answer, yet once again, he was being non-committal, and, she decided, defeatist.

'You'd better find out, one way or the other,' she said. 'Ask your heart. And if you find you don't love her, why stay with her? Why not liberate yourself entirely instead of existing in this halfway state that is clearly not doing you any favours.'

'I'd never consider a divorce. She'd have a fit.'

'Let her. You need to develop a backbone, if you'll pardon my bluntness. Decide what it is that you want and put that first. If writing is your passion, be led by that. If she refuses to cooperate, and by the sound of things she will refuse, then you have no choice. You just need some courage, Richard.'

She didn't expect him to answer. She wondered if she'd come across too strong. The older she got, the more forthright she became, and besides, she'd lived alone all her adult life and saw nothing wrong with it. A spinster, not that anyone used the term these days. She liked to think of herself as a fiercely independent woman. Too fierce for most men. She was adamant in her conviction that marriage was not the be all and end all to life, and that women, and men, could be perfectly happy without a partner. Intimacy she'd always found overrated. She only had to think of her sister Ingrid for confirmation. Married beneath her, denied she was dissatisfied, and then one dreadful day she walked in front of an oncoming bus. A brutal and fatal wake-up call. Poor Ingrid. Poor Claire.

But not poor Richard, who was too sensitive by half.

Without conversation, the silence crowded in. She knew she'd offended her companion with her unbidden lecture, and that he needed time to assimilate her words, mull them over. Perhaps she had even been of some help. It was impossible to know. His breathing was shallow and he didn't seem to move a muscle, not that she could hear.

She listened, staring into the dark, her mind drifting. She was down in the bunkers then up in the attic. She couldn't help imagining macabre goings on in that weird kitchen. Gustav Winter had had a wife and young boys. What a place to raise a family. Inhospitable is an understatement. The villa was creepy in every respect and she couldn't imagine what it would have taken to live here. Then again, Winter was a military man, a general. And his wife might have been his greatest ally, happy to be cut off from society, happy to spend her days corralled in the courtyard of this monolithic house, protected from the fearsome wind, or out on the front terrace, taking in the magnificent coastline, the cliff. It was the late 1930s and into the 1940s. There would have been little on the island back then. No tourist resorts.

No shopping centre. Were the locals compliant? Were they happy to have a portion of their island annexed as German territory? Were there benefits? Roads? Electricity? At Villa Winter, there would have been servants. The Fumero family. They probably lived in the huts she'd seen out the back of the courtyard. Or they'd come up from Cofete. How would they have felt, working here? Not bored. They might have been rushed off their feet. The airstrip meant the comings and goings of military personnel. How often? The villa might have enjoyed plenty of visitors other than those destined for the bunker rooms. How many bedrooms did the farmhouse have? Four? And then the attic rooms. The Nazis were known for revelling in off-duty recreation. This place with its courtyard and large wide terrace out the front could have served as something of an exotic pleasure palace as Helen had mentioned over lunch, somewhere secluded to escape the German winters, the perfect retreat. With Gustav's wife the perfect hostess. Bizarre.

No matter what those people came here for, some of them ended up dead. She'd heard there was a cemetery here of unmarked German graves. Her mind shot to the incinerator. To ash. More dead and no evidence. Convenient.

Her grim musing was interrupted when Richard snorted and then proceeded to snore. It was a loud snore that echoed around the walls. She didn't have the heart to wake him, but she needed him to stop. With that racket going on she would never hear if anyone approached the villa. Grateful the painkillers had started to work, she heaved herself to her feet and fished her phone out of her pocket. Not wanting to wake him up right away, she took a few cautious steps in the direction of the table before switching on her phone torch. A harsh white beam illuminated the path ahead, casting strange shadows across the walls. As she headed past the chest, an image of the dead woman flashed into her mind, her face, that peculiar series of numbers on her collar bone. Clarissa hurried on by, keen to get to the window in the corner of the southwest wall. Once there, she killed the torch, checked the time – it was eight fifteen – and peered outside into the night. At least here, she could leave Richard to sleep while she stood guard.

The temperature was still falling. She pulled her jacket tighter around her chest and shivered. She was at risk of catching a chill. She marched on the spot, pumped her arms, tried to get the blood flowing. It wasn't enough exercise to get the warmth to her fingertips. She pumped her arms faster, then tried some lateral raises. She gave up after her fist thumped a cupboard door. Pain shot through her knuckles. A second later, as she nursed her hand, she heard a soft swish, the sound of something lightweight like paper shifting. She peered out the window to make sure no car was approaching and then switched on her phone torch, pointing it at the ground before directing it at the cupboard. She saw it wasn't a door she had thwacked, but a drawer. She pulled it open and found it empty. Then she pulled it right out and set it down on the floor and shone her torch into the cavity. At the back was the edge of what appeared to be a letter or document of some kind. She reached in and extracted the find. She only had time to replace the drawer before a tiny flash of light outside caught her eye and she killed her phone torch. She tucked the letter in her bra and pressed up against the window, peering out.

Moments later, there it was again, flashing in and out of sight. There was a long pause of nothing. Then, not one but two light beams illuminated the track from Cofete. A vehicle was heading this way.

6

UNWELCOME COMPANY

She turned and attempted to bolt through the room in the blackness, managing to stub her toe on the side of a trunk on her way by. She slowed and took a few more steps. Once she was reasonably confident she was out of the path of the window, she switched on her phone torch and ran over to the armchairs.

'Richard!'

He was still snoring. She shone the torch in his face and shook him awake.

'What on earth,' he said, covering his eyes.

'Get up and get moving.'

'Just hold on a minute,' he said, easing himself to his feet.

'We don't have time to muck about. We've got company. We have to get out of here.'

She went and kicked out of the way the jacket they were using as a door sausage, then thought better of it and picked it up. There wasn't time to put it back where it came from. There wasn't time to replace the metal pail Richard had fetched either. Still, it was unlikely to arouse suspicion unless whoever it was carried an inventory of every item in the room and its precise location. They were out the door in no time, Clarissa leading the way.

'What about our food?' Richard said.

'It'll have to stay there. Hurry up.'

The crunch of tyres on gravel grew ever closer. Light appeared at the entrance to the courtyard as they entered the tower room.

Clarissa raced over to the stairs.

'Where to?'

'The bunkers.'

'You have to be kidding.'

'We've no choice. If we climb the stairs to the tower there's every chance we'll be seen. Follow me. And be careful,' she hissed. 'Don't make a sound and don't, whatever you do, trip.'

They hurried down the stairs. Clarissa pressed her hands to the walls to steady her descent, daring to switch on her phone torch as they turned the first corner. At the bottom of the stairwell, Clarissa tapped Richard's arm and brought a finger to her lips. They both froze. Clarissa killed her torch and made an effort to slow her breathing. There were no footsteps crunching on the gravel beneath the loggia. Whoever it was moved about with stealth. Then a door closed with a thud. The visitor had gone into the living room.

Clarissa turned on her torch and headed down the passage. Richard was close on her heels. She gauged the distance, stopping where she thought the chest would be situated. Richard bumped into her.

'Sorry.'

She entered the third cell and pointed up at the ceiling.

The Ghost of Villa Winter

'Have you considered whoever this is could be trying to rescue us?' he said.

'I very much doubt that, Richard. They'd have called out, not sneaked around scarcely making a noise.'

She put on the yellow jacket and then killed her torch again.

'What did you do that for?' Richard hissed.

'Conserve battery.'

And the dark sharpened her hearing.

Although, there was little noise for a while. Then, a barely audible thwack. Had to be the lid hitting the floor. After a few moments of silence, she thought she detected the sound of something being dragged. It was faint, muffled, the concrete too thick to be sure. She thought it more likely she was imagining the sound. She waited.

After a short while she heard movement in the stairwell. A man grunted. She poked her head out the door. A distant light appeared at the end of the passage. There was a soft tapping sound, and another, and then another. She couldn't make out what the sound was and then she realised it was the heels of shoes. The killer was dragging the body downstairs.

That was unexpected and certainly idiotic, unless... And she pictured the incinerator.

Her blood curdled at the thought.

She bundled herself back in the cell and groped around for Richard. When her hand touched the fabric of his shirt she reached out and gripped his arm and stepped closer.

'We're going to have to find a way of getting up to the attic,' she whispered.

'Shouldn't we hide in one of these bunker rooms? The bathroom at the end?'

'And what if the killer decides to take a stroll while he's dealing with the body?'

'But we have to walk right by the kitchen to get to the stairs. How will we do that?'

'Pick our moment.'

She suspected the killer would need to head back upstairs. It would be quite an effort heaving a body and the necessary tools all at once. What would he need? A saw, at the very least. And fuel for the incinerator. She wasn't the praying type, but in that moment, she wished she was. Or that she had a closer connection with God. Now was the time for divine intervention, if ever there was one.

She felt her way back to the doorway and peered down the passage. A figure appeared, backlit. Must have left a torch in the kitchen. The shape didn't move for a few moments and Clarissa sensed the man staring down the passage. She was not that confident she couldn't be seen.

The figure turned and walked away and she heard footsteps going up the stairs. Her logic served her well. And she was grateful, too, for the now heavy-footedness of the killer, his shoes, the acoustics of the stairwell.

'Come on,' she hissed, switching on her phone light.

They raced out of the cell and down the passage. As they reached the foot of the stairs, she glimpsed the body, still wrapped in its blanket, on the slab. She wasn't about to stop and check it over. She didn't bother checking Richard was right behind her either.

She took the tower stairs with caution, pointing the light down at her feet and back towards Richard. She hurried, leaning into the wall, hoping neither of them would trip. At the second bend in the stairs, she killed the light. They continued on up, fumbling, gripping the wall, feeling their way.

The Ghost of Villa Winter

At the top of the stairs, she took a few tentative steps into the space and gazed through the archway at the courtyard. There was no light. She heard a car door close. She couldn't be sure they had enough time to make it up to the tower but it was a risk they had to take.

She couldn't use the torchlight. Adrenalin coursed through her veins as she groped her way to the foot of the stairs and took the first treads two at a time in a sudden burst of confidence. After that, she slowed her pace, feeling her way with her feet and leaning against the wall for a sense of balance.

The moment she reached the top, she skirted the narrow landing, noting a creaking floorboard or two as she laid down flat at the entrance to the tower room, peering down at the foot of the stairs. Richard made it onto the last tread when the light of the killer's torch lit up the courtyard, sending a faint beam of light into the stairwell. He stepped onto the landing and froze.

The light in the stairwell grew brighter.

She pulled in her head and sat up on her haunches, looking up at Richard, hoping to catch his gaze, ready to mouth to him to leap onto the concrete floor of the tower, but he didn't look her way. Instead, he inched his way forward and when he neared the doorway there was a soft creak. He heard it too. He hurried on by, leaving her crouched on the floor.

She crossed her fingers that the light downstairs would fade as the killer descended the bunker stairs, but it didn't.

The light below brightened and moved around illuminating first one wall of the attic, then another as the killer shone his torch up the stairs.

She waited, frozen, her breath caught in her throat.

After a long pause the light dimmed and she heard the distinct sound of footsteps heading down the bunker stairs.

She eased herself to her feet and backed away. She had to reassure herself many times that he couldn't have seen her. That he could not have heard her heartbeat or her breathing. She could certainly hear Richard breathing behind her. Surely not loud enough to be heard below. But she knew the killer had heard that creak and he'd sensed something. Or was wary.

As the light faded, she backed into the tower. She'd managed to get as far as the doorway to the attic of the north wing when the light disappeared altogether.

'Richard,' she whispered. 'Hold on to me.'

She waited, expecting to feel the pressure of his hand on her arm. Instead, he managed to grab hold of her left breast. She swiped at his hand, managing to grip his wrist. As she turned, she placed his hand on the back of her shoulder. From there she was forced to inch her way forward in the black.

She took a few small steps and then a few more, holding out her hands hoping to make contact with a wall. Another small step forward and there was a thump as Richard's head hit a rafter.

'Sorry about that, Richard.'

She waited. No sound emanated from the kitchen two floors down and she was grateful for that. She took three sidesteps and kept walking in what she hoped was the right direction, holding out her hands.

Soon she felt the cool smoothness of glass. Another three sideways steps and her hands met with wood. She'd found the door to the balcony. The toe of her right shoe met something solid. It was her stubbed toe and she stifled a gasp.

'There's quite a threshold,' she said as she passed through the doorway onto the balcony, pausing for Richard. 'And mind your head.'

She was fairly sure there was no furniture out here, but she couldn't count on her memory. She was about to shuffle along beside the wall with her hands outstretched, but the roof rafters were set too low. Even she was in danger of whacking her head.

'What do we do now?'

'Find the little doorway. Probably best to crawl on our hands and knees.'

She went first, crawling, groping about, at last finding the doorway. She entered first wincing as large pieces of grit dug into her knees and palms. It was to be a night of pain, that much she knew, a high price to pay for attending a sightseeing tour.

As Richard entered, he managed to catch his foot on some rubble and she took in the unwanted sound of rock skittering on concrete.

'Shit.'

She drew back as she felt him squeezing through.

'Is all of you in?'

'I think so.'

She eased the door shut.

'Do you think he heard?'

'I doubt it.'

'What'll we do now?'

'We wait.'

'I could do with a light.'

'Not sure we should risk it.'

There was a long pause.

'I feel like a sitting duck up here.'

'Then what would you have us do, Richard? Make a run

for it? You can't spend much time outside what with the dust. And besides, he has no idea we're here.'

She didn't mention the risk she'd taken closing the cadaver's eyes. She didn't mention the creaking floorboard on the landing either. It would only terrify him more.

They fell silent, broken only by the occasional cough from Richard, which he thankfully did his best to suppress.

Clarissa shifted position until she could lean back against the wall. Then she brushed the knees of her trousers. The painkillers were working, and she was grateful for that small mercy. But the concrete of the floor was cold and uncompromising. As was the wall. It didn't take long for her buttocks to start complaining and a dull ache to grow in her hip. And her back was quick to join in. She imagined Richard was feeling the same. Neither of them was capable of sitting hunched on the floor like this for long without enduring considerable discomfort. She was too old for this sort of caper.

She wondered how long it had taken them to reach this strange attic space. A couple of minutes? She conjured an image of the killer in the kitchen below. He'd have to light the incinerator and wait for it to generate enough heat, if that was his plan. That could take quite some time, depending on the fuel. Assuming the incinerator was functioning and the chimney unblocked. It was also assuming the killer knew those things. Perhaps he didn't. Perhaps this plan of his was not going to work out. In the meantime, he would be kept occupied butchering the body. That task would be easier if the body was naked. She tried to visualise the process, how long it would take. How long to joint a human body? Not long, depending on the implement. How long would it take for the various body parts to burn? Much longer. There wasn't room in the incinerator for anything like the whole body at once. You would only be able to incinerate a few small parts at a time. Not incinerate either. For on reflection, it would take about half a day to heat that old furnace up to the required temperate. The killer must be using it as an oven. As she thought it all through, she realised with considerable annoyance that the process would take many hours and possibly all night. There was no way her own living body would tolerate this amount of discomfort cooped up in a claustrophobic and distinctly uncomfortable space for an entire night.

Her thoughts were interrupted by a distant and intermittent revving followed by a lengthier whine. A chainsaw. She wished she could have shielded Richard from the macabre reality of what was taking place in the bunker kitchen. Maybe he thought the killer was sawing wood. She left him to his own thoughts and pushed away the goings on two floors below.

She wondered who the dead woman was. A local? A tourist? She had a pretty face. A little pixie-like, from memory. Too young and too sweet to be killed. Clarissa regretted not searching the corpse. She shouldn't have let Richard's horror impede her own natural curiosity. That poor woman. She'd suffered a violent death. Strangled by bare hands. Smacked of an act of violent passion, of rage. The husband or partner perhaps. What of the peculiar tattoo? Then again, these days lots of young women covered themselves in all kinds of tattoos. It was probably meaningless.

The letter tucked in her bra dug into her flesh. She adjusted its position, curious to see what it was and reluctant to use a second of her phone's charge to make the discovery. Besides, she was not predisposed to divulging her find to Richard. Whatever it was would have to remain tucked against her flesh, warm and snug.

What felt like hours passed. Hours of suspicion and doubt and shifting about to alleviate the excruciating discomfort. She wasn't certain the incinerator was the killer's preferred method of hiding the evidence until a faint whiff of smoke hit her nose. She steeled herself for what was to follow.

Sure enough, about an hour later there it was, wafting up from the kitchen, the meaty smell she'd anticipated. This killer wasn't incinerating the evidence, he was roasting it as she'd surmised.

Unless he had an exceedingly poor sense of smell, Richard must have realised what was happening but she couldn't bring herself to broach the topic.

Before long he said, 'What on earth is that smell?'

Her response was indirect. 'At least we have a good indication of when it will be safe to leave this hideout.'

'Whatever do you mean?'

'When that smell dissipates, I imagine our killer will be on his way.'

It took him a while to cotton on to what she meant.

'Good god, you don't think he's...?'

'I very much do, Richard.'

'And in the meantime?'

'We wait.'

The cramp in her buttocks was threatening to lock her hips. And the painkillers were wearing off. She hauled herself to her feet and engaged in a few light stretches. She was reluctant to take more of Richard's meds. He didn't have that many tablets and there was no telling how long she'd have to make them last. She raised her arms and touched the rafters, using their height to feel her way around the space. Richard had taken to lying flat out on the floor near the door and she avoided where he lay. As she slowly moved around, she forced herself to become accustomed to being unable to see. It was a strange experience and proved distracting for a while.

When the pain in her back and hip had subsided, she sat down again, staring at nothing, doing her best to ignore the return of the pain in her stiffening limbs until it became too much and she shifted and stood and stretched and sat down again. And as she sat, she thought of what it would have been like for anyone else shut in this room and hoped she was wrong about this place. And she thought of poor Trevor imprisoned in a small cell in Tahiche, away from his family in England, away from his culture, his life.

It was a violent place and he wasn't cut out for prison life. Thus far, he had avoided the worst of all prison fates, but for how long? Especially now two thugs known for their violent debauchery had been transferred from a prison in Tenerife. It seemed too cruel a punishment for a man as sensitive as Trevor to endure that particular humiliation, that degradation, when his only real crime, other than stealing the proceeds of crime, was to make use of written material of an unknown source to craft a story about a prison which incarcerated young men because they were gay. No, no, she had to double her efforts and get the man out of there before anything heinous happened to him.

It felt like another hour went by. Perhaps two. She had developed a headache.

She switched on her phone and switched it off again, checking the time. It was three in the morning. Surely by now the killer had had ample time to conduct his gruesome operation?

'Can you move away from the door?'

Richard rolled over.

'Don't make a sound. And whatever you do, don't cough.'

She went down on her hands and knees and eased open the door. She received a blast of wood smoke and roasting meat for her trouble. The balcony beyond was black.

She pushed the door to and said, 'We need to take turns to watch for any light coming from below. That will give us an idea of when he's leaving.'

'What if he comes up here?'

'Then we shut ourselves in and lean hard against this little door,' she said, thankful the door opened inwards.

Clarissa took the first shift. She wasn't sure how long she could lie prone on the hard and rough concrete which seemed to jab her in various places from tip to toe. She had no choice but to keep shifting position. It just wasn't possible to keep still.

The main consequence of the open door was the roast smell, which was so intense in other circumstances her mouth would have watered.

About ten minutes went by and her body rebelled and she had to ease herself back into the room.

'Your turn.'

He obliged. She heard him shift position as he, too, suffered the cold hard concrete. Neither of them had much endurance.

It was on her third watch that a light appeared in the stairwell, illuminating the tower with a weak shaft.

The light moved from the stairwell to the courtyard and disappeared. A short while later the light returned, headed back to the stairwell and disappeared. He was packing up, preparing to leave. At last!

He made three trips. Minutes passed. The light didn't return but there was no sound of a car leaving. Just when she thought they could at least prepare to head downstairs, the courtyard lit up, stronger now as though the killer was shining his torch up at the little balcony. There was a moment of hesitation and then the light faded before illuminating the stairwell. Dread filled her as the light grew stronger. He was coming up to the attic. He must have heard that floorboard. Richard caught the expression on her face as she closed the door.

They both leaned up hard against it.

And waited.

Footsteps on floorboards. Just a few. Then nothing. The killer was in the tower.

It wasn't long before the footsteps were on floorboards again, this time coming closer and closer still. Then the soft thud of footsteps on concrete, footsteps that sounded so close and stopped and she knew the killer was right outside the little door.

The handle turned and Clarissa fought against the pressure of the killer's push hoping Richard was doing the same. Then, just as Clarissa feared the killer would attack the door with his chainsaw and they'd end up in the same state as that poor woman, she heard a faint electronic beep.

There was a long pause. The killer was checking his phone. At least, she presumed that was what he was doing.

She waited, her shoulder still pressed hard against the door, just in case. Then, more footsteps, this time heading away.

They waited and waited, neither of them feeling brave enough to open the door and look out.

Not until the sound of a car engine removed all doubt.

But the recent terror had rattled her nerve.

'Go and have a look, Richard.'

'You look.'

Anger flared. He really was a coward. She lost all respect for him at that point.

'We'll go together.'

She yanked open the door and went first, crawling on her hands and knees. As she stood, she turned and said, 'Don't put your light on, Richard. We are not out of the woods yet.'

She made her way in the dark without waiting for him. With outstretched hands she headed across the balcony as fast as she dared. When she reached the doorway, she recalled the threshold and felt her way with her foot to make sure she didn't trip. She carried on through the attic room with arms outstretched, her confidence building, judging the distance. She felt around for the tower wall when she thought it should be near, and when her hands met cold render, she then felt along for the doorway. She was at last in the vestibule. From there, it was relatively easy to make her way into the tower. She reached one of the windows in time to see the taillights of the departing car as it disappeared on its way back to Cofete. She waited a few moments longer before switching on her phone torch, directing it at the attic where Richard emerged, limping.

'I tripped over that blasted threshold.'

She stifled her reaction. Even though he was proving a liability, she would rather have him for company than any of the others on the bus, and she supposed anyone was better than no one in the circumstances.

'Back to our armchairs, I suggest.'

'You think it's safe?'

Ever the doubter. She would have to get to the bottom of that pervasive fear of his. Rooted in childhood, she expected. Fancy a grown man behaving in such an unheroic fashion. He was all but emasculated. She summoned her patience and said, 'There was only one person in that car and he's gone. If he comes back, we'll hear him.'

She led the way down the stairs, taking her time, leaning against the wall for balance, the lack of a banister more disconcerting than ever, given her fatigue and the now searing pain in her hip.

Back in the living room she shone her phone torch around and noticed the lid had been put back on the wooden chest. Richard went straight to their food stash and extracted his water bottle.

She was thirsty too, but curiosity had the upper hand and she went over to the chest. The lid had not been nailed shut. The nails lay in a pile on the floor nearby. Her eyes went straight to the nail Richard had bent and to the hole he had nailed it into, the soft wood of the lid sporting the nail's indentation. She slid off the lid, let it clatter to the floor and surveyed the contents. Appeared to be a number of blankets under the cadaver as she had earlier anticipated, and they were all neatly folded.

'Can't you leave that alone?' Richard said from his favoured spot over by the fireplace.

She ignored him. If a clue was to be found, it would be in here. She took an antique trowel off the wall, knelt down and, with one hand shining the phone torch into the chest, she lifted up the edge of the nearest blanket, eager to see what lay underneath. She found nothing other than the base of the chest. She proceeded to lift the sides of that blanket and then another, working her way around the inside perimeter of the chest.

After exploring the front and left side, she tackled the back, her knees complaining with every move she made, her hip joining in. If pain could talk it would be yelling. It was when she shifted along and her right knee made contact with a small pebble that dug into her knee cap and she almost cried out in pain that a gold chain caught her eye. She pulled back and sat down, breathing through the agony. Then she gave her knee and the surrounding floor a good brush with her hand.

A quick glance over at Richard who seemed to have his back to her – although she couldn't be sure as he was standing in the dark – and she used a spare tissue to pick up the chain. She popped it in her pocket before continuing the hunt for clues. She found nothing more. Satisfied she had thoroughly if cautiously searched the chest, she stood up and wiped the trowel clean of fingerprints and hung it back on the wall. She wasn't sure whether to divulge her find to Richard. Would he be discreet or blab? More's the point, would he be of any use to her at all in solving the crime? She thought not.

She went into the other room out of his line of sight and examined her find. On close inspection it was a gold ankle bracelet. Judging by the weight, it was cheap. Crescent moons and five-pointed stars hung from the chain and the word "Anna" had been incorporated into the links. It was the sort of ankle bracelet worn by a young woman, possibly of teenage years, although Clarissa was certain the woman had been older than that. She went into her photos on her phone and examined the face. It was hard to fathom, but she would hazard a guess at early-to-mid-twenties.

She pocketed the bracelet and went over to the window. There was nothing to see, although the night had started to give way to day. She checked the time. It was five to seven.

She used the torchlight to cross the room. When she reached Richard she announced, 'I'm going down to the bunker. Coming with me?'

'No, thank you,' he said, taking up his favoured armchair

and clutching himself, shivering. 'I'd rather remain here where I am.'

'Then I'll go alone,' she said, peeved that he allowed his cowardice to trump any chivalrous bone he had in him.

She made her way outside, making sure to close the door behind her for the sake of Richard's breathing, although she was not about to relinquish the yellow jacket.

7

A STRANGE ENCOUNTER

All was still in the courtyard. There was scarcely a whisper of wind. She inhaled and her mouth received a fresh coating of dust. The faint light of dawn struggling through the calima backlit the cliff that towered up beyond the house, an imposing giant of a cliff ensuring no one would ever take Villa Winter by surprise.

She went and stood in the middle of the courtyard and scanned the rooftop, her gaze resting on where she and Richard had hid for hours through the night, taking in what she could see of the window situated in the first room of the north wing, then observing the tower. She sensed the presence before she saw it. There, framed by one of the arched windows on the second and inaccessible level, was the shape of a man. He was uniformed and wore a military hat. It was the ghost of Gustav Winter. She was sure of it. He didn't seem to look down at her and as he walked away from the window she wondered where he was off to.

It was with some trepidation that she went into the hall and passed the staircase that led to the tower. She turned on her phone torch and descended the stairs, her stride tentative as she made to enter the kitchen.

At first, she stood in the doorway and shone the torch around. The killer had been thorough. There was not a droplet of blood to be seen. She went and opened the incinerator to find both the oven and the firebox empty. The bricks were still warm. The only other sign there had been anyone down here was a faint whiff of pine air freshener, as though the killer had wanted to leave no odour that could suggest the gory tasks that had occurred only hours before. No blood on the stairs or passage, either. And the blanket was gone. She could have been forgiven for believing she had imagined the whole episode.

Aware of the spirit presence in the tower, she had to force herself to inspect all of the bunker rooms in search of clues. The absence of another human made her senses acute. She took her time in each room, pausing, soaking in the atmosphere. Nothing good had ever happened down here in these windowless cells. She was sure of that. She reached the end of the passage. After a quick look down the passage to nowhere – a space that made her blood curdle – she entered the bathroom and tried turning on the taps. They were stiff, as were the bath taps. She eyed the toilet covetously, succumbing to an urgent need to release her pee. Without a second thought she lifted the lid, undid her pants and emitted a long sigh as her thighs touched the rim. Once finished, she closed the lid and pressed the lever. Nothing happened to the water flow, but she experienced a sudden rush of suffering as she stepped away. She knew her imagination, overstimulated by the conspiracy theories and unsubstantiated speculations, coloured her impressions, which meant she couldn't rely on her psychic abilities. There was too much interference. What she did know was the ghost upstairs hadn't joined her. Had anyone died down here? She didn't doubt it. But was the bunker haunted? She thought not. She was drawn beyond the walls, drawn towards the ocean, and, she surmised, to the cemetery of unmarked graves. If the ghost of some tortured soul tramped this terrain, it preferred to do so outdoors and not in the confines of this horror chamber. She fully intended on paying that particular ghost a visit, whether Gustav Winter up there in the tower liked it or not. Although she had no idea how unless someone, Pedro Fumero probably, indicated its location. For now, finding no clues in any of the rooms, she began to make her way back.

She'd only made it a quarter of the way down the passage when her phone torch went out and she was plunged into darkness. Fear bolted through her. She had to be firm with herself. There was nothing down here. Her phone battery had died, that was all. Obviously, the torch had drained the battery. She groped her way back keeping a hand against the passage wall, counting the doorways, and when she thought she was near the stairs she called out to Richard.

There was no response.

She yelled three more times and waited.

Nothing.

Leaving the passage wall, the darkness was disorienting. She edged her feet forward, her hands outstretched. Taking small steps, she felt about, hoping to make contact with a wall, guided by the smell of pine air freshener. She knew how easy it was to steer off course in the dark.

She kept going but there was still no wall to be found. Then, she stopped, certain there was some presence right behind her. She swung around, hands flailing, scooping up nothing but air. The moment she stopped, an unearthly draught whooshed between her legs. She looked down, not that she could see anything. But she did sense something, a supernatural being, and whatever it was wanted her to pay attention to the ground beneath her feet.

That's all very well, General Winter, she thought. But she wasn't about to go searching in the pitch blackness. She kept going. Her hand met with the timber of a doorway. It had to be the kitchen. She'd come too far. She turned around and inched forward, kicking out a foot in search of the bottom stair.

When her foot met with concrete and her hands with air, she knew the stairs were in front of her. She reached down and felt for the bottom step to make sure. Climbing the stairs in the dark was a slow process. She was exhausted. Her hip started complaining again. It was only on the second corner that daylight lit her way.

She paused in the hall and took two more painkillers, working up enough spit for the swallow. They were Richard's, she knew, and in that moment taking them felt like spite.

All was still in the courtyard, the hazy gloaming adding a preternatural air to an already eerie situation. When she entered the main room, she found Richard hiding behind his armchair.

'Didn't you hear me call out?'

'I did hear something,' he said evasively.

'And you didn't think to come and see if I was alright?'

'I thought maybe you were being attacked.'

'And you felt no compulsion to come to my aid?'

He gave her a pleading look. She lost patience with him.

'What on earth are you doing writing crime. No wonder your books are not selling.'

That remark stung. She could see it in his face. He had the emotional age of a child.

'Let's eat,' she said, deciding a change of topic in order and finding she was ravenous.

Also, she was livid.

She removed the hessian basket from the wall and tipped the provisions out onto the table. There was no cup to drink out of. She tore open the carton of juice and gulped down a generous amount before offering it to an aghast Richard who'd managed to come forward out of his hiding place to hover behind a dining chair. Too bad if he didn't want to go second; she would drink the lot. She set aside the potato crisps and one block of chocolate, and put the nuts, the second chocolate block and the protein bars in her canvas bag for later. The jelly babies she left where they'd landed. Then she picked up the magazine, the chocolate and the crisps and went and sat at the other end of the table. There she munched her way through half the crisps before pushing Richard the packet. He wasn't so fussy dipping his hand into an opened packet of crisps.

Pointedly ignoring her companion, she brushed her hands on her trousers and leafed through the magazine, arriving at a feature article on tattoos. One of the photos displayed the same tattoo as that of the dead woman, a series of Gothic numerals. Masking her reaction, she nonchalantly turned the page.

'We're leaving this place, Richard,' she said, breaking into the chocolate block and shunting his half down the table before diving into her share, 'So make yourself ready.'

He left the chocolate and disappeared outside. She hoped he wouldn't come back gasping for air. While he was out of the room, she reached into her pocket for her phone, recalling as she swiped the screen that it had no charge. In

The Ghost of Villa Winter

the split second she was returning the phone to her pocket, she noticed the screen had lit up. Extraordinary. She quickly photographed the pages of the article in case the phone died again, before viewing the battery. It still had about ten per cent charge remaining. Then why had it suddenly died on her down in the bunker? She had no time for poltergeists interfering with electronics.

She went and put the yellow jacket where she thought it had come from and then hung the hessian basket back on the wall, returning the magazine to its depths. Richard re-entered the room and without a word shoved the family-size pack of jelly babies in his backpack, along with his water bottle. He appeared to be sulking. He hadn't touched the juice. She offered him the carton again and he waved it away. Not one for waste, she downed the remaining contents, enjoying the sweet fruity tang.

After taking a final look around the room, she poked her head outside. The calima showed no signs of abating. They would both need a face covering. As Richard folded up his spare shirt, she removed her jacket. She tied his makeshift mask and he tied hers. A quick scan to make sure they were leaving nothing behind and they set off.

The painkillers she'd taken earlier had started to work, which proved the only blessing. She hadn't walked more than twenty paces and already, her mouth was dry. She wasn't sure the makeshift mask was working all that well, if at all. She had to keep shoving it back in place. The only thing it did do was humidify her face. She wanted to hurry but knew any increase in breath intake would trigger Richard's asthma. She trudged on. Richard trailed behind. At least the first two-hundred metres was downhill. After the first big bend, the track meandered as it followed the coastline south.

When they cornered the next bend and headed towards Cofete there was a slight rise to the track. That is, what she considered a slight rise. For Richard, it was a mountain. Not ten paces on and he started wheezing and complaining he needed to stop. Clarissa encouraged him to keep walking. About halfway up the slope, he said between wheezy breaths that he really had to stop. He sat down on the side of the track. Then the coughing began.

'Slow your breath. Try to ignore the tickle in your throat.'

It was no use. She stood over him, wondering what she could do to help. He couldn't sit there, coughing and wheezing. Going back to Villa Winter was not an option. Not only was it uphill almost all the way, they had insufficient food and were low on water. And should anyone else arrive at the house on that calima-laden Sunday, it would not be anyone she would wish to encounter.

Was it clutching at straws or a flash of instinct? She wasn't sure, but she unzipped his backpack and extracted the packet of jelly babies. In her haste to tear open the plastic, she almost spilled the lot. She steadied the contents and proffered the pack. Richard continued wheezing and coughing. She shoved the pack at him again and he dutifully took an orange one.

'Chew it.'

He obliged. And as he chewed, he reached out and took a red one. Followed by another orange one. The chewing slowed his coughing and eventually the wheezing. It was an astonishing if apposite cure. She eased him to his feet and fed him jelly babies all the way to Cofete.

8

A SECOND BREAKFAST

THE VILLAGE AT THAT EARLY HOUR OF A SUNDAY MORNING WAS deserted. There was no sign of movement and not a sound, not even a barking dog, among all of the twenty or so dwellings. Bracing herself for the door-knocking task ahead, Clarissa eyed the sprawl of low, flat-roofed buildings, many of them unrendered stone, arranged higgledy-piggledy and fanning up towards the cliff. She could only hope that inside one of those dwellings there were folk indoors, still asleep or waking up. The woman with the donkeys, perhaps.

As they entered the empty car park, Clarissa decided that the woman with the donkeys had to reside in the fenced-off allotment to their left, where there were a few small trees and sheltered areas where vegetables grew. She made a mental note to knock on the farmhouse door as her second port of call. First, she would try the restaurant.

The allotment and the restaurant were shielded from the ocean by the low dome-shaped hill that began its rise on the other side of the car park. With the car park empty, the hill had gained in prominence. Whoever had originally created this village had not done so to enjoy the vista.

Although perhaps the hill afforded some shelter, mitigated the sense of exposure. In all, Cofete was a wild-looking place that appeared to offer no comfort, especially after that night spent in Villa Winter.

With Richard trudging behind her, she approached the restaurant door expecting it to be closed.

'There you are!'

So unexpected was the sound of another human voice, she almost leaped out of her skin. Fred Spice stood there outside the al fresco dining area, hands on hips in his I Love Fuerteventura t-shirt with Margaret right beside him. With Richard not fully himself, there was no time for pleasantries.

'I need to get Richard indoors. Is the restaurant open?'

'I believe so. They said they'd open early just for us.'

He pushed open the door and they bundled inside, Clarissa steering Richard to the nearest table.

'Close the door, please.'

'Whatever's the matter?'

'It's the dust.'

'Sounds asthmatic. Go get your puffer, would you Margaret. There's a love.'

Margaret scurried off, returning about five minutes later with her puffer. By then, Clarissa had removed the face covering and given Richard three more jelly babies. The packet was half empty.

Clarissa took the puffer and gave it a few shakes.

'Have you used a puffer before?'

He shook his head.

'Breathe in as you press down here. Hold your breath then exhale and repeat.'

While Richard took his dose of Ventolin, Clarissa's curiosity could wait no longer.

'Remarkable that this place is open,' she said. 'Never known a restaurant opening for two patrons.'

'I meant all of us,' Fred said. 'The bus broke down so we spent the night here.'

'Not here exactly,' Margaret said with a nervous giggle.

'We were billeted in various huts. Those the restaurant owner had keys for. He is in charge of the holiday lets here.'

'Convenient.'

'Incredibly.'

'And here is the man himself,' Fred announced and Clarissa came face-to-face with the shifty-looking man who had received a package from the woman with the donkeys. He was tall, wiry, his curly black hair on the cusp of being too long for cooking, and he wore a cocksure smile on his face.

'Meet Salvador.' Fred introduced him as though he owned him.

'You must be Clarissa and Richard,' he said, his gaze slithering to-and-fro between them. 'Made it back then.'

He gave Richard a manly wink. Richard's face fell in response.

Whatever had the tour party been saying about them? It appeared neither Salvador nor the Spices were about to enlighten them.

'Come and sit down over here.' Salvador ushered them to an already laid table at the back of the restaurant. Clarissa chose a seat with her back to the wall and Richard sat beside her. Fred and Margaret took up the opposite chairs.

'Now what can I get you?' Salvador said. 'Bacon and eggs? Coffee?'

It was yes to everything on offer. Despite having ordered, Margaret proceeded to study the menu while Fred told

Richard what he'd learned about the history of the restaurant.

Clarissa paid him no attention. She had no energy for more of Fred's information. She recalled when she was last here, the crowds, the noise, the chatter. That time, the tour party had dined outside. Now she saw that the room itself – a rectangle seating about sixteen at best – had a rustic feel, with large tiles covering the walls to waist height. An array of artefacts and photographs adorned the walls of yellow ochre above. Wooden tables and chairs were arranged along the wall opposite the bar. The view of the cliffs drew the eye out of the glass-panelled front door. As she took in the surroundings – immediate and afar – a heavy fatigue swept through her. Her hip complained despite the medication. Not surprising, after their ordeal the night before. She wanted nothing more than a soft bed to lie in. The last thing she needed was more company, but as Salvador brought over the coffees Vera and Carol appeared.

'We wondered what happened to you two,' Carol said, smiling mischievously at Richard as she sat down on the far side of Fred, her gaze flitting over Clarissa as it would an uninvited fly.

'...after you went off by yourselves,' Vera said, finishing Carol's sentence and pointedly ignoring Clarissa as she squeezed around the far end of the table, plonking herself beside Richard and giving him a playful nudge. 'We thought maybe you were having a romantic liaison.'

The friends both laughed. They'd clearly cooked up their little fantasy and were bent on milking it. As to motive, Clarissa hadn't a clue, unless it was simply a wind-up. Fred looked a touch embarrassed but nowhere near as embarrassed as Richard.

Clarissa had to quash her own reaction. She put on her

bland face and as she stirred her coffee she said, 'And you didn't think to come and test your theory?'

'We did think of walking back, didn't we Fred,' Carol said, avoiding Clarissa's gaze and choosing instead to pay close attention to her napkin. 'Then we decided the dust was too much.'

'It was getting late by then,' Fred said in Carol's defence.

'You mean to tell me there is no other vehicle in Cofete?' Clarissa said, overtly flabbergasted and inwardly cool. She knew full well there had been another car.

Carol and Vera exchanged glances.

'We haven't seen one,' Fred said, looking at Margaret who shook her head.

'We never thought to ask,' was all Vera came up with. She sounded defensive. 'Like Carol said, we thought you two had stayed behind on purpose.' She paused, her face breaking out in a smirk as she eyed Clarissa derisively. 'After all, spending the night with a successful author, we didn't want to cramp your style.'

Richard sank lower in his seat. There was an awkward silence. Salvador, who was standing beside the coffee machine and must surely have heard Carol's last remark, leaned over the bar and said, 'There is no car here. My wife Catriona took our car into Morro Jable for the weekend.'

It seemed bizarre they didn't have a car each.

'What about the other people in Cofete?'

'There's no one living here in the village at the moment. Most of these houses are used for holidays and the calima has kept people away this weekend.'

'And the woman with the donkeys?'

'Merida?' He smiled. It was a discomforting smile and Clarissa had no confidence in the veracity of anything the man said. 'She only has her donkeys. Sometimes she takes the public bus into town.'

'There's a bus?' Richard said with amazement, his eyes filling with hope.

'Runs twice a day through the week.'

'And it's Sunday,' Richard said despondently.

'The island is incredibly well-serviced, don't you think?' said Fred. 'We'll try the bus next time, won't we, Margaret.'

His wife didn't look all that enthusiastic.

The conversation faded. Once Salvador had brought over coffees for Vera and Carol and taken their order, he disappeared into the kitchen. Soon they were distracted by the smell of frying bacon.

Clarissa wrapped her hands around her coffee cup with relish. As she sipped the hot, strong brew, she wondered when the others would drift in. She didn't have long to wait. Next to appear was Francois who acknowledged her and Richard with a most indifferent hello, as though he couldn't have cared less for their welfare. When she got back to Puerto del Rosario, she would be lodging a complaint. She wasn't sure who to, but there had to be someone. She wanted to quiz him over his duty of care there and then, but held back. Francois was not the sort of tour guide who would embrace criticism.

'What exactly is wrong with the minibus?' she said instead.

'The starting motor.'

He plonked himself down in the seat beside Margaret and scrolled through whatever App he had open on his phone.

'Salvador said he would have called a mechanic for a spare part but the shops are closed,' Fred said informatively.

'He'll get someone to drive one down from Puerto del Rosario tomorrow.'

'And where is it? I mean, I thought it would be in the car park.'

'Behind the restaurant. There'd been a discussion as to whether to head straight back to civilisation when Helen took a turn for the worse.'

Just as Clarissa absorbed the information in walked Helen, looking remarkably healthy, for her.

'You're here,' she said, eyeing Clarissa and Richard as she pulled out the chair at the head of the table.

'The same might be said of you,' Clarissa said, smiling sweetly as her thoughts raced back to the medical emergency at Villa Winter.

There was a brief moment of unease that seemed to ripple around the table. Helen showed no sign of responding to the remark.

Yet again, it was Fred who advanced the conversation. 'You mean the sudden departure,' he said, stating the obvious.

'She had a panic attack,' said Vera.

'Often mistaken for a heart attack, apparently,' added Carol.

'Delayed reaction, wasn't it?'

'To the cliff path.'

'No, it was the bunkers. She gets claustrophobic.'

'Anyway, the nurse here sorted her out.'

Richard's mouth fell open. 'Cofete has a nurse?'

'Why sound so surprised?' Vera said.

'It's just that commuting to work from Cofete seems, well, astonishing.'

'You'd be amazed,' Carol said as though she knew all about it.

'Merida isn't practicing, though,' said Vera. 'I guess she's retired.'

'Prefers the simple life.'

Salvador came and took Helen's order. Clarissa asked for a second coffee. As she finished her first, she took in the group. They were all there, minus Simon and the lads.

'Will Steve and Dave be joining us?'

'Afraid not,' said Fred. 'A pity. I rather liked them.'

'Whatever happened?'

'Cocky fellows decided to walk back to Morro Jable. Walk! In the calima, too. I ask you!'

'They probably made it to the lookout and then hitched a ride,' said Helen.

Clarissa tried to imagine the lads walking back up the path in the dark, inhaling the dust. It would have been a punishing ascent, even for fit lads like them. She could only hope one of them had a torch.

In a sudden back-and-forth flurry, Salvador brought out plates loaded with bacon, eggs, bread and tomatoes, along with more coffees. The tour party dived into the meal, Richard with particular gusto. Everyone focused on their food, yet the atmosphere seemed strained. The explanations offered up in response to her questions failed to satisfy Clarissa's inquiring nature, the absence of a car in the village and Helen's miraculous recovery uppermost in her mind.

Without the presence of the lads, Fred had lost his allies and might have benefited from holding his tongue. But it appeared his fondness for being the expert was boundless and he broke into the conversational silence with, 'Did you know Villa Winter is exactly west of Morro Jable?' He turned to Vera and Carol who didn't look the least bit interested but at least graced him with a glance. 'If you felt brave

The Ghost of Villa Winter

enough to take the cliff path between here and the house you would end up in one of those deep valleys, the next one down from the one with that hairpin bend.'

'Is that so?' Vera said with a hint of sarcasm.

No one else was paying attention. Richard was too busy eating and Helen had bowed her head, concentrating on the food on her plate. There was no response from Francois but that was to be expected. Clarissa loaded some of her egg and bacon onto her fork.

Fred was undeterred. 'Maybe Gustav was planning on tunnelling through.'

'Doubt it,' Francois mumbled.

'Interesting thought, though.'

The scowl on Francois' face was enough to make Clarissa recoil and she was glad Fred hadn't seen it. What had Fred said to cause that reaction? Perhaps it was Fred himself. After all, he seemed to trigger a similar response in everybody.

The silence resumed, interrupted by chinks of cutlery. It felt like a reprieve. Clarissa focused on her meal, her thoughts straying to the bracelet, the magazine, the letter tucked inside her bra. And to the cadaver in the chest and what had become of it, her. She wanted to feel safe, wanted reassurance their nightmare was over, but she knew it wasn't. For a fleeting moment she even thought of Trevor, of his ordeal with the backpack and how it had ended with his arrest, of how frantic he must have felt with all that indecision, and temptation. What would anyone do if they found a backpack full of cash? Keep it, most likely.

As they finished scraping plates and draining cups, Vera leaned forward in her seat, her face wearing a provocative smile as she said, addressing Richard, 'Where did you sleep?'

'In the armchairs by the fireplace,' Clarissa said quickly, annoyed by the woman's manner.

Richard shot her a puzzled look. She kicked him under the table. He seemed to get the message.

'Not in the bunker rooms, then?' said Carol, her face creasing into what could only be described a sneer.

A murmur of laughter rippled around the group who were all now listening with interest. Richard sat frozen in his seat.

'We thought about it,' said Clarissa, taking charge of the conversation, 'but there were no mattresses.'

'True.'

The two women looked thoughtful for a moment, their attention shifting back to Richard.

'Wouldn't have been that comfortable, sleeping in a chair,' Vera mused, nudging him.

'We managed,' he said.

'I would have found sleeping there really spooky,' said Margaret.

Clarissa gave her an acknowledging smile. 'It was a bit.'

'Anything odd happen?' said Helen.

It was a strange question, but then again, she was asking about Villa Winter.

'I am afraid to say we had a most uneventful night.' Clarissa's gaze travelled around the table. There was a little too much curiosity in all the pairs of eyes staring her way, and she found it disconcerting. Hoping to deflect further scrutiny, she sat back in her seat and announced with a sweep of her hand, 'Delicious food.'

'We think so, too, don't we Margaret,' said Fred, his garrulous tongue suddenly an asset. 'I was only just remarking earlier that the goat stew is the best I've ever tasted. And not too greasy. Salvador must go to a lot of trouble cutting off the surplus fat. Usually, goat stew gives me a bit of indigestion, but not here. You must ask him for the recipe, Margaret. Although he might not give it to you. Chef's do like their secrets.'

For once Clarissa was pleased to have Fred in the room. He rattled on about the various goat dishes he had eaten in Fuerteventura and Lanzarote, digressing to the virtues of al fresco dining by the sea. No one took much notice, but no one talked over him or tried to interrupt. It occurred to Clarissa that Fred's monologue might be his way of diverting the awkward conversation. Perhaps he wasn't socially inept after all. Indeed, he might prove an ally in this peculiar situation they found themselves in.

After he'd cleared away the plates and the others had drifted off, Salvador took Clarissa and Richard across to one of the terraced dwellings close to the restaurant where they could shower and rest. Clarissa would have preferred one of the detached cottages further uphill, where she could observe the comings and goings of the others, but the terraced house would have to do.

After showing them around, Salvador made to exit the front door.

'Are you leaving the key?' Clarissa said, holding out her hand.

He laughed. It was an oddly unpleasant laugh. 'This key is mine,' he said. 'No one locks their doors in Cofete.'

He walked away as she closed the door. There was no latch or means to lock the door from the inside. Clarissa resisted the idea of creating a barricade.

9

PUZZLING EVIDENCE

The layout of the holiday let was basic. A central passage led through to the back with rooms to either side. The first two were bedrooms. Then an internal living and dining room – simply furnished – and a kitchen and bathroom with windows looking north. It wasn't the sort of indoor space inhabitants would be inclined to spend a lot of time in. Clarissa had never been fond of windowless rooms. At least there were fresh towels and toiletries in the bathroom.

Clarissa showered first. She was quick, thinking of the hamlet's water supply or lack thereof, and she had never been one to luxuriate in bathrooms. Besides, there seemed little pleasure in the act when she had to put back on clothes in need of a good wash. Once dressed, she reinserted the letter into its bosomy hiding place. On her way down the hall, she found Richard hovering in the dark living room.

'All yours.'

Leaving him to get clean she claimed the bedroom on the left and laid down on the bed for a few minutes to rest her hip before changing her mind and getting up and heading to the kitchen to sit on a hard, wooden chair. She had to stay focussed and if that meant in discomfort and pain then so be it.

Richard seemed to take an age in the bathroom. Her impatience grew and with it, misgivings. She needed to talk the situation through with someone and that someone was him. Yet she was ambivalent. How much should she mention? What should she hold back? She took out her phone to find the battery was well and truly flat. So much for a ten per cent charge. She reached into her blouse and fished out the letter, the one item she felt reluctant to divulge to anyone. Opening the folds, she eyed the neat cursive, the official-looking letterhead, the date. She knew enough German to ascertain the letter had been sent from Berlin and the date: June 1944. Pity those lads had gone. They spoke German. Although she wouldn't have shown them. She needed a German-English dictionary. Until she had one, she would have to remain in ignorance.

She heard the squeak of a door and quickly tucked the letter back into her bra. Richard appeared in the doorway with a towel draped over his shoulders and his hair still dripping wet. He looked around, embarrassed, and scuttled down the hall, returning with a razor and a small vile of what she presumed was cologne. After he disappeared into the bathroom, she stood and paced back and forth, tentatively stretching the muscles around her hip. The painkillers didn't seem to be doing much but at least they masked the worst of the pain.

The door squeaked again, followed by the pitter-patter of bare feet. A strong smell of expensive perfume hit her nose well before Richard entered the kitchen, clean shaven with his wet hair combed back from his face. He was dressed, as she was, in the clothes they had on before, and no doubt that was a source of annoyance for someone who paid so much attention to their appearance. Perhaps he was washing away recent memories. He was naïve if he thought all this was over.

'I need a nap,' he said, yawning.

'I would prefer it if you stayed awake.'

'What on earth for? We are away from that blasted villa, safe and sound and taken care of. There is nothing to do except wait for the minibus to be repaired or the public bus to arrive, whichever comes first.'

'You think?'

'What else is there to think?'

'If you'll take a seat, I'll tell you.'

'Why not sit in the living room where it's comfortable?'

He looked askance at the table. It was old and battered with stains embedded in the pine. The chairs were no better. But what difference did any of that make? It was a room lit by daylight and contained the sort of barely comfortable upright chairs needed to stay awake. She gestured for him to sit down.

'I need us both to concentrate.'

He obliged with a sigh, taking up the seat opposite hers. After brushing away a few flecks of dust, he placed both elbows on the table to prop up his head. His eyes were heavy and there were dark rings beneath them. She began to wonder if it was worth voicing her concerns to someone who looked like they would fall asleep standing up. But she had to air her thoughts or she would burst, and besides, she didn't share his confidence that all was well. Yet could she trust him to keep quiet? She hesitated. She'd already decided she had to trust him. She would probably need him before the day was through.

The Ghost of Villa Winter

'Now promise me you'll keep what I'm about to say to yourself.'

'What are you talking about?' he said to the table.

'Promise?'

'If you insist.'

'I'm serious. I made two discoveries at the villa.'

He looked up with sudden interest.

'Discoveries? What discoveries? Why didn't you tell me before?'

'I'm not altogether sure I should be telling you now, but if I don't, I fear for your, for our safety.'

A look of slow shock appeared in Richard's face. At least he was starting to take her seriously.

'Back in the restaurant,' he said. 'Is that why you lied about our night?'

At last, he gets it. She leaned forward in her seat hoping to reinforce the gravity of the situation. Her hip wasn't happy with the move and she leaned back again. While she had his full attention, she hammered home the gist of things. Perhaps his adrenalin would kick in and wake him up some more.

'We have a murderer in our midst and I'm afraid we haven't a clue who it is.'

His jaw fell open.

'You don't really think it is any of those people on the bus?'

'I very much doubt it. But I don't know what to think. Except that something very strange is going on here and I am determined to get to the bottom of it.'

'You haven't told me what you found.'

'An ankle bracelet belonging to the dead woman.'

'How do you know the bracelet belongs to the victim?'

'I don't. But I found it tucked in the blankets in that chest so it is a fair assumption. Besides, everything is worth investigating.'

She fished the bracelet out of her pocket and held it up for them both to inspect.

'Interesting.'

He relinquished his elbow prop and reached out a hand. She gave him the necklace.

'We have a name, Anna. I doubt the moons and stars mean much.'

'It's girlish. The sort of thing a teenager would wear. How old do you think the victim was?'

'I wish I could tell you. I did take a photo of her. But for my phone,' Clarissa said lamely. 'Battery's flat.'

'Does this joint have power?' Richard said, getting up and flicking on a light switch.

The single light bulb in the centre of the ceiling lit up. Finally, a moment of luck.

'I heard a generator, back at the restaurant,' he said. 'And there's a lot of solar about.'

Richard left the room and came back with his fanny pack. He sat back down as he unzipped the main pocket and ferreted about at the bottom, extracting a phone charger and a Spanish plug adapter. He held out his hand for her phone. They both exhaled with relief when the charger lead worked. There was a wall socket beside the table. He plugged in the adapter and they waited. When the phone had enough charge, a few deft swipes and they were both gazing at the photo of the dead woman's face. The eyes were closed and she looked serene, but Clarissa recalled the fixed gaze, the terror that was written into those eyes, that poor woman. She was pretty, with features more typical of Spanish than Canarian. It was hard to view the image for very long without recalling what had happened to her post mortem.

'Probably early twenties, I'd say,' Richard said.

'Maybe. The trouble is, as we get older, young people all look the same age. I expect they see us like that, too.'

'I think it has to do with our degrading eyesight.'

They both laughed. Then Clarissa gave him a serious look.

'We have to figure out who killed her.'

'This really is a matter for the police.'

'We are here and they are not.' She paused. 'We can at least try.'

'We don't know a thing about her,' he said doubtfully.

She pointed at her phone's screen.

'What about that tattoo on her neck?'

He leaned further forward and peered at the photo before sitting back in his seat.

'Tattoos are commonplace these days. Numbers especially.'

Clarissa felt deflated. Then she recalled the magazine. She scrolled past the photo of the woman to the photos she'd taken of the article on tattoos.

'It might be coincidental, but I found a magazine in that hessian basket we used for our food and in it was this.' She passed Richard her phone. 'I've yet to read it.'

He took in the image before flicking back to the photo of the dead woman and returning to the article. His expression changed from mild indifference to complete engagement as he read.

'What does it say?'

'Anna's tattoo is identical to the one in the magazine.'

'I know that much.'

'The article is talking about a deviant quasi-Satanic cult

with groups dotted throughout Europe. They seem to have Germanic roots. They're Holocaust deniers who tattoo themselves as a form of branding.'

Clarissa sat back and rubbed her arms as a chill whistled through her.

'I forgot to look at the date of the issue.'

Richard took another look at the photos.

'Last month. You managed to capture the date in one of the photos.'

Their gazes met.

'Not an old magazine, then. Not a magazine that had been put in that hessian basket donkey's years ago and forgotten.'

Richard rubbed his chin. 'What are you getting at?'

'Don't you see? The magazine and the murdered woman are connected. I'm not sure how. But it's too much of a coincidence to just be chance. What if the magazine belonged to the woman? Maybe she put it in the hessian basket to hide it, in the same way that we hid our food. After all, the basket was right by the front door. You'd put something in there for easy access or if you were in a hurry.'

'Or you'd put it there to hide it from the inquisitive eyes of tourists who would no doubt poke around in all those drawers and cupboards.'

'You mean the magazine might belong to the murderer?'

'It's possible. The woman had the same tattoo. Maybe the killer confronted her with the awful truth. Slayed her for being part of that cult.'

She hadn't thought of that. She'd assumed the magazine belonged to the victim. She viewed Richard with fresh respect. It was the most sensible thing he'd said since they met and she saw a glimpse of Richard the crime writer. She was still processing the possibility of that particular motive when he said, 'Did you know Satanism used to be practiced on the island?'

'I did not,' she said, shocked to hear it. 'But given Fuerteventura's dark history, nothing would surprise me.'

'If we're dealing with a cult, that puts a different complexion on things.'

'How so?'

A distant crash followed by a shout caused Clarissa to jump up from her seat and rush to the window. Richard was about to join her but she waved him back. She saw Vera marching off up towards the cliff away from Merida's farmhouse. She looked furious, and, with her combat-hat haircut and her uniform-style dress, menacing. What had upset her? Clarissa wasn't game to go and find out. As Vera disappeared out of view, Carol appeared in her stead, marching down in the direction of Merida's, her stride as determined as Vera's. What was going on? She was about to pull away from the window when Carol stopped in her tracks. She seemed to be looking at the ground at her feet. She stood up and looked around. As her gaze neared the terraces, Clarissa stood back from the window. She was sure Carol couldn't see her, not through the glass. Then Carol bent down and picked something up. The object was small in size, that was all Clarissa could make out. Carol then headed off to Merida's. Once she had disappeared, Clarissa backed away from the window. She was about to join Richard at the table when movement caught her eye and Vera appeared, this time much closer, heading straight towards the rear yards of the terraces. Clarissa couldn't duck out of the way fast enough. Vera pinned her with her gaze and waved, her face lighting in a cheery grin. Even from this distance Clarissa could see it was fake. Clarissa waved back before taking up her chair, a touch breathless.

'What was all that about?'

'I really have no idea.' She filled Richard in.

'Obviously someone, probably Vera, dropped something and Carol found it.'

'I figured that much.'

'We mustn't allow ourselves to get overwrought. In my novel *Haversack Harvest* my lead character was prone to that tendency and it really mucked up the investigation. I used it as a device, which is, I suppose, why I know so much about it.'

He sounded sage, but Clarissa had enough insight to know he was drawing on the self-same quality lurking in him. But he was right. She already had a headful dealing with the identity of the slain woman, and the bloodcurdling awareness that after their hike back to Cofete, it was possible whoever disposed of the body knew or assumed they knew Clarissa and Richard were witnesses to the act. Clarissa regretted pretending at breakfast they had slept in those fireside chairs. She would have done better pretending they had got stuck in the attic. At least then, there might have been a chance the killer presumed they remained unaware of the body and its disposal. Although that was not very likely. She should never have closed the cadaver's eyes. Then there was Richard's poor hammering leaving a bent nail in the chest. Small details, but glaringly obvious to the observant eye.

They sat in companionable silence for a short while. It seemed as though they were both waiting for her phone to charge. Then an unexpected rush of wind rattled the kitchen window and Richard cleared his throat.

'How's your breathing?' she said.

'Perfectly fine,' he said, standing.

He exited the room and she decided to leave him to his

own devices for a while. She thought about relocating to a more comfortable chair, but she felt a need to be near the window, the natural light, despite the discomfort of her hip. It was a small impediment, she knew, as her thoughts drifted to Trevor and her scheduled visit tomorrow. Even though she was due in Tahiche at two in the afternoon, it was a visit she was doomed to miss. She would never manage to get from one end of Fuerteventura to the other, and then from one end of Lanzarote almost to the other without her own car. Poor Trevor, incarcerated in what seemed to be the only dismal-grey building on the island. He would be crushed when he discovered her absence. She was his hope, his encouragement, his lifeline. Without her, who did he have to look out for him? No one.

It was the insistent dull ache in her hip that made her stand and walk up the hall. She found Richard in his bedroom, but thankfully not asleep on his bed. He was sorting out the contents of his backpack. She stood in the doorway and watched. He popped the last of his things inside the main compartment and did up the zip.

'It's hard to know what to do,' she said.

'About what?'

'The body, this place, everything.'

'We are rather trapped.'

They made their way back to the kitchen.

'At least the weather seems to be fining up,' she said, taking another look out the window before resuming her seat.

'Something occurred to me while I was tidying up my backpack. Can you send me that photo of the girl?' he said, digging into his fanny pack and pulling out his phone. 'I'll upload it and do a reverse image search and see if we can identify her.'

Reverse image? She'd never heard of such a thing.

As he gave her his email address, she paused and said, 'But I have no phone reception.'

'This place is connected to the internet. I found a modem in the dining room. Here are the details.'

He handed her a laminated card. She reached for her phone and typed in the username and password. Then she got him to repeat his email address, and she sent the photo. She waited, intrigued, as he did whatever he was doing.

After a few minutes he said, 'Damn.'

'What's up?'

'I drew a blank.'

'Oh well,' she said, thinking it was most unlikely the woman would be identified in such a simple fashion. Who needed detectives when the internet made it anyone could be a sleuth?

Richard was still fiddling about with his phone.

'There's one more thing we can try. It's a facial recognition site.'

'Everything's online these days. I can scarcely keep up.'

He laughed and showed her the site he'd loaded.

'Social Catfish?'

'It's used to help verify people on dating sites. Make sure they are legitimate and not scammers.'

'How do you know all this?'

'I'd like to say it was research for a novel. But I found out all about this when I delivered a creative writing workshop at a literary festival on the elements of the crime genre. I was introducing aspects of the police procedural when a student piped up saying there was no longer any need to know anything about detective work unless you were writing historical fiction. Laughable, and of course I was thrown as I knew nothing about reverse image searches and ended up looking like a complete ignoramus.'

He put the phone down on the table and she watched as he loaded the photo of the corpse onto the social catfish site. In seconds they were both staring at the woman, Anna, named as an undercover police officer in a long rant about how she was a slut. Clarissa was horrified.

'Why would anyone want to reveal her true identity?'

'Probably an ex-boyfriend trying to get back at her, going by the sound of what they've written. Happens a lot, apparently. Something else I learned in that workshop.'

Clarissa stood. The painkillers seemed to have worn off. That or the pain in her hip was worsening. Either way, she felt a need to walk about. She went over to the window and looked out at the scruffy yard, the cliff, the ocean. A strong northerly wind was busy clearing the air of dust. Vera appeared again, heading downhill and entering Merida's place. What on earth was going on with those women? Clarissa returned her gaze to the room and observed Richard, bent over his phone. Her opinion of him had risen considerably and she decided he might even turn out to be an asset, at least when it came to the cogitation side of sleuthing.

'If Anna was undercover,' she said, opening the fridge to find it bare, 'there's only one conclusion to draw from this.'

'She infiltrated some weird group or cult and, thanks to the boyfriend, got found out.'

He was spot on. And yet it seemed too simple, too one-dimensional for a murdered body in a chest at Villa Winter. Besides, they didn't know for sure she really was an undercover cop. They only had the disgruntled ex-boyfriend's word for that. Still, given the paucity of evidence, they needed to rest their inquiry on an assumption and it might as well be that.

Since in all likelihood Anna had infiltrated a cult, the last thing she would have in her possession was that magazine expose. It was looking more likely that horrible ex-boyfriend followed her to Villa Winter and confronted her with the evidence. After all, he was on some sort of vendetta and, if his claim was true, he definitely had an issue with her working as a detective. Jealousy, no doubt. Come to think of it, he was the most like suspect. Weren't deranged former partners the usual perpetrators of crimes against women. He probably lured her to Villa Winter knowing it was secluded, an ideal location for a murder.

A few laps of the room and she sat back down. She'd have to come clean about the painkillers at some point. There were only six tablets left. She needed to make them last until sometime the following day, assuming Richard had no need of them in the interim.

'Whoever killed that woman came back and destroyed the evidence,' she said, thinking aloud.

'And then presumably he took off,' Richard said. 'I mean, why hang around? The perpetrator would have driven away in his car, surely?'

'Or abandoned it in the village and walked.'

'Walked?' he said.

'The others said Steve and Dave walked back, so why not the killer? Besides, he could have dumped his gear somewhere it wouldn't be found and taken the shortcut up the cliff. There's a path.'

'A cliff path?'

'Yes, Fred mentioned it at breakfast. Remember?'

'I must have wandered off.'

'Anyway, I saw it before, on a map.'

She pictured the killer hiking up the cliff and dismissed the idea as highly improbable. No one in their right mind would scale a treacherous path like that in the dark. It was tantamount to suicide.

'There's something we haven't considered,' she said slowly. 'The killer could just as easily be hanging around here, in hiding.'

'How likely is that, do you think? I mean, if I were the killer, I'd be in a big hurry to get far away as fast as possible.'

'But that's you. And not everyone has your disposition.'

She was being as tactful as she could. Anyone who was able to return to the scene of the crime and dispose of the body in such a gruesome manner did not have a fearful bone in their body.

She was in two minds whether to stick with the ex-boyfriend theory. On the one hand, it did mean he was probably nowhere in the vicinity, having succeeded in executing his crime and disposing of the evidence. On the other hand, what if she was wrong? She didn't want to give Richard an excuse to relax and take a nap, just in case. And she couldn't shake the feeling that something very strange was going on. All that toing and froing to Merida's. In fact, the very strange behaviour of both Vera and Carol ever since they'd arrived at Villa Winter.

Daggers shot through her hip. She couldn't remain seated any longer. She went and stood by the window, her mind settling on the matter of transport as the crux of the inquiry. At least investigating the getaway gave them something tangible to do.

'The others claim there's no car in the village,' she said. 'We need to find out if one of them heard or saw a car drive off.'

'Surely they'd have mentioned it at breakfast.'

'Maybe. But we didn't ask and not everyone was present. Merida wasn't there and Simon didn't show up. The lads have apparently headed off back to Morro Jable. And we do know that the workman who was in the courtyard when we arrived had a car. He took off in a hurry, too. If I had to put my money on anyone, it would be him.'

Was the workman the boyfriend? Was he pretending to be a workman to mask his true identity? Satisfaction rose in her as she thought she may have solved the crime.

Richard scuttled her theory when he said, 'A bit obvious, don't you think? In all the crime fiction I have ever written or read or seen on television, the most obvious suspect is never the culprit.'

'This is not fiction,' she said dismissively, as pride gave way to irritation. 'This is real life. And if we are considering all those we know were at Villa Winter, then I think we can rule out the women. None of them look strong enough to heft a body down to the bunkers or wield a chainsaw.'

'True. Although we are yet to meet Merida.'

'I saw her briefly and she didn't look big-boned.'

'What about the lads?'

'Steve and Dave have been on my mind as well.' They hadn't, but perhaps they should have been. Although they seemed to be a unit and only one person returned to dispose of the body. And besides, Australia was a long way to come to commit a murder. She went on. 'I have a lot of questions around the whole scenario. Why was the undercover cop at Villa Winter? And how did she arrive? By car? Then, where's the car? Did she get a lift and then walk from Cofete? Must have walked from the village, unless she came down the cliff path. In a calima? Not likely. Or the bus. We mustn't forget the public bus.'

'Which doesn't run on Saturdays.'

'Maybe she arrived on Friday. We do know she could have arrived in any number of ways. Did the killer travel with her? He must at least have had prior knowledge that she was coming here.'

'True. This was not a random killing.'

'I think we've established that. They had to have known to each other. Or she was under observation.'

Richard snapped his fingers.

'We are assuming the killer committed the murder at the villa.'

'You mean he might have bundled the body in that chest for storage, with the intention of making full use of the incinerator?'

He slumped back in his seat. 'You're right. Not that likely.'

'There's too much we don't know and will probably never know.'

'And you know what? This isn't any of our business. I, for one, am looking forward to a relaxing afternoon, a big long sleep, and a bus ride out of here in the morning.'

She'd suspected as much. Well, there was nothing for it. She didn't want to scare him, but what choice was there?

'That's all well and good,' she said, 'but there's something else I haven't told you.'

He gave her a pleading look.

'I don't think I can take much more.'

'I don't think you are taking in the gravity of the situation.'

'Meaning?'

'When we got to the top of the attic, you put your foot down on a squeaky floorboard. I am pretty sure the killer heard that.'

Richard froze.

'I wondered that,' he murmured.

'Hence he searched the attic rooms.'

'And didn't find us.'

'But the point is if the killer is still in Cofete, he would no doubt by now know we were at the villa.'

Her blood curdled as she said it. As though she had been trying to hide the stark fact even from herself.

Richard was slow to take in the full impact.

'I suppose word would travel fast. And in any event, he would have seen us arrive at Villa Winter.'

'You're missing my point.'

'Which is?'

'Do I have to spell it out for you?'

He stared at her blankly.

'The killer may well have seen us all arrive for the tour, but my point is he now knows for certain that we didn't leave with the others.' She paused, watching his expression change.

'You mean he saw us arrive in Cofete this morning?'

'Exactly. It puts us both in mortal danger.'

'Dear god.'

'Like I said, I'm not planning on falling asleep anytime soon.'

There was little chance of that in any event; her hip would make sure of it.

They were jolted from their worrisome tête-à-tête by a knock on the door. Richard went to answer it. He returned seconds later announcing, 'Lunch is served.'

'Already?'

She unplugged her phone and put it in her pocket, handing Richard his phone charger and adapter as she stood.

'I'm not sure I'm all that hungry,' Richard said.

The Ghost of Villa Winter

'We can't hide ourselves away in here. We can't even lock ourselves in since Salvador has retained the only key. Besides,' she said, looking around at the tired and flaking paintwork and the rustic furniture, 'it would be good to get out of this mausoleum of a place, don't you think?'

She gathered together her belongings and shoved everything in her canvas bag. She was about to open the front door when she saw Richard was planning on leaving without his backpack. She grabbed his arm and said with some force, 'We take everything with us.'

'Won't that look suspicious?'

'If anyone asks, we'll say we're going for a walk on the beach right after lunch. Besides, the tour bus crew are not our main concern.'

10

AN INTERRUPTION AT LUNCH

They stepped outside to find the calima had all but cleared. Would that mean visitors, tourists, locals would start flocking into Cofete? At least it meant a beach walk would appear authentic. Because it had just dawned on her that since they had no idea of the identity of Anna's boyfriend, he could be any one of the men here in Cofete. Perhaps it was the workman they'd seen in the courtyard. Or it could be Simon or Francois or even Salvador if he was given to having affairs. Although she had to rule out Simon; going by his rainbow embroidered shirt, he identified as gay. Francois was a tough pick, too, but she shouldn't let appearances cloud her judgement.

At the restaurant, a table had been laid for lunch on the patio outside. They were the first to arrive, Clarissa choosing two of the chairs with their backs to the wall and a view of the car park and indicating to Richard to sit beside her. Salvador appeared with a carafe of water as they sat down. He wore a welcoming smile on his rugged face and she knew instantly beneath that smile lurked some other emotion, some other thought. He was simply too upbeat not to be hiding something.

'Fabulous to have fresh air again,' she said cheerily, matching his demeanour.

'These calimas can disappear fast.'

'Does that mean we can expect an influx of visitors?'

'Just us here today. I heard on the radio there's been an accident on the cliff road. Some idiot tried to turn around and the back wheels of his vehicle overshot the edge of the road. An oncoming car slammed into him.'

'Fatalities?'

'Not that I know of. Wouldn't have been going fast so I doubt it, but it means all traffic to Cofete has to turn back. They've cordoned off the road.'

All optimism Clarissa had harboured vanished. Salvador had to be telling the truth. He had no reason to lie and there was no evidence of anyone arriving in the village to contradict him. Once Salvador had retreated to the kitchen, she helped herself to water and passed the carafe to Richard who filled his glass to the brim. As he drank his water, she leaned towards him, giving him a nudge to make sure he was paying attention before telling him to be on his guard.

'And watch what you say.'

'Don't worry, I will.'

It wasn't long before the others filtered in. First came Vera and Carol who plonked themselves down on the other side of Richard. Seemed they still had no interest in getting physically let alone cordially close to her. Since she and Richard had returned from their nocturnal ordeal at Villa Winter, the attitude of the two women had changed, and Clarissa was in danger of losing all respect for them. Gone two intelligent, engaging and feisty women holding their own in a conversation with male strangers. Women she might have enjoyed conversing with, perhaps even confiding in. Instead, they had taken to teasing Richard and ostracising her whenever they could. Then there was the matter of their little visits to Merida's, probably to issue various complaints. Now they had descended even further, carping and bitching to each other about Fred in his absence and then complaining about their dirty clothes.

'Next time I go on a tour I'm packing a spare outfit,' Vera announced.

'A pair of fresh knickers would be nice.'

Clarissa chose not to comment. There was an all too short moment of silence, broken by Carol who turned to Richard and said, 'Enjoy your little lie down?'

She gave him a wink. He stiffened. Clarissa leaned forward and spoke for them both.

'We took it in turns to have a good long shower and a well-deserved rest.'

'Funny,' Vera said, staring daggers. 'I saw you peering out the kitchen window earlier, so I thought maybe it was only Richard who was resting.'

'Oh, you can never tell what these two lovebirds get up to when they're by themselves, hey Richard.' Carol nudged his arm again. 'A little hanky-panky, I don't doubt.'

The two women burst into raucous laughter. Richard's cheeks reddened. He really should learn some retorts. His emasculated manner left him wide open to those sorts of jibes. Women picked up on his crushingly low self-esteem. His fastidiousness. Mind you, Clarissa could think of nothing to fire back with either. They were saved from further humiliation by the appearance of Helen, who wandered over and sat opposite Vera and Carol. It was as though she, too, was avoiding close contact with Clarissa.

She chose not to be hurt by it, reminding herself she was much older than any of them and she had a visage some found intimidating, a visage hardened, no doubt, by the enormous discomfort she found herself in with her hip. Still, she thought she'd at least try to strike up a conversation. She waited for Helen to lift her gaze.

'How are you faring?' she said sympathetically.

'Perfectly fine, now, thank you. Yourself?'

'Never felt better.' Richard shot her a quick sideways look which she ignored. There was no way she was going to admit to her current incapacity, not to Richard and not in the face of so much hostility. She went on. 'Especially after that hearty breakfast. I think now the calima has gone, I might take a long walk on the beach. What do you think, Richard?'

'You can always leave him here with us,' Carol said. 'We'd gladly take care of him for you.'

'Yes, gladly.'

Were there no limits to these two? It was only when Francois entered the walled dining area and took up the end of the table that the conversation settled down. He seemed to have gained authority over the group, authority he surely did not have back at the villa, and, Clarissa noted, it was authority gained despite being incompetent and irascible and the cause of their predicament.

He acknowledged Clarissa with a grunt and proceeded to study his phone.

A few moments passed and then Simon appeared, striding across the car park. He came and sat down opposite Clarissa and, like Francois, bent his head over his phone. There were two places laid in the middle of the table for Fred and Margaret. She began to hanker for their presence. Fred harmonised the group with his monologues, not that anyone wanted to hear them. It was just that the Spices filled a gap that very much needed filling and not with the nonsense coming out of the mouths of Carol and Vera.

Clarissa stared at Simon until he lifted his gaze. What was it with these men and their phones?

'We didn't see you this morning. Don't you eat breakfast?' she said lightly, not wanting to appear she was prying.

He stared at her through cool eyes.

'Fruit, and I had it in my shack.'

He supplied her with a weak smile. It wasn't enough to warrant further dialogue but she persisted, determined to find out more about him. She followed up with, 'I expect you are keen to get back to civilisation.'

'As keen as the rest of us.'

'What brought you here? I mean, you haven't taken much of an interest in the tour and you seem distracted.'

'I've a lot on my mind. One of my clients has chosen this weekend to threaten suicide and I've been trying to save his life.'

'You're a psychologist?'

'Social work. But this is after hours.'

He was the most unlikely looking social worker she had ever encountered. But at least his profession explained his preoccupation. The poor man must be feeling terribly burdened. His remark didn't explain why he had come on the tour in the first place, if he was having to deal with that terrible drama. And what of his wandering off while they were up at Villa Winter? What of his little exchanges with Francois? She wasn't satisfied with his response and dearly wanted to probe further but now was not the time or the place. She needed to talk to him alone.

Salvador appeared with a basket of bread and a platter of tapas. He was about to set the food down on the table

The Ghost of Villa Winter

when they were distracted by a distant scream, followed by a lot of shouting. The shouts grew louder and Fred appeared on the far side of the car park, his arms waving frantically, followed by a transparently terrified Margaret. Fred came barrelling towards the restaurant, red-faced and breathless. Margaret hung back.

'There's been an accident,' he gasped.

The others looked up, shocked. Salvador put down the platter he was holding. Vera and Carol stood at once.

'What is it?' said Helen.

'A man. I think he's dead.'

'Dead?'

'Well, he doesn't appear to be breathing.'

Francois was first to react, standing abruptly and making to leave the patio. Fred stepped out of his way. Prompted, the rest of the gathering followed Francois, passing Margaret – who stood like a stranded waif wringing her hands – and hurrying across the car park to where a path beside the hill led to a swathe of gravel fringed by a low dry-stone wall. The area, which afforded a sweeping view of the coastline to the north, was given over to two bronze statues, a man and his dog, each on its own stone plinth. The man, Gustav Winter, stood triumphantly looking out over his farmhouse in the mid-distance. Eyeing the figure was confirmation of her ghostly sighting; Gustav Winter was haunting the villa. The statue of his dog stood looking loyally up at his master. Slumped over the dog's back was a man.

Voices rose hysterically as everyone spoke at once. Near the start of the gravelled area, Fred tried to comfort Margaret who couldn't contain her shock. The other women hovered beneath the Gustav Winter statue, consoling each other. Simon watched on from a safe distance on the far side of the statues. Richard positioned himself near the dog, about four paces from the dead man's feet. Clarissa joined him. She was about to take charge of the situation when Francois and Salvador went over and lifted the body off the dog and laid him down on the ground face up. The head tilted to the side. The mouth hung slack and there was no sign of breathing, but at least the eyes were closed. He'd never been a handsome man. He had a distinctive face with thick eyebrows, an upturned nose and a pronounced underbite obscured to a degree by a thin moustache. Although as dead bodies went, this one wasn't gruesome. Clarissa noted the smart clothing, distinct from yesterday's overalls. And his shoes were polished. He appeared to have been going somewhere. She wondered why he hadn't turned up at breakfast that morning. Maybe he wasn't invited. Perhaps, like Simon, he was self-catering, or he'd eaten with Merida. It was only the tour party who lacked provisions. Did he live in the village or was his home elsewhere? Salvador had failed to mention him earlier, when he said there was no one except himself and Merida around. An oversight? Or ignorance? In her side vision, she saw Richard staring in disbelief. She kept close to him, monitoring his reaction.

Salvador was standing at the head end of the body. His face wore a bland expression.

'It's Alvaro,' Francois said, taking a step back.

'You know him?' Richard said.

'He does a lot of work up at the house. Construction.'

'He was in the courtyard when we arrived for the tour,' said Clarissa. 'Headed off in a hurry, too.'

'He didn't want to disturb us,' Francois said without shifting his gaze.

'He won't be disturbing anyone now,' Salvador said grimly.

'Are we sure he's dead?' said Clarissa.

The Ghost of Villa Winter

Without so much as bending down to check for a pulse, Francois turned to the others and said, 'Go get Merida.'

'I'll go,' Vera said and rushed off up the path.

Everyone else stood around. It felt like an age before the hearty and wholesome woman Clarissa had seen when they'd arrived in Cofete the day before came rushing over carrying a medical bag, a look of concern in her face. She had on a vivid red T-shirt beneath the same dungarees and her voluminous hair was scarcely contained in a large comb, with long wavy tresses blowing about in the wind.

She knelt down beside the man, felt for a pulse and shook her head. Then she inspected the body. Everyone watched. No one seemed able to move. They were all frozen where they stood, in varying states of shock and disbelief. The anticipation was palpable. Eventually Merida rose to her feet and said, 'Alvaro's dead.'

'How?' said Clarissa.

'Blunt force trauma.'

'Meaning?' said Carol who had edged closer, terror having given way to fascination.

'Someone clobbered the poor fellow on the back of his skull.'

A number of the party gasped.

'Poor Alvaro,' Salvador said. Clarissa, whose gaze had barely shifted from his face since Merida arrived on the scene, studied him closely. Did she detect sincerity?

'Murder?' Vera said, joining Carol as she edged even closer to view the body.

'I thought he'd just collapsed,' said Fred, clearly distressed. 'Who would do such a thing?'

Merida picked up her bag. 'Someone very angry and very strong, I imagine.'

Everyone looked at each other with a measure of doubt

and suspicion and disbelief. Clarissa was reluctant to reveal too much about herself but she felt she had no choice.

'Do you mind?' she said, kneeling down as Merida stepped away. 'I used to be a mortuary attendant.' She felt the skin of the dead man's cheek and moved his arm. Flesh still warm and no rigor mortis. He'd been dead less than two hours. She would hazard a guess at within the hour. She heaved herself to her feet, doing her best not to appear stiff and preventing her face from wincing.

'And?' said Merida.

'I'm no expert, but it seems fairly clear he was killed very recently.'

She held back on the whole truth in case it led to unforeseen consequences, not least a raft of accusations amongst the group. She'd witnessed a similar episode in her mortuary attendant days, when a groom was murdered at his wedding. All hell broke loose in the wedding party when the pathologist at the scene announced he'd only been dead an hour.

Fred left Margaret's side and joined the men near the body.

'Someone should contact the police,' he said emphatically.

Salvador looked at him with derision. It was an unexpectedly strong reaction. Had Fred managed to irritate him to that extent in the short time they'd been acquainted? Or was it instant dislike? Either way, there was loathing in Salvador's eyes and Clarissa found it disconcerting.

'How are we to do that?' he said sarcastically. 'Phone reception is appalling at the best of times.'

'But Francois and Simon have been using their phones here the whole time. How can they do that without reception?'

The Ghost of Villa Winter

Richard opened his mouth to speak. Before he did, Simon said, 'I've been reading articles I downloaded the other week.'

'And I've been practicing my English.'

At least one of them was lying, unless Simon had an internet connection in his billet and was using that to counsel his at-risk youth. Or perhaps that was a lie as well. Clarissa wouldn't put it past him.

'But the calima has cleared,' Fred said, not knowing when to desist. 'Surely that means reception will have improved.'

Salvador yanked his phone out of his trouser pocket and switched it on.

'No bars. See?' In a token move, he held the phone up to Fred, but did not allow him time to properly see the screen. 'Do you have any bars, Merida?'

'Nope.' She didn't even look.

'It goes like that here.'

'It's why we like it.'

Clarissa wasn't convinced the pair were telling the truth. They might not have phone reception, but they probably had Wi Fi which meant they could at least send an email to the nearest police station. And either one of them could have committed the murder. But there was no point in challenging Salvador.

'What are we going to do?' Vera said, her arms wrapped around herself. 'We can't leave the body here.'

'We should leave the body right here, until we can fetch help,' Clarissa said authoritatively.

'No, we better move it,' said Salvador.

'Usually, you don't disturb a murder scene.'

'Yeah, but there are a lot of wild dogs in the area and we want a corpse, not a half-eaten carcass.'

155

'Wild dogs?' Fred said. 'It's the first I've heard of it.'

'You're not from round here,' Merida said dismissively.

'We get vultures, too,' said Salvador.

'And eagles,' Merida chimed.

'Plenty of kestrels.'

'They eat carrion, too, right?'

'They'd rip the poor fellow to shreds.'

'Oh, please!' said Margaret. No one took any notice.

'And what about the flies,' said Merida.

'Especially the flies.'

'But it's winter,' said Fred.

'There are still flies. Just not quite so many.'

'We can cover the body in a blanket,' Clarissa said, trying to be practical.

'A blanket,' said Merida flatly. 'Fat lot of good that will do in this wind.'

Clarissa took a sudden dislike to the woman.

'A blanket is what is needed,' she said again. 'And we can organise a rota and keep watch.'

'I'm scared of dogs,' said Helen.

'Me, too,' said Vera. Clarissa thought that highly unlikely.

Salvador resumed his spot at the head of the body.

'You're overlooking the main point. This is a prime tourist area and when the sightseers do come tearing down the cliff in the morning, the last thing we want them to see is a corpse.'

Clarissa could scarcely believe what she was hearing.

'Then, tape the area off.'

She was ignored.

'Why don't we load the corpse onto one of your donkeys and take the road back to Morro Jable?' said Fred.

He was serious. It wasn't a bad idea, assuming the car

blocking the road allowed for people and beasts to pass by. At least whoever accompanied the donkey would get to leave this cursed location. Perhaps they should all go, and leave Salvador and Merida to deal with their problematic little village of Cofete. But it was not an idea that met with much approval. Salvador and Merida exchanged a mocking laugh.

'Are you serious?' Francois said with a scoff.

'Drop it, Fred,' said Merida.

She was right. Fred's suggestion meant borrowing Merida's donkey and she had already revealed she would fall in with Salvador's wishes. Clarissa recalled that package they exchanged in the car park yesterday. The pair were in cahoots in some fashion, no doubt about it, but murder? Maybe not.

'Then what are we to do?' said Carol.

Clarissa shot a quick look behind her and saw that Carol, too, was distressed. Vera wrapped a friendly arm around her shoulder and offered Clarissa a thin smile. Clarissa turned back to the corpse.

'I still think my suggestion is the best option,' said Fred, plainly offended by all the rebukes he had been receiving of late. Clarissa began to feel sorry for the man. He went on. 'Unless, anyone can come up with a better idea.'

Salvador was quick to come up with, 'I'll put him in the cool room. When my wife gets back, I'll drive the body into town.'

He gestured to Francois and together they lifted the corpse. The women all headed back up the path ahead of the two men, with the exception of Margaret who clung to Fred, her head buried in his shoulder as she waited for Francois and Salvador to pass them by. The party walked away like a funeral cortege with Simon bringing up the rear.

Clarissa stuck by Richard who hadn't moved from his spot. They waited for the others to disappear around the side of the hill. Simon glanced back at them as he entered the car park and slipped from view. He was too far away for her to read the expression on his face, but she didn't care for his faux-nonchalant attitude.

With the others safely out of earshot, she said, 'I'm not liking this one bit.'

'Me neither,' Richard said with sudden relief. 'All that nonsense about moving the body. Even I know you don't interfere with the crime scene.'

'Not unless you've something to hide.'

He was looking out at the ocean and the long, deserted beach. The wind blew his hair back from his face. Standing tall, all cleanshaven, he was suddenly handsome in her eyes and she glimpsed the life he had led as a result of those classic features coupled with his crippling anxiety. It was a challenging mix. While others expected an inner nobility to blend with his superior manly looks, he could offer nothing but stuck on charm thinly masking a bundle of neurotic insecurities. No wonder he clung to his wife.

'Do you think the two murders are linked?' he said, coming out of his own reverie and stating the obvious.

'Have to be. We'll talk later,' she said, beckoning for him to accompany her back to the restaurant. 'Careful what you say, Richard. Something strange is going on here and it's fairly obvious Salvador and Merida are in cahoots.'

'This doesn't fit the ex-boyfriend theory.'

'I haven't given up on that yet.'

'How well do those two know Francois?'

'Reasonably well, from what I've observed. Why?'

'He's the only one of us who visits here regularly.'

'As far as we know.'

'Definitely not Fred and Margaret.'

'They are not contenders.'

'As for Simon and the three women, we don't know the first thing about them.'

'Except that they don't know each other.'

'Vera and Carol are friends.'

'True. But they don't know Merida and Salvador. At least, that's how things appear.'

She thought back to when she saw Vera and then Carol heading to Merida's place. But that could have been for any reason at all. A friendly invitation. A cup of sugar. A plaster for a cut. It was important not to get paranoid.

'We can't go suspecting everyone,' she said. 'We'll drive ourselves insane.'

'What about those lads?'

'Steve and Dave?'

He stopped in his tracks and she was forced to do the same, taking a step backwards. The heel of her foot landed on a large pebble and slid off it, turning her ankle. A hot dart shot through her hip. She suppressed a gasp.

'Those lads could be in hiding,' he said. 'If you ask me, I bet that's what's going on. And you know what else?'

'What?'

'One of them could be the boyfriend.'

'I hadn't really considered that.'

Because they were from Australia, which just felt too far away. But the world was a small place these days. Yet again, his reasoning impressed her.

They continued walking. As they neared the restaurant, they slowed their pace. Richard stopped again, requiring her to stop as well. She wished he wouldn't stop dead in his tracks whenever he had something important to say. She was about to continue when he tapped her arm. She was about to caution him not to speak too loudly or appear too furtive in front of the others now seated at the lunch table and all looking their way, but she needn't have feared.

'Fred has the right idea,' he said. 'Why don't we do what Steve and Dave apparently did and walk back to Morro Jable?'

She scanned the cliff towering above them and pictured that wriggly snake of a road clinging to its side. She laughed, more for the benefit of the others than to mock him.

'It's too far, Richard,' she said gently.

He didn't contest the fact. She didn't mention her hip. There was every chance he'd offer her the painkillers tucked in her trouser pocket.

Clarissa eyed the two vacant seats at the table and approached with considerable reluctance. The others were tucking into the tapas and chatting quietly. Merida had taken up a chair between Francois and Simon at the table's end.

'Ah, the lovebirds have arrived!' said Vera, looking straight at Richard, a grin plastered across her face. She gave him a pronounced wink. The joke was well past its use by.

'We got distracted by the view,' Richard said awkwardly.

'That's what they all say.'

Carol and Vera both laughed. It was more of a cackle. No one joined in.

'Vera, stop it,' said Fred. 'Leave the poor man alone. Can't you see he's been through enough.'

'He hasn't been through anything, as far as I can tell,' Carol snapped. 'No more than the rest of us.'

Richard didn't care for the attention from either direction. He sat down and took a long draught of his water. Once he'd set down his glass, he kept his gaze pinned on the table.

'I think we are all overwrought,' Clarissa said, taking up

her chair beside him and adopting a peacemaker role. 'It's never easy confronting a dead body especially when they've been murdered.'

Carol screwed up her face. 'Don't.'

Clarissa gave her a cool stare. 'We have to face the truth. I'm just glad we are all here to support Merida and Salvador. Imagine how they would be feeling right now if we weren't here.'

'Exposed and in danger, most likely,' said Margaret grimly.

'Are we in danger, do you think?' Helen said, wide-eyed.

'Not sure,' said Clarissa. Finding herself the centre of attention, she added, 'But I do think we should all stick together, or let each other know our whereabouts. That sort of thing.'

'Sounds like a plan.'

There was not much tapas left. Fred proffered the platter and Clarissa took some olives and what was left of the mushrooms, leaving Richard with a few meatballs in tomato sauce. He took the last of the bread. As they consumed what they had, Salvador gathered up dirty plates and replaced the tapas with a hearty-looking meat and lentil stew served with little potatoes and more hunks of white bread. He held his arms wide with obvious pride and said, 'Enjoy.' He grinned. There was no sign he was at all troubled by the ordeal of Alvaro's death, which was remarkable considering he had the corpse in his storeroom. Some people were not fazed by death.

Plates were passed around as Vera served. Clarissa did not have much of an appetite after the enormous breakfast but she forced herself to keep eating the tapas on her plate. Exhaustion had started to kick in the moment she'd picked up her fork and stabbed her second olive. She was surprised at the appetites of everyone else. Perhaps they were comfort eating. They were certainly showing no signs of trauma, other than Margaret.

As much as she would have loved to dull her senses and numb her hip pain, Clarissa forwent the wine circulating. She had to kick Richard under the table as he was about to accept a glass. He accepted it anyway but he refrained from taking more than a sip. When Salvador reappeared, she asked for a coffee.

'Make that two, and strong, if you please.'

Richard said nothing. He seemed resigned to let her take control. Her appetite grew stronger when she set aside her tapas plate and tasted the stew. It was delicious, the meat tender, the sauce rich with layers of flavour. As she ate, her gaze travelled around the group. Helen ate slowly and she appeared entirely absorbed in her food. Vera and Carol were deep in a side conversation which seemed to pertain to a member of Vera's family. Fred kept glancing at Richard, but he chose not to speak. Margaret was a bundle of nerves. Clarissa caught her eye and offered her a reassuring smile. Simon was as self-absorbed as ever. Merida ate methodically, keeping her focus low even as she reached for her wine. Francois reached for his as well.

'Alvaro will be missed,' he said, addressing Merida.

'He will. Such a pity. He only got out last week.'

'Out of where?' said Richard.

No one answered. There was only one place you got out of, Clarissa thought. Two, if you included a mental hospital.

'Who is going to tell Pedro?'

No one answered. Since Pedro and his family had a close and enduring association with the villa, he'd find out soon enough.

The first to finish, Merida set down her fork and pushed

The Ghost of Villa Winter

away her empty plate. 'I just don't get it. He was a really lovely man,' she said with genuine sadness. 'He fixed my yard just the other day. Always ready with a hammer or a saw.'

'He was a local?' Clarissa asked.

'He lived in that lone shack right up the back. He was a solitary guy. Never talked much about his past, but I know he'd had a difficult life. Unhappy childhood and an unhappy marriage.'

'What drew him here?'

'The surf.'

Merida fell silent. She was the only one in the group to look genuinely aggrieved.

There was a brief pause in the conversation, most returning to their stew. Before long Salvador came out with the two coffees. After setting them down, he drew up a chair, positioning himself behind Merida and Simon who shifted their seats to make room. Clarissa finished her stew and reached for her cup, eager for the caffeine. Richard, who didn't have the energy for his usual fastidiousness, took a slurp of his before stabbing the last of the meat on his plate.

Fred, who had been subdued for the duration of the meal, set down his fork and said with gravitas, 'You all realise this means there's a killer on the loose.' He looked around at the others. Reactions were slow and mixed. Alarm appeared in Margaret's face.

Fred, don't,' she said.

'It's alright, love. But it needs to be said.'

'Fred's right,' Helen said, leaning forward. 'We should face up to this.'

'Could be a hiker come down from Morro Jable,' Merida said.

'We get a lot of those,' said Salvador.

'Or someone heading down the beach.'

'Up the beach, maybe.'

'Those hikers are everywhere.'

'You get all sorts here.'

'A mugging, you mean?' said Fred.

Salvador and Merida both looked at him at once.

'Could be.'

There was a lull in the exchange as everyone absorbed the possibilities.

Then Vera sat up tall and wide-eyed as though a light bulb had gone off in her head.

'What about Steve and Dave?' she said, snapping her fingers. 'They said they were walking back to Morro Jable, but did anyone see them go?'

'Even if they did,' said Carol, 'the lads could have doubled back.'

'I never considered that,' Helen said, as if she had been privately cogitating suspects.

Perhaps she had. Clarissa didn't know whether to feel relieved she and Richard were not the only ones to harbour suspicions, or irritated at the competition. She hadn't realised how attached she was to solving the crime. She did have one up on the competitor. Helen knew nothing about Anna. No one did, other than the killer, and her and Richard.

From that moment, the lads became the subject of intense suspicion among the group.

'I always thought that pair were shifty,' Carol said. 'I reckon they're poofters.'

Clarissa couldn't suppress a gasp. She shot Simon an apologetic look but he didn't react.

'Oh, I don't know,' said Fred, rising to their defence. 'I found them personable and intelligent.'

'You would say that,' said Vera. It was clear from the expression on her face that she held Fred in complete contempt.

'Whatever do you mean?' he said indignantly, the colour rising to his cheeks.

Vera pinned him with her gaze.

'You only have a high opinion of them because they sided with you at lunch.'

'And on the tour,' added Carol, knocking back her wine.

Everyone else watched on, waiting for Fred's retort. He was slow to respond. When he did, he surprised everyone by saying, 'Have it your way. Now is not the time for bickering.' Then he slumped back in his seat and reached for Margaret's hand, defeated.

'Did you hear Steve speak German?' Carol said, determined to whip up the speculations. 'Maybe that pair have more invested in Villa Winter than they let on.'

'I've never had much time for conspiracy theorists,' Vera said, no doubt realising that Fred's resignation had weakened the impact of her own attack. 'All that rubbish about U-boats and secret tunnels and a second bunker.'

Clarissa recalled the ghost she'd encountered in the bunker and the way it had guided her to pay attention to the ground below.

'Did they mention the second bunker?' said Richard. 'I don't remember that.'

Carol nudged Vera and sniggered.

'Yeah, that must have been when you two took off up to the tower.'

Ignoring the teasing, Fred caught Richard's gaze and said, 'They went on and on about some secret...'

'I think Vera's got a point,' Merida cut in. Heads turned.

'The lads could well be hanging around here. If not them, then someone else.'

'Oh, my good god, do you really think so?' Carol said, a look of shock appearing in her face.

'We'll soon find them if they are still here in Cofete,' Salvador said, oozing confidence.

'You mean...?'

'We'll mount a search.'

There were nods and murmurs of agreement, and Salvador instantly took charge.

'I suggest we head off in groups. Me and Merida know the area the best so I think we should pair up with the rest of you. Merida, you take this man here,' he said gesturing at Simon. 'Go right up the back on the north side.'

'You okay with that, Simon?' Merida asked.

'Sure.' The pair locked gazes and the corners of his mouth lifted a fraction in what amounted to a smile. Typical predator male scoping the possibilities and locking one in for later. And he was gay? No way! Bisexual maybe. Clarissa wasn't sure she was capable of disliking him any less, and she wouldn't let the idea of prejudice cloud her judgement. She had always held an aversion to the playboy type.

'And Francois, how about you take that woman at the end.'

'Me?' Helen said doubtfully.

Salvador gave her a hurried nod and turned back to Francois. 'You cover the houses close to the cliff road.'

'No problem'.

It was hard to fathom what use Helen would be should they stumble on the killer. Stick her foot out should he pass her on his way by?

Salvador turned to Fred. 'You and Margaret might as well stay together. Go over to those houses at the front of yours. I'll take Vera and Carol with me and search the houses up the back on the south side. And you two,' he said, catching Richard's gaze. 'You can search around your place here.'

People began to shuffle out of their seats. Clarissa drained her cup and stood. Richard did the same.

'How will we sound the alarm if we find him?' Fred said.

'Don't you mean them?' said Vera in the same derisory tone she had taken to using when speaking to Fred.

'We don't know if it is Steve and Dave.'

'A dead cert, if you ask me.'

'Fred has a made a good point,' Salvador said. 'I have some whistles. I'll get them.'

'Whistles?' Carol said after he'd gone. 'That man sure is well-equipped.'

'It's his wife,' said Merida. 'She's a coach.'

While they waited, the group fell into a furtive discussion about how to apprehend anyone they should find.

'Hey, what about weapons?' said Vera. 'Shouldn't we be armed?'

Merida nudged Francois. 'She's right. Come with me.'

Salvador returned with a clutch of the sort of whistle used in a school's physical education class. Then Merida and Francois appeared, loaded with two oars, a garden fork, a shovel and a hoe.

Fred looked doubtful as Merida handed him an oar.

'What am I supposed to do with this?'

'It's better than nothing.'

'Salvador would have plenty of knives,' Simon with an ironic smirk. 'Would you prefer one of those?'

Fred took an interest and Helen looked aghast.

'Weapons can be counter-productive,' said Carol quickly.

'I don't know how many times I've seen a knife knocked out of an assailant's hand.'

'That's the movies,' said Fred.

'So?'

Richard accepted the hoe Merida proffered. Everyone hovered as Salvador divvied out the whistles and door keys. Clarissa took charge of their set, Richard having already proven he had no luck with keys.

11

A SEARCH OF COFETE

With the village carved up between them, the killer couldn't possibly avoid detection. That was the thought everyone carried with them as the little groups assembled. Since Clarissa and Richard had been assigned the area around the restaurant and the short row of four terraced dwellings nearby, they had the easiest portion of the search. As the others wandered off, Clarissa took the opportunity to use the restaurant bathroom, leaving Richard standing around on the patio.

When she returned, she thought Richard was looking haggard and fit to drop. He needed to get his adrenalin pumping. She sidled up to him and said, 'Has it occurred to you that there are only two possibilities. Either the killer is in hiding in the village as the others seem to think or he was seated right here at this table only a moment ago.'

'You don't think...?' he said, instantly aroused as the thought sank in.

'It's possible. We need to keep an open mind. And I daresay the weapon used on Alvaro is here in Cofete somewhere. Could even be hanging on one of the walls of this restaurant.'

Richard glanced inside.

'How likely is that?'

'You never know.'

They entered the restaurant and started scanning about.

'What are we looking for?'

'Something to bludgeon with.'

Out of the array of artefacts on the restaurant walls there was nothing that fitted the purpose. Although they couldn't be sure the weapon hadn't been hanging on one of the walls since in two portions of the display there were gaps beneath the nails. One gap in particular caught Clarissa's attention, two nails side-by-side and a gap of about three centimetres between, a perfect arrangement for a hammer, especially considering the negative space afforded by the framed photos above and below, the wooden ladle to the left and the small guitar on the right. She took a photo. Then one of the framed photos below caught her eye. She was surprised to find a photo of Alvaro proudly showing off his surfboard. She took a photo of the photo, only because he was easily the strangest looking man she had ever encountered. It was his underbite, all the more prominent due to his grin.

'I'm not quite believing this is happening,' Richard said as they wandered outside.

Clarissa looked around to make certain the others were out of earshot.

'It's a farce,' she said. 'But we have to play along. And you never know, Salvador might be right. The killer might be lurking in one of these houses.'

'I hope it isn't Steve and Dave.'

'Why's that?'

'There are two of them.'

She let out a grim laugh.

'I think we can be certain no one would be so stupid as to hide out so close to the restaurant.'

Clarissa inserted the key labelled One and they entered the first of the terraced dwellings and were greeted by a strong odour of the sea. The place had been painted entirely in blue, a sort of bright maritime blue, the space decked out with all manner of seafaring items. There were old fishing nets adorning the walls. Upturned chests served as side tables. Framed photos of grinning men holding up their prize catch. Clarissa and Richard stayed together, tentatively entering each room and making their way through to the back of the house, Richard armed with his hoe. The last room they entered was the kitchen, and although spotless, it felt dirty. It was probably the fishy odour, which was stronger in there. A quick search through all the rooms a second time and they exited the house, locking the door and moving on to the next.

The rooms were smaller this time and there was no hall, each room opening onto the next with the bathroom tacked on the back. The walls were sensibly painted white, but even so, most of the space was gloomy. Clarissa went over to the large kitchen window and surveyed what she could see of the village. She wondered what the others were up to and how seriously they were taking the search. She spied Fred clutching his oar and creeping around the side of a stone hut not far off with Margaret tiptoeing behind him. In the distance she glimpsed Simon and Merida entering a hut on the edge of the village. No sign of anyone else.

Passing their own place, they inspected the house at the terrace end. Again, there was a lack of windows and the rooms were small. Surveying the surroundings, Clarissa saw that Salvador had given them the best pick of those particular holiday lets. The furnishings in the end terrace were worn and the place suffered a hint of mould. The rustic kitchen comprised a narrow bench with a curtain strung across the shelves below, an old fridge and a battered Formica table with four plastic chairs. A ladder, an empty paint pot and a small collection of tools indicated someone was doing some renovations.

'Who would bother staying in a place as rough as this?' said Richard, voicing her own thoughts.

'I imagine a lot of those stone huts are worse. Low roofs and small windows. I suppose most people stay here either for the surf or the isolation. Or both. Probably attracts the occasional artist or writer, too. This place does have a fascinating quality to it. Enchanting, almost.'

'If you like towering cliffs and pounding waves, then yes.' He paused. 'I find it desolate.'

'You are a man who likes his comforts.'

'Am I that obvious?'

'I'm afraid you are.'

Having conducted their portion of the search and, as anticipated, found nothing, they went back to their accommodation. This time, there was no need to use the key. Salvador had made sure their place remained unlocked. She was relieved to find there was nothing untoward to see. Everything was as they'd left it.

She went and looked out the kitchen window which, although offering a limited outlook, provided a much better view of the north side of Cofete than the other houses in the terrace. She was surprised to see Carol and Vera leaning against the back wall of a hut on the high side of that portion of the village. They were laughing. Then Salvador came into view. He appeared to be enjoying a cigarette. She could only assume they had completed their area of the search. After all, with four groups involved in the search party, they each had only four or five dwellings to inspect. Perhaps the absence of anyone using their whistle was a clear sign that no one suspicious was about. A thought confirmed when she saw Merida joining Simon and waving to Salvador who waved back.

Clarissa left the window. She was poised to enter the bathroom for a quick scan when Richard called out. He sounded perturbed. She about faced and hurried down the hall.

When she entered his bedroom, he said, 'Someone has been in here. I left my toiletries bag under my pillow with the drawstring extending to the right. See?'

The drawstring extended to the left.

'You're quite sure.'

'Positive. I did on purpose. I always do when I stay anywhere, ever since my hotel room was robbed.'

Clarissa didn't doubt him. If there was one thing Richard could be relied on to get right, it was knowing how he'd left things.

'Why would anyone search through our things? And more's the point, who?'

She thought back to when they had left for lunch and was disappointed to realise they had been the first to arrive at the table. Anyone could have searched their place, although they would have needed to enter through the back since the front door was visible from the restaurant patio. Only just, but it would have been an enormous risk. Clarissa's skin prickled. There was no time to contemplate the situation.

'Richard, we better get going.'

They left their accommodation and joined the others regrouping at the restaurant. Fred and Margaret were sitting in their earlier spots at the table. Merida and Simon had taken up the table behind them. Vera and Carol emerged from inside the restaurant with long glasses filled with something fizzy.

'Thirsty work, sleuthing,' said Carol with a giggle.

Fizzy, and alcoholic.

Salvador appeared behind them as Helen came running around the corner of the restaurant building. Not long after, Francois rushed into the patio holding a steel meat mallet, the handle wrapped in cloth. Clarissa pictured the two nails on the restaurant wall denoting a missing item.

'I think this is what killed Alvaro,' he said, holding out the mallet and showing it around. There was blood on the mallet end.

'Where did you find it?' Salvador said.

'Under the sink in that yellow farmhouse on the edge of the village.'

'That's right by the cliff road.'

'Whoever it was planned a fast getaway,' Merida said grimly as Helen seated herself down near Vera and Carol. The two women remained standing, wide-eyed and sipping their drinks. Helen was flushed and out of breath. Clarissa feared she might be about to have another of her turns, but no one else took any notice. They were all focused on the mallet.

'We'd have seen or heard any car heading off up the cliff road,' said Salvador, reaching and taking the mallet from Francois. 'That yellow farmhouse is only a hundred metres from here. You can't just drive off without someone knowing.'

'It's them. I just know it,' Vera said.

'Steve and Dave? We have no proof of that,' Clarissa said doubtfully.

The Ghost of Villa Winter

Vera gave her a withering look.

'Who else can it be?'

Salvador went and stood between the two tables. Fred and Margaret turned.

'Is that human blood?' Margaret said, horrified.

'Impossible to tell, but it's fresh.'

'Salvador, is the meat mallet yours, by any chance? I mean, could they have taken it out of your kitchen?'

Salvador handed the meat mallet to Merida before heading off to check. When he reappeared, he said, 'Mine is still there. I have no idea who that one belongs to. The farmhouse is rented out. Anyone could have left it there.'

'If it's the murder weapon,' Merida said, asserting control, 'we need to bag it up and take it to the police when we deliver the body.'

There were murmurs of agreement. Salvador returned to the kitchen, emerging with a clear plastic bag. Everyone watched as he eased in the mallet, including the cloth wrapped around the handle.

'I'll go and put it with the body,' he said.

Clarissa's gaze drifted towards the missing item on the restaurant wall. Could that really have been the meat mallet? She doubted it. A meat mallet was not the sort of implement to be hung on a wall.

'What do we do now?' Vera said. 'I mean, surely we can relax knowing the murderer is long gone.'

'We don't know that for sure,' said Merida. 'Like Salvador said, we would have heard a car. The only way they could have left the village is on foot. The road up the cliff is very exposed. And so is the beach. Whichever way they went they would have risked being seen. My feeling is they are still lurking somewhere nearby.'

'We haven't searched everywhere,' Francois said slowly.

'I was thinking that,' Merida said. 'We haven't been back to Villa Winter. Those lads could be hiding out there.'

'Down in the second bunker, maybe,' said Richard.

'Ah yes, the second bunker,' Clarissa said with interest, recalling her ghostly encounter.

'It's a myth,' Salvador said emphatically. 'There is no second bunker.'

'And we don't know it's them,' Fred said, without directing his remark at Merida seated behind him, and instead glancing at Vera.

'Will you shut up already? Of course, it's them.' Vera slammed down her glass. It was near empty. She brimmed with sudden fury, fists clenched, her eyes glaring rage beneath her combat helmet haircut.

'Steady on,' Fred said, alarmed, turning back to his wife for reassurance. Margaret didn't look capable of reassuring anyone.

Carol patted Vera's arm.

'Get a grip, love.'

'He drives me nuts,' Vera said between gritted teeth.

'He drives everyone nuts, I imagine.'

Neither of them cared that Fred could hear them. They collected their glasses and retreated into the restaurant. No one else moved. An atmosphere of unease pervaded the group. Salvador saved the situation from descending any further when he said, 'Francois, Simon, let's go check out Villa Winter. Merida, you keep an eye on things here. Everyone needs to stick together as much as possible. Safety in numbers.'

The men headed off on foot, armed with an oar, a garden fork and a shovel. A most unlikely trio that would have been comedic under other circumstances. As it was, the absence of those strong and fit men left everyone remaining behind vulnerable. Not that everyone was bothered. Instead, all cohesion was lost and the group fell into disarray. Helen joined Vera and Carol who seemed to be having a merry old time inside the restaurant, drowning their sorrows in whatever was to hand behind the bar. Merida said she needed to do a few things back at hers. And Fred said he was taking Margaret back to their billet for a lie down. Clarissa was left with Richard and no one inquired or cared about what they chose to do.

12

A VISIT TO FRED'S

Clarissa grabbed her canvas bag, tapped Richard's arm and said, 'We have to get to the bottom of this. Come with me. Time to pay someone a visit.'

'Where are we going?' he said, trailing behind her with his backpack slung over one shoulder as she headed off past their digs and cornered the end of the terrace.

She waited for him to catch up.

'To talk to Fred. He is the only one we can trust around here, as annoying as that may be for you. I can't bring myself to have any confidence in the others.'

'Do you know which place is theirs?'

They faced a cluster of dwellings on the low side of the road. On the high side were the huts searched earlier by Merida and Simon.

'Let's take a punt.'

They approached the first of the cluster, walking down a short gravel drive to the front door of an unrendered stone hut. Richard knocked and they waited. There was no sound coming from inside. Clarissa peered through a window. The interior looked unlived in.

The Ghost of Villa Winter

'I don't think this is the place,' she said. 'Let's try the one next door.'

They headed off up the track and entered another gravel driveway. The hut at the end was also made of rough stone and the windows were set at varying heights in the walls. Richard held up his hand to knock when the door flew open and Fred appeared.

'I saw you coming. Get inside before anyone else sees you. Quick,' he said.

It was an odd thing to say. Paranoid almost. Who was Fred hoping to avoid?

There was no entrance hall. They walked straight into the sitting room and Clarissa was pleasantly surprised to find the décor modern and spruce. The owners had taken a lot of trouble styling the arrangement of furnishings and wall hangings. There was a touch of India about the space and a faint hint of incense. Fred stood in the centre of the room. There was no sign of Margaret.

'Are you two alright?' Clarissa said with genuine concern.

Fred's response was stiff. 'Been better. Margaret is still in shock after the incident with the body. She found it. We were having a walk around the base of the hill and I'd stopped to remove some grit from my shoe.'

'I didn't know that,' Richard said.

'We're all looking forward to getting away from here,' said Clarissa for want of something to say. 'By the way, is there any reason you didn't want us to be seen coming here?'

'It's Vera and Carol. They were trying to get Merida to persuade Salvador to evict us because they prefer this holiday let to theirs. Merida refused to intervene. I don't want to make matters worse by appearing as though we have formed some kind of alliance with you.'

'I see what you mean.'

At least she had an explanation for the strange marching back and forth to Merida's earlier.

'I'd offer you tea,' said Fred, 'but we don't have any. I have some whisky.'

Richard opened his mouth to speak but Clarissa was quick to decline for both of them.

'I think it's best we all keep a clear head.'

Without waiting to be invited, she sat down in one of the armchairs to relieve the persistent dull ache and occasional sharp twinges in her hip which she had been steadfastly ignoring, and Richard took one end of the sofa. Before anything was said, Margaret entered the room and sat herself down in the other armchair. She looked forlorn and avoided Clarissa's gaze. Fred remained standing.

'You must be done in, Richard. That blasted Vera and all her teasing. I don't know how you put up with it. Has she no respect for who you are? An acclaimed author of bestselling novels, no less. She should show some grace.'

Richard emitted a short laugh. 'I try to ignore her.'

'Fred,' Clarissa said, unable to contain herself. 'Sorry to cut in, but we're here to ask a few questions.'

As Fred's eyes darted from Richard to her his expression morphed from warmth to coolness and she wondered at his opinion of her.

'Go right ahead,' he said with strained politeness.

She smiled at him hoping to ease the tension.

'Did any vehicle leave the village last night?'

'Last night?' He sounded confused. 'Alvaro was killed at lunchtime. You said so yourself.'

She hesitated, not wanting to give too much away.

'This is about something else,' she said, hoping she wasn't sounding evasive.

'When you were stuck in Villa Winter?'

She inhaled to speak when Richard said, 'It occurs to us that if Steve and Dave did head off, they might have stolen a car.'

Fred seemed satisfied with that remark and Clarissa filled with gratitude.

'Not that I know of,' he said, plainly delighted to now be addressing his hero. 'And I would have heard it. Or at least seen it. We have a direct line of sight up the cliff road, see.'

They turned to the window and found themselves staring straight at the cliff and the road snaking its way into the distance.

'What time did the lads set off?' Clarissa asked.

Fred turned to his wife.

'It was just after afternoon tea, wasn't it?'

Margaret perked up a little, no doubt relieved to have something to think about other than Alvaro.

'That's right. We'd all got settled and suddenly they announced they were leaving.'

'So, before sunset.'

'Oh yes, well before then.'

'And did you actually see them head off?'

'We saw them walking up the road, yes. We'd left the others and headed back here to get out of the dust. I watched from this window until I could no longer see them.'

'And you heard no vehicle drive in any direction after that?'

'No. But then, Salvador laid on an elaborate dinner and we were sitting inside out of the calima for quite some hours.'

'Was everyone present?'

'Yes, the whole tour party, except the lads and you two.'

'What about Merida?'

'She was there.'

'We'd have seen taillights, though, don't you think?' said Fred. 'If a car had been heading to Villa Winter, if that's what you mean.'

Clarissa stood and made for the front door, announcing, 'I'll be right back.'

She headed down to the bottom of the lane that ran past the Spice's and stood at the corner of the car park. She looked up the road heading to Villa Winter and then back in the direction of the restaurant. She discovered it was not possible to see the road at all from the restaurant thanks to the high wooden fence around Merida's place obscuring the view. She rushed back to Fred and Margaret's, not bothering to knock on her way in. Fred appeared shocked at the sight of her sudden entry as though she had taken a liberty.

She didn't have the patience to mollycoddle his sensibilities. Without offering an explanation she said, 'Richard, we better get going.'

He left the comfort of the sofa a little reluctantly, she thought. Now was no time for dozing in Fred's living room.

'One more thing,' she said, addressing Fred and Margaret on her way to the door. 'You didn't hear a car in the early hours of the morning, by any chance?'

They both shook their heads.

'No,' said Fred. 'Although we do tend to sleep soundly. But why all these questions? You don't think the lads killed Alvaro, surely?'

'We're just trying to figure out if it's true that no one here has used or seen anyone else use a vehicle this weekend.'

'If we'd heard a car, everyone would have heard it. So why ask us?' Fred said with surprising irritation. 'Margaret has been through enough.'

'She has. I can tell.' She gave Margaret a sympathetic look. 'We'll leave you to rest. Sorry to disturb you.'

As they walked back to their digs, Richard said, 'Why didn't you trust Fred enough to tell him what happened at Villa Winter?'

'You heard him. Margaret's been through enough,' she said sourly. 'Besides, we need to keep that ordeal to ourselves.'

Perhaps if she had divulged the truth, she would have gained Fred's sympathy, at least a fraction, but she couldn't risk it. As it was, he was hostile. Jealous, obviously. He would no doubt have dearly wished to monopolise Richard.

Once they were inside their accommodation, confident no one else could hear them, Clarissa said, 'We've established something, Richard.'

'We have?' He sounded doubtful.

'It comes down to means, motive and opportunity.'

'Of course.'

She followed him to the living room.

'Based on Fred and Margaret's testimony, it appears no one had the opportunity to dispose of Anna's body since they were all seated in the restaurant throughout dinner. No one had the means since no one had access to a vehicle. As for the motive, discovering the victim was an undercover cop, if true, is all very well, but what was it exactly she was investigating?'

'You mean,' he said, sitting down, 'was it really some weird satanic cult? Or something else?'

She remained standing in the doorway.

'I'm not sure how to approach the crimes from the angle of motive. Not yet. What we do know is a vehicle managed to sneak up to Villa Winter while the party were at dinner and sneak back when everyone was asleep. That same vehicle could be long gone by now, were it not for the death of Alvaro.'

'Assuming there was only one killer.'

'Exactly. How likely is it there are two killers?'

'It really is looking likely those lads are the culprits.'

'Except that Margaret watched them disappear up the path.'

'They could have waited and then come back.'

'Retrieved a hidden vehicle and lay in wait until they were sure everyone was in the restaurant and then made a dash for it.' She paused for a moment, absorbing the possibility. 'It's plausible.'

But she couldn't erase a nagging doubt that they had nothing to do with any of it, despite their conversing in German, which seemed to link them to Villa Winter but only tenuously, and despite their disappearing acts.

She visited the bathroom and while there, downed another two painkillers. When she returned Richard had slumped in his armchair with his eyes closed.

'I don't know about you, Richard,' she said loudly, 'but I think a brisk walk is in order.'

He opened his eyes and yawned. 'I really could do with a nap.'

'Nonsense. You're coming with me.'

'Must I?'

He looked up at her in disbelief. But he obliged, heaving himself to his feet. As they made their way to the front door he said, 'Can't we leave our things here?'

'Nope. You saw what happened earlier. Whatever we have in our possession stays with us.'

'You are a hard task master,' he said with a grim laugh.

'I wish I didn't have to be.'

13

A BEACH WALK

Clarissa took them round the back of the terraced houses, veering off before they reached Fred's and taking the track behind Merida's. When they reached the T-intersection on the outskirts of the village, Clarissa headed north for a short stretch before leading them down the road to the beach. The wind was fresh but not unpleasant and it was downhill all the way.

About ten minutes later the road curved and on the bend was a sandy rectangle given over to a makeshift cemetery. Formal access to the cemetery was through double wooden doors set in a small section of high stone wall. They didn't enter. They could see all there was to be seen from behind the low perimeter wall edging the bulk of the area. It was the most desolate cemetery there ever was. Basalt boulders were strewn across the sand, and here and there were weathered wooden crosses marking graves. Clarissa thought it likely there were more graves than crosses and the sand, driven by the wind, was banking up and slowly reclaiming the site.

'Locals are buried here,' Richard said. 'I read there is

meant to be a second cemetery of German graves but I've no idea where.'

'Closer to Villa Winter, no doubt.'

The cemetery reinforced the isolation of the place, those who chose to live on this wild and windswept coast allowed to remain here after their deaths.

They carried on past the cemetery and stepped onto the soft creamy sand that stretched on endlessly in both directions. The tide was low and the waves moderate. They both bent down and removed their shoes to find the sand was pleasantly cool. She led them to the harder, wetter sand which was easier to walk on.

'Which way?' Richard said.

'South, I'd say.'

Richard chose to stay beachside, leaving Clarissa to field any unexpected wash from a large wave. Chivalry was not in his DNA. Although she suspected if she had been young and pretty, it would have appeared in an instant.

Far away from anyone and with the waves crashing and the wind carrying away their voices, there was not a chance they could be heard.

'Let's make it to that low cliff,' Clarissa said, pointing ahead of her.

'Don't you think it's a bit far.'

'We'll be there in no time.'

She looked forward to the painkillers kicking in. Until that happened, she hoped the exercise would help her strained hip. Surely, the rhythmic walking motion would do it no end of good. They walked in silence for a while, Richard lost in his own reflections. It was liberating to be away from the others and if there were any possibility of maintaining that distance, she would be all for it, but she

The Ghost of Villa Winter

was too old for sleeping on a beach, and besides, it was the wrong time of year, the nights too cold.

'Under other circumstances, I'd be enjoying this,' Richard said, as though reading her thoughts.

'I'm sure we both wish we were doing something else.'

Even as she spoke, she realised she hadn't meant to sound that despondent. He unexpectedly stopped in his tracks and she was forced to follow suit. He gave her a penetrating look.

'What is it?' she said.

'You seem troubled.'

She sighed. There was no point holding back. 'I have an appointment tomorrow and I'm not going to make it.'

'Can it be re-scheduled?'

'Not easily. I was heading up to Tahiche prison to visit an inmate.'

'Can you tell me who?' he said with sudden interest.

She was disconcerted by his directness.

'We should keep going,' she said, and they continued on in silence, maintaining a slow and steady pace.

She began to feel guilty at not sharing with him something she freely told others. It was his authorly status that caused her reticence. She wasn't sure how much she should tell him. But then, what was the harm? 'Trevor Moore,' she said at last.

'I thought so. I've heard a bit about him. We share a publisher.'

'Astonishing.'

She resisted the urge to stop walking. It was not a habit to be encouraged. A wave crashed and she eyed the wash, veering towards Richard as the cold salty water approached and wetted her feet up to her ankles. Now they shared something in common – Trevor – she felt instantly closer to

Richard, bound to him somehow, through happenstance. She wished she'd brought it up before. It would have gone a long way towards building a friendship out of this unlikely alliance. Given them something to talk about other than recent murders and imminent danger.

'Angela hasn't told me much about Trevor, of course,' Richard volunteered. 'But I read about his case in the newspapers.'

'What you will have read is unlikely to contain much truth.'

She waited, but he didn't divulge what he'd read.

'I'm trying to get him released, or at least his murder conviction overturned.'

'Why the interest? You don't strike me as a do-gooding Christian.'

She emitted a sombre laugh.

'My niece is involved in the case. Trevor stayed at her place for a few days and she believes he is guilty. There were two deaths, as you know. The priest, and the lad that drowned. The lad is a relative of Claire's husband Paco.'

'That doesn't explain why you got involved.'

'I suppose it doesn't. I don't like to see an innocent man in prison for something he didn't do. Especially when it's partly my own flesh and blood who put him there.'

'I always thought it unlikely he had committed those murders. He didn't seem to have a motive.'

'And writers don't tend to profile as murderers.'

'Unless your name is William S. Burroughs.'

They both laughed again.

'Trevor Moore is no Burroughs.'

'From what Angela tells me, he's neurotic.'

'A lot of writers are.'

He stopped in his tracks again. She wished he wouldn't

The Ghost of Villa Winter

as she was forced to stop as well. She forgave him when he said, 'I'll be driving back to Lanzarote when all this is over. You're welcome to come along. See if you can schedule another prison visit.'

'That's very kind of you.'

'Better than the bus.'

She had to agree with him.

They walked on in silence. Three large waves crashed near the shore in quick succession and they were forced to veer up the beach quite a distance to avoid the wash. Clarissa thought the tide was coming in.

'And what about you?' she said as the wash of the last wave receded and she went back to walking on the wet sand. 'Any ideas for a plot?'

'I'm too tired to think.'

'I daresay when you get back home and rested, ideas will flow.'

'I daresay.'

There was a long pause. Then he said, 'Trish always phones on a Sunday afternoon. She'll be expecting me to answer.'

'I shouldn't worry about Trish. She'll cope with not knowing where you are.'

Even with the wind and the waves she could hear him sigh.

'I doubt it. The last time I was out of reception when she called me, she had a fit of histrionics.'

Clarissa felt her impatience rise. She never could accommodate those choosing to stay in dysfunctional marriages to their own detriment.

She moderated her voice to mask her feelings when she said, 'If she's that bad, Richard, you know what the answer is.'

'What is that?'

'Do I really need to spell it out?'

'No, I mean, look.' He was pointing at the head of the beach where something plastic was sticking up out of the sand. They went over and discovered it was a broken surfboard. Richard tried to move it but it was buried too deep. As they were about to walk away, Clarissa spotted something small and shiny nearby and went to investigate.

'Find something?'

'Only a button.'

She picked it up and studied it. The brass was embossed and looked official. If she was not mistaken it was the sort of button that appeared on the uniform of a police officer. How strange to find such a button here? She popped it in her pocket.

The sun was getting lower in the western sky and the temperature was dropping. A sudden gust of wind lifted the hem of her blouse. She shoved it down and buttoned up her jacket.

They had reached their destination too soon, although walking on the sand was tiring and she doubted she would have managed much further even with the painkillers. She thought they'd walked about a mile. As they neared the low, beachside cliff, the beach narrowed. Clarissa slowed her pace, keeping a wary eye on the ocean, the incoming tide. The mountainous cliff was closer too, towering beside them. This time she was the one who stopped. Richard looked thoughtful. She led him over to a ridge of sand at the head of the beach and sat down. They watched the waves roll in, one upon another, and fell into companionable silence. It felt like they were sitting at the end of the earth with the beach stretching on and on to the north. The setting afforded no sense of protection. It was wild and exhilarating and as far from civilisation as it was possible to be. They might be in the plains of Namibia or outback Australia or the Russian taiga. And yet on the other side of that mountain range, huddled in the steep-sided valleys, was a tourist resort. It scarcely seemed possible.

One day the road might get widened and sealed with crash barriers and tourists would arrive in their droves. A luxury resort would be built right where they sat, and another and then another, all the way up the coast. No. That wouldn't happen. This place was too wild and windy and untameable. Tourists wanted to holiday in comfort. They wanted safe beaches and all the facilities. Not this level of exposure. What an extraordinarily special place this was. And what a terrifying place to be stuck in.

Her mind drifted back to Anna and Alvaro, two souls who'd lost their lives in the most brutal manner. What on earth was going on here?

'I keep thinking about the murders,' Richard said at last, he too, caught up in the reality they faced.

She kicked at a pebble. Then she picked it up and stood and hurled it into the ocean.

'It's hard to think about anything else.'

She searched for another pebble. There were few about. She wandered on a few paces, picked up a small flat pebble and hurled it as the wash came in.

'It feels like we've been over it and over it.'

'That's because we have.'

She soon tired of her game and since Richard had chosen to remain where he was, she joined him.

'The big question is, are we sure the two murders are linked?' he said.

'They would have to be.'

'But this second killing makes no sense.'

'It doesn't. Especially as Alvaro was one of my prime suspects.'

'There's something else that bothers me. What do you make of that accident that blocked the cliff road?'

'Rather a coincidence, don't you think?'

'But why would anyone want to isolate us all in Cofete?'

'I am not sure I like the answer to that.'

'Meaning?'

'Richard, you can be exceptionally dim-witted sometimes.'

'I'm sorry.'

'No, it's me who should be sorry. I didn't mean that to sound harsh. It's just that if we have all been corralled in this village, there is every chance the killer will pick us off one by one.'

'Then let's hope that isn't the case.'

'Indeed.'

They paused to watch a large wave roll and crash, the wash rushing up the beach almost to their toes. Another one of those and Clarissa decided they would they head back. They didn't have long to wait.

'The bottom line for us is everyone is a suspect,' she said, getting to her feet.

She chose the ocean side once more, not trusting Richard not to crash into her and bowl her over should a large wave threaten to wet his ankles. The wind blew hard into her face and she knew the walk back would be arduous. Richard fell in with her stride.

'Everyone's a suspect except Fred and Margaret,' he said.

'I think we've established they're ruled out.'

'The whole tour bus is ruled out. No one here could have gone to Villa Winter to dispose of the body. And that leaves only Steve and Dave that we know of.'

The Ghost of Villa Winter

'I think we're missing something.'

'I think we need to get back to means, motive and opportunity.'

'Perhaps.'

Richard stopped in his tracks. She was about to gently remonstrate him when he said, 'Hang on. What if Alvaro did kill Anna and did dispose of the body, and then someone else killed Alvaro?'

She grinned at him.

'Richard, you are the perfect Watson! I believe you may be right. After all, he wasn't at the restaurant or Fred would have said. It's the only alternative if we are to dismiss the lads as suspects, assuming they had nothing to do with Alvaro's death.'

'Does add a layer of complexity, though. I mean, two killers.'

'A most unusual situation.'

They resumed walking.

'I've no idea how we'll solve the mystery.'

'What we need, Richard, is evidence.'

She shifted swiftly to her right ahead of Richard as the wash of a wave rushed towards them. Richard veered to the right as well. They found they had to dodge many more waves as the tide came in, but both were reluctant to labour through the softer drier sand. By the time they were halfway back, Richard had slowed his pace.

'Do you think we can take a shortcut back to Cofete?' he said. 'That beach road does seem like the long way round?'

'I don't think it makes much difference.'

He persisted, slowing his pace even more. 'There has to be another track somewhere. Besides, the terrain isn't too bad. We can pick our way through the scrub.'

'I'd rather stick to the way we know.'

It was her hip. She didn't want to risk a misstep. And she preferred taking the other road for another reason. The road led back to the north side of the village, out of sight of the restaurant, the locus of all the drama, and for the most part hidden from view. They could sneak back to their digs and pretend to the others they had enjoyed a long lie down, assuming no one had spent the last hour or two staring out of windows on watch duty. If they entered the village from the south, she felt they would have no choice but to reveal themselves. Perhaps the approach to the village was not as exposed as she imagined. Perhaps she was just a creature of habit. Or it was fatigue muddying her thinking. She didn't like cross-country treks. That was the real reason, she told herself.

He seemed resigned to let her have her way. A short while later, he pointed and said, 'Look up ahead. Aren't they farmhouses?'

She saw what appeared to be buildings, low lying, to the south of the hill sheltering Cofete.

'I didn't notice them before,' she said.

'The hill hid them.'

A large wave crashed close to shore followed by another, and the wash surged up the beach, causing them both to make a dash for the dry sand.

'Farmhouses means a road or track,' he said, eyeing the ocean with caution. 'We only need to make it that far cross country.'

She needed no further persuading, despite her earlier misgivings. She was done with the rising tide, the huge surf, the sand. Besides, there was something new to investigate. It was possible, not likely but possible they might find a clue. They dusted the sand off their feet and slipped on their shoes and headed in the direction of the farmhouses.

The Ghost of Villa Winter

The ground was uneven and littered with small rocks. She took care where she put her feet. Desert plants – various kinds of euphorbias, she thought – were dotted about, dusty and wizened due to the drought. The land rose steadily towards the cliff, that natural barrier between east and west, both looming and magnificent, drawing the eye with its ragged, undulating edge. The wind blew and blew, unrelenting.

Richard walked a few paces ahead. He had a rigid, upright gait and for the first time she realised how he was compensating for his bad back. That posture was all very well but it made him look wooden and a touch unstable. There was not enough mobility in the hips. Not that she had the luxury of flexible hips either, but she was a darn sight more mobile than him, even with her injury. She wondered if he was in any discomfort, if he would need his painkillers. She dared not ask.

They kept the farmhouses in sight. A hundred yards further on and the sand gave way to gritty soil and she saw a gravel road up ahead. Richard was triumphant. He turned to her and grinned. It was a small success.

The going was much easier once they were on the gravel track. She no longer needed to pay quite so much attention to where she put her feet.

About two-hundred yards further on they saw the remains of a dry-stone wall and the ruins of a farmhouse. It was Richard who suggested they have a snoop around.

There was not much to see. The dwelling itself consisted of a single room fronted by an undercover area, and a walled yard. At the other end of the yard was an outbuilding. The windows had no glass and all the timber had been removed from the doorways. The ruin looked like it would fall down at any moment. She didn't like the feel of the place, although she could see it would at one time have been a going concern for someone eking out a living here. Cofete enjoyed good soil and the run off from the cliff when it rained was evident in the stormwater erosion that was everywhere.

They headed up to the second ruin which appeared to be in an even worse state of repair than the last. They entered the compound through a gap in the wall and wandered around. A larger area was given over to walled animal pens. After poking around inside each of the pens, they arrived at the farmhouse which consisted of a single room. Again, no doors or windows and the roof was on the point of collapse. The farmers here might have enjoyed relative abundance in good years of above average rainfall, but it would have added a new dimension to any notion Clarissa had ever had of a peasant farmer. A tiny hut and some animals in a yard tucked on a narrow plain between the ocean and the cliff, what sort of a life would any local have led? A short one, she imagined.

Another gap in the wall beside the single room meant there was no need to double back. Clarissa made her way towards what would have been the main entrance, through which she could see that another hut had been built on the other side of a small area of gravel. It wasn't until she exited the compound that she saw a vehicle parked to her left and sheltered from view on all sides by a stone wall higher than its roof.

Richard was close behind her.

'Well, I never,' he said with a gasp.

'Let's not get too excited. It could be in the same state as this ruin.'

It was an old Mazda hatch. A 1990s model, she suspected, as it closely resembled her old blue car that she'd sold to her neighbour. The rear bumper was dented and pitted with rust, but the tyres looked new. She tried the passenger-side door and found it open. Richard opened the driver-side door and they both got in.

'The key is still in the ignition,' he said.

'Doesn't surprise me.'

She found herself bracing in case he turned the key. He didn't. Instead, he popped the boot and got out.

She stayed where she was. For the shortest of moments, it was pleasant to sit out of the wind enjoying the comfort of a car seat, although the car's interior carried a faint smell of cigarette smoke. Thankfully the ashtray was clean. She opened the glove box and was about to rummage inside when Richard called to her.

'Take a look at this.'

It was with some reluctance that she exited the car. Richard was using his arm to prop up the hatch door. He pointed inside. There, crumpled in the corner, was an olive-green blanket. There were traces of blood on one of the edges and the colour was unmistakable.

'You recognise it?'

'There's only one conclusion to draw from this, Richard. We've found the killer's car.'

He eyed her apprehensively.

'I think we better get well away from here,' he said nervously. 'If the killer sees us, if anyone sees us and then lets that slip, we're done for.'

'Let's not panic. We need to search the vehicle thoroughly before we go anywhere. You deal with the boot.'

She left him standing there propping open the hatch door and got back in the passenger seat before he could disagree. After a quick scan of the dashboard, she emptied the contents of the glove box into her lap. An old pair of sunglasses, a cloth – slightly soiled – no cigarette lighter or matches. The smoker was probably not the driver. There was a bunch of old bills and receipts, business cards and a few letters. She sifted through the letters. Some of them were very old. One carried a 1980s postmark. She knew she was tampering with the evidence, if evidence was what it was, but she slipped it into her pocket. She felt vindicated when she scanned some utility bills addressed to a Mr Banks who, she noted, also appeared to be the 1980s letter's addressee. Also scattered through the pile were assorted ferry tickets and three soiled serviettes. This Mr Banks used his glove box as a dustbin.

Richard called out for her to hurry up.

'Just a moment.'

She was about to ignore the business cards, but one caught her eye. On it was written Simon Slava, psychologist. Listed beneath were his specialisms, including social work and corrections counselling. And the card carried a photo of Simon. He didn't have a stubble beard and his hair was cut in a more conservative style, but it was him. She felt queasy as she pocketed the card and riffled through the rest of the papers. At the bottom of the pile were the car's registration details. Registered to Mr Banks. She took a few photos of the details and then sifted through the paperwork one more time and extracted one of the old utility bills carrying Mr Banks' home address, taking a photo before slipping it into her pocket. The rest she shoved back in the glove box, attempting to arrange the contents how she found them.

'Find anything?' she said as she joined Richard who closed the hatch door on her approach.

'Not a thing. You?'

'I'll tell you on the way.'

The track curved to the north after a short stretch and

The Ghost of Villa Winter

cut a diagonal path up towards Cofete that was obscured from view thanks to the hill. Her calves were aching a little from the exercise but her hip felt a lot freer after the long beach walk which was a blessing. Perhaps she wouldn't need any more of Richard's painkillers. Although the incline and the headwind made for heavy going and she was soon out of breath. About twenty paces into this final leg of their walk, Richard, who'd walked on ahead, came and walked beside her.

'Well?' he said with impatience.

Fatigue fogged her brain and she had to rouse herself to focus.

'The car belongs to a Mr Banks. I found the registration papers.'

'He's the murderer, then.'

'I expect so.'

'Where is he?'

'Good question. Although if the keys were always left in the ignition, anyone could have taken the vehicle to Villa Winter last night.'

'Not anyone, remember. They were all at the restaurant except Alvaro, and Steve and Dave.'

'Which puts the lads back in the frame.'

'Is that all you found?'

'Let's wait till we're back at the digs.'

They were rounding the base of the hill. Not long and they would be entering Cofete from the southwest. She could see the back of the restaurant up ahead. She scanned the village. There was no sign of anyone. The tour bus stood out like a beacon with its zebra stripes, reinforcing their predicament and the long wait until the morning when they could leave.

With her new knowledge she was furtive and eager to

escape detection. By now everyone would be in the village, Salvador, Simon and Francois having had plenty of time to complete their inspection of Villa Winter.

She wanted to hurry but her legs felt like lead. Richard trudged on a pace or two ahead. She pressed on, focussed on the bus, watching it get nearer with every step. It wasn't long and they were right beside it. They were about to veer off to skirt around the southern wall of the restaurant when she stopped in her tracks. Richard kept on walking and she was forced to hurry up to him.

'Wait,' she whispered.

He turned. 'What is it?'

'I thought I heard voices. Come.'

They went and leaned their backs against the restaurant wall and listened. It was Salvador and Merida and their voices were raised. Sounded like they were arguing although that could have been the acoustics. The concrete walls of this section of the building served to amplify their voices.

'I told you before,' Salvador said. 'There was nothing to see up at the house.'

'Except for that yellow jacket.'

'We have no idea when the jacket was moved.'

'What did they need a jacket for?'

'Beats me. To keep warm, maybe.'

'And the pail?'

'I bet they did that.'

'The point is, where the hell were they?'

'That's what I would like to know.'

All went quiet. Clarissa nudged Richard and beckoned him away.

'They know we moved the pail and the jacket,' he hissed.

There was raw terror in his eyes. 'Which means they know we were snooping about in the living room.'

'Relax. They think it was Steve and Dave.'

'You reckon? Then maybe we should let them have their delusions.'

'I think you're right.'

As they rounded the rear wall of the restaurant and made their way across to the row of terraced houses, a glint in the distance caught her eye and she scanned the shacks on the high side of the village. There was no telling which were empty and which were housing one of the tour party. No one had said where they were staying. She only knew Merida's and Fred and Margaret's. Another glint didn't manifest but she was sure she hadn't imagined it.

The moment they entered the house, she closed the door and said, 'We're being watched.'

'I wish I could say you're being paranoid but I just saw someone disappear into a house up above here and I thought the same.'

She hoped it was the same person. They knew who it wasn't, but not who it was.

They went straight through to the living room to sit in comfort in the gloom. Time was getting on and they were no closer to solving the mystery. She wanted to feel safe, but any one of the tour party could knock on the door, or worse, march right on in. She should have demanded that key off Salvador. With night approaching, the prospect of sleeping here in Cofete felt less and less appealing, especially knowing there was a murderer on the loose, a murderer who might have already killed twice. She was so tired she could hardly keep her eyes open but sleep was not an option.

She shifted in her seat, adjusting the cushions behind

her. Richard slid off his backpack and swigged the last of his water. Forcing herself to be practical, she made a mental note to fill her water bottle in the restaurant and told Richard to do the same.

'You should charge your phone.'

'I'll do it later,' he said, flopping into the other armchair.

'Do it now, please.'

He made a show of hefting himself upright and slumping to the kitchen. While he was out of the room, she emailed herself the photos of the documents. If anything happened to her, Claire would have access as next of kin. She shouldn't think like that, but given the situation, it was warranted. She then tucked the old letter in a secret pocket in her capris. She'd sewn the pocket inside the waistband last year as she thought it ideal for those occasions when she found herself in a rough area on her travels and wanted to hide her cash and bank cards. It was large enough to hold a passport and was the perfect size for a small letter.

Richard re-appeared as she was examining the business card. She flipped it over and found on the back of the card was scrawled in the worst handwriting she had ever seen an appointment date and a name. It took her a few moments to make out all the letters and when she was confident she had, her jaw fell open. Trevor Moore.

'I don't believe it,' she muttered.

'What is it?'

She looked up. Richard hovered, his eyes a little wider.

'I didn't tell you before because this is a huge find. I wasn't sure if it was a clue, but now I suppose it is.'

She showed him the card.

'Simon Slava,' he read aloud. A look of astonishment appeared in his face. 'This is Simon on the tour. What is his business card doing in Mr Banks' car?'

'Wouldn't I like to know.'

He made to hand back the card.

'Turn it over,' she said.

She waited. He had the same trouble reading the lettering as she did.

'It says Trevor Moore,' she said at last, her patience worn thin.

'What on earth?' he said.

'That's what I thought.'

As he went to sit down, he held out the card. This time she took it back.

'Stands to reason if Simon is a prison counsellor that he would have Trevor as a client,' she said. 'But I'm still gobsmacked.'

'That his name should be written on the card?'

'A card shut in a Mr Banks' car.'

He paused, thoughtful.

'This doesn't mean that much though. Anyone could have written Trevor's name on that card.'

'True,' she said. 'It's just that it has started to make me wonder if the deaths of the priest, the drowned lad, and Anna and Alvaro are all connected.'

'I'm always wary of joining the dots,' Richard said. 'Writing crime has taught me that much. You've no idea how critical crime fiction readers can be. Means, motive, opportunity, they all have to be plausible, logical, with as few wild leaps and happy coincidences as possible.'

She was slow to respond. Her hip had started aching again. So much for the painkillers.

'There is one thing, though, Richard. Someone, and presumably it was Mr Banks, had Simon's card in his possession and that same someone, presumably Mr Banks again if it wasn't Simon himself, had written Trevor's name on the back.'

'Meaning?'

'There's a link between the killer, Simon and Trevor.'

'Far too circumstantial,' he said dismissively. 'Besides, there's a different modus operandi between three of the killings. Alvaro was whacked on the head, Anna was strangled and that lad drowned.'

'And the priest was stabbed multiple times with a kitchen knife.'

'That would make four killers.'

'That's ridiculous.'

She hated to admit Richard was right. Even so, she would interrogate Simon the first chance she had. If he did know Trevor, then he might have an opinion on his innocence.

Sitting in the windowless living room with the weight of the mystery on her shoulders and the menace of a killer or killers on the loose, she felt like her head would explode. Such a scramble of evidence. All they knew for certain was the first name of the woman in the chest, identified as an undercover cop, and that her killer was a Mr Banks, unless someone had borrowed or stolen his car. Nothing concrete to go on. They didn't even know if Anna had been killed because her cover was blown. She could have been murdered for an entirely different reason. What were the chances of finding out anything more? Doubts swirled. Her discomfort and fatigue weren't helping. The two of them should hunker down, barricade themselves in and have a good long sleep. Then, in the morning they could depart and leave it to the police to solve the murders. She was no sleuth. She didn't even have a game plan.

As her thoughts swirled and she closed her eyes hoping

The Ghost of Villa Winter

to relax, it occurred to her in a flash there was no guarantee that Social Catfish site had in fact revealed the real Anna. She wasn't sure how much it mattered, but while Richard dozed, she extracted her phone and searched for the site in her history. She re-uploaded the photo of the cadaver and this time a different version of the woman's identity was given. There was mention of the earlier version being taken down as fake. Now Anna was revealed as a travel journalist and photographer interested in dark tourism. The person announcing the information had provided links to several websites featuring Anna Trower's articles. Poor woman. Did anyone know she was missing? Had the police been notified? Clarissa was certain of only one thing, she had been murdered because of what she had discovered, not who she was. No more vengeful ex-boyfriend. She checked through her photos to see who had written that article on tattoos to discover she had managed to leave the author's name out of the frame.

Clarissa switched off her phone and settled back in her armchair. The soft seat pad meant her hip caused her less pain. Exhaustion consumed her. Richard was already snoring. She rested her head on the backrest and closed her eyes.

14
———

DINNER

Her eyes shot open. The room was black. She was disoriented, her mind fuzzy. Something must have startled her out of sleep. She heard Richard snoring and realised where she was. She reached for her phone. It was a little before six o'clock.

She was putting away her phone when someone hammered on the door. She waited, holding her breath.

Then a voice called out, 'Are you in there?'

She recognised the voice in an instant. It was Fred.

Relieved, she eased herself to her feet and used her phone torch to light her way to the hall where the diminished daylight managed to enter. She opened the front door to find Fred peering in her bedroom window.

'Come in,' she said, and he gave a little start.

Touché!

'I won't,' he said, the colour rising in his cheeks. 'I just came to tell you dinner is soon to be served and we are invited for drinks.'

'I'll go wake Richard and see you there.'

She waited for him to walk away before closing the door.

She remembered the house had power as she made her way back down the hall. When she reached the living room doorway, she groped about for the switch, flicked on the light and emitted a short cough. It was a cruel act, the light proving brilliant, and Richard shielded his eyes as he woke. He looked as disoriented as she did moments earlier and she regretted having to stir him, but she doubted the others would let them sleep and besides, she wanted to talk to Simon and more food would be good after their long beach walk.

'We have been summoned to dinner. Drinks first, but I suggest we both refrain from anything alcoholic.'

He avoided her gaze and fumbled about with his backpack.

'I think I could do with a stiff whisky or two. You should as well. We need to unwind and sleep. Forget all this sleuthing. There is nothing to be done other than wait for tomorrow to come and get out of here.'

'Have it your way,' she said.

He was a grown man who could make his own decisions. She, on the other hand, would remain stone cold sober. Someone had killed Anna and Alvaro and that person was on the loose.

While Richard freshened up in the bathroom, she fished out the old letter tucked in her capris, curious to read the name and address. The utility bills and registration details had only carried an initial for the first name. A. The envelope had been subject to some mild water damage and the writing was smudged. The surname of Banks was legible enough but she couldn't make out the first name. She held the letter up to the light and studied each letter in turn. That was when she made out enough letters to see it was Alvaro. Alvaro Banks.

She sat back down in her chair with a thump. Her heart began to race. It was too much of a coincidence, although he must have been young when the letter was written. Why had he never opened it? Even if he had, why had he kept it? She doubted she would ever know.

She did know, in as much as it was possible to know anything in this peculiar situation, that Alvaro owned that car. Which put an entirely different complexion on things. It now appeared it was Alvaro Banks who had disposed of the body of Anna and then he himself had been murdered. What for? Not doing an adequate job? Of course, he might not have murdered Anna, but that would mean someone else had killed both Anna and Alvaro, albeit using a differing method each time. Unless Alvaro had in fact killed Anna.

Who was this Alvaro Banks? She would ask a few questions over dinner. Sound casual. See what she could find out.

She heard movement and quickly pocketed the letter. Better Richard knew nothing of this twist. He would pour cold water on it and leave her deflated. Seemed to be a habit of his. He had just about poured cold water on his entire life.

When he reappeared, he held up his red backpack and said, 'Do we have to?'

'We most certainly do.'

She watched as he slipped an arm in a shoulder strap.

'Seems bulkier than before,' she said.

'I put the toiletries back.'

'Have you got your phone and the charger?'

'It's all in here,' he said, tapping his fanny pack.

'Then let's get going.'

A rich smell of stewed meat greeted her nostrils as she pushed open the restaurant door. She was hungry again in an instant. All this fresh air and exercise had given her quite an appetite. It felt like a lifetime had passed since they were last gathered together around the far table in the restaurant interior devouring a much-needed breakfast. The others were all there, quaffing wine and spirits, and laughing and joking as though nothing untoward had happened that day. As she made her approach, misgivings rushed to the forefront of her mind. She was alert and hoped Richard was as well. A car did drive to Villa Winter and that car contained Alvaro Banks who was later murdered. The tour party, along with Salvador and Merida, were all a little too keen to blame Steve and Dave. There was something going on here, something someone was keeping hidden.

They walked down past the bar, feeling the gaze of Salvador as he made drinks for the others. She stopped and caught hold of Richard's arm.

'Salvador,' she said, resting her elbows on the high counter. 'I wonder if you would mind filling our water bottles.'

'Sure,' he said with a perfunctory nod.

She extracted her water bottle from her canvas bag and then turned to Richard as he retrieved his.

'Better to do it now than forget and end up parched in the night.'

Salvador made a point of filling both bottles to the brim, Clarissa's pint-sized plastic bottle and Richard's giant, three-pint affair. He'd be peeing all night if he drank that lot. Richard deposited his bottle in his backpack and they went and joined the merrymakers.

Francois, Merida and Simon were seated at one end of the long table. Fred and Margaret had chosen the middle of the table and had their backs to the wall. There was an empty seat opposite Margaret which was reserved for

Salvador – he'd left his drink in the centre of the table mat – and Helen sat opposite Fred. There were two vacant chairs facing each other and then Vera and Carol shared the table's far end.

All heads turned on their approach.

'You two never go anywhere without your bags,' Carol said mockingly. 'You can leave them in your accommodation, you know. Anyone would think you were frightened they'd get stolen.'

'Bit of a habit of mine,' Clarissa said, feigning an apologetic excuse, 'ever since my hotel room was ransacked. I lost an old photo of my sister who died and a gold ring that belonged to her. Even the toiletries were sentimental. After that, I vowed never to go anywhere without taking my belongings with me.'

'And what about you, Richard?'

'That's me again, I'm afraid. I persuaded him to do the same.'

'Hilarious.'

The remark, her expression altogether implied Carol found the explanation anything but.

'You always do what women tell you?' said Vera sarcastically.

Clarissa could see Richard cringing. He needed to learn some defences, develop a thicker skin, not leave it to others to protect him. 'Will you leave the man alone,' Fred said with some force. It was all the confirmation Clarissa needed. If Richard didn't want the attentions of the likes of Fred Spice, he needed to dredge up some fortitude.

Carol and Vera both looked daggers at Fred but the teasing stopped.

Richard pulled out the chair beside Helen and sat down facing the wall, leaving Clarissa to ease behind the two

The Ghost of Villa Winter

women and take up the remaining chair. Finding herself sandwiched between Vera and Fred was not the best of circumstances. Simon, who she had been hoping to be near, was too far away to talk to privately. He appeared to be flirting with Merida. Francois competed for her attention. Helen wore an impassive expression on her face, but Clarissa detected beneath the surface a swell of emotion. She reached for her drink with lowered eyes.

Carol guzzled whatever she was drinking and held up her glass.

'Salvador, my good man, we need replenishing over here.'

'There's wine on the table,' he said. 'Drink that.'

He dumped a tea towel on the counter and went through to the kitchen. Carol put down her tumbler, reached for the open bottle of red and poured herself a glassful.

Vera slugged her drink, keen to keep pace.

'Meet any murderers on your beach walk, then?' she said, her gaze flitting back and forth between Clarissa and Richard.

'Not funny,' said Fred.

'It wasn't meant to be.'

'I'll be so glad to get out of here tomorrow,' Margaret said in a lull in the conversation at the other end of the table.

'Let's toast to that,' Vera said, raising her glass.

Carol waved down her friend's hand.

'Wait a moment. Richard and Clarissa don't have drinks. Richard, hold out your glass.'

Carol poured with an unsteady hand, filling his glass almost to the brim with red wine. Without hesitation, he took a large gulp.

'You?' Carol said, addressing Clarissa.

'I'm fine with water.' She smiled thinly as she reached for the pitcher in the centre of the table.

'Suit yourself,' Carol said, plonking the wine bottle down.

'Three cheers for Salvador!' yelled Vera, standing and swaying a little. 'Salvador! Get your ass out here!'

All eyes were on the door behind the bar. There was a short pause and then he emerged, surprised. A cheer broke out.

'We can't thank you enough for all you've done for us,' said Fred, taking command.

'It's nothing,' Salvador said, laughing to himself and disappearing into the kitchen again.

Clarissa wondered who was footing the bill.

When the group settled back down, Vera started on Richard again.

'You two enjoy your afternoon?' she said, leaning towards Richard as much as she could with Carol in between them. Richard's response was to slug more of his wine. The glass was already half empty.

Vera persisted. 'You went for a walk. I saw you come back. Where did you go?'

So that glint of light Clarissa had seen as they cornered the restaurant was her.

'We headed down to the cemetery, then took a long walk on the beach,' Clarissa said.

Three pairs of female eyes bore into her, Carol and Helen now taking a keen interest. Richard was staring down at the table.

'Which direction?'

'South, to the cliffs.'

'Wow, you made it all the way down there.'

'It wasn't far.'

'Is that right?' said Helen disbelievingly.

'You didn't come back that way though,' Vera said. 'I saw you come up behind the restaurant.'

Heads turned. It was Merida who spoke. 'Then you'd have gone past those two abandoned farmhouses.'

All eyes fell on Clarissa, Richard's with undisguised alarm. Her heart started pumping hard. She thought fast. 'We didn't see any farmhouses. At least, not up close. We got a bit lost, if you must know. Richard wanted to take a short cut back hoping to find a path and not finding one. In the end we used the hill as a point of reference to get back.'

She had no idea if she'd convinced anyone her account was true. Merida looked especially doubtful. Clarissa began to inwardly question who knew the location of Alvaro's car. Merida and Salvador, surely. Unless Alvaro had left it there in hiding from all pairs of eyes.

The arrival of the food ended the interrogation. Large bowls filled with another of Salvador's aromatic stews were placed in front of one and all. More wine appeared and Carol refilled Richard's glass. Clarissa wished he had more sense than to drink it, but it seemed he had developed a thirst.

She dived into her stew, happy to ride out the meal staring into her bowl, ignoring the company as much as she could. Chunks of meat were accompanied by carrot, courgette, red bell pepper and potatoes. The onion had melted into the gravy. Salvador was an excellent cook. She vowed she would recall her time in Cofete in its culinary context and try to obliterate the rest. She had always found it best to cultivate good memories out of difficult experiences, rather like a sculptor might perfect a work of art out of a shipwreck.

After the food and the wine came the liquors and

Salvador put on some lively dance music before disappearing once more into the kitchen. It wasn't long before the inebriated Vera and Carol got up to dance. Merida joined them. Helen did too. For someone of frail health, she was remarkable agile suddenly.

All of the men stayed seated. Vera broke away from her dancing buddies and came over to try to drag Richard to his feet. He refused, endeavouring to extricate himself from her tugging grip.

'Loosen up, will you.'

She gave up when he turned away from her, and she joined the others whooping it up to a salsa tune. Simon and Francois watched with expressions of mild admiration and amusement. Peeling his eyes from the bouncing bosoms and bottoms, Francois turned to the table. 'In your absence this afternoon,' he said, addressing Clarissa, his face breaking out into a supercilious smile that contorted his already contorted face, 'we came to a consensus that the best response to the situation was to enjoy ourselves.'

'We did? I wasn't part of any consensus,' Fred said, puzzled and indignant.

Francois eyed him with bristling contempt.

'You weren't here either for some reason.'

'Margaret needed a rest.'

Having made his announcement, Francois settled back in his seat, leaving Fred to squirm with humiliation. He fumbled with his napkin before searching for Margaret's hand and giving it a squeeze as though she was the one in need of reassurance. She whispered something in his ear. Clarissa imagined it was Take no notice.

The dancing continued. Clarissa was in two minds whether to seize the opportunity to relocate to the chair next to Simon, her urge to question him vying with a pervasive sense of caution. Curiosity won and she left her seat and took up Salvador's. Considering Simon was a man of few words, she decided against any sort of preamble in favour of a direct approach. She turned and gained his attention.

'You said you were involved in social work. A psychologist.'

'I am,' he said cautiously, eyeing her with suspicion.

'You don't by chance take on prison clients?'

'Corrections counselling is one of my specialisms.'

She should have heeded his arrogant tone. Here was a man who liked to patronise from a position of self-appointed superiority.

'Have you come across Trevor Moore?'

The remark threw him. She detected a moment of uncertainty in his manner. He quickly covered it up.

'I'm not permitted to discuss individual clients. Confidentiality, you understand.' He paused. 'Why the interest?'

'I'm trying to get him freed.'

'Some people should know when to leave well alone.'

Indignant, she ignored the implied threat.

'I happen to believe in his innocence. There is no way he could have killed that priest or that lad.'

'The police and the courts don't agree.'

'The police and the courts can be wrong, as well you know.'

She could see she was getting nowhere. He'd revealed nothing and she'd revealed too much. Or perhaps she'd revealed nothing at all.

She returned to her seat. Richard drained his glass and reached for the bottle of sweet brandy for a refill. His eyes were glazed and his hand swayed a little as he poured. Not a man used to his drink. He was no doubt hoping to knock himself out, obliterate all thought of the weekend in a liquid haze, stagger to his bed and snore until sunrise.

Time seemed to drag, although it was still light outside. Clarissa reached into her pocket for her phone. It was just past seven o'clock. Salvador emerged from the kitchen. The music ended as abruptly as it began and the women staggered back to their seats. Vera clutched the edge of the table to steady herself.

Clarissa wasn't enjoying the close proximity of her foe. She glanced down, groping for her napkin that was sliding off the edge of the table, when the fabric of Vera's wrap-around dress parted. She took in Vera's fleshy suntanned thigh and her eyes fixed on a small tattoo. A row of numbers. It seemed at a glance to be identical to the tattoo she had seen on Anna's collarbone. Vera, now seated, was quick to re-arrange her dress. As Clarissa leaned back in her seat their eyes met. Clarissa quickly looked away, sensing with considerable force that her sighting of that tattoo was a terrible mistake.

In the following few seconds, the mood at the dinner table changed dramatically. First, Vera whispered something to Carol, who attracted the attention of Helen. The three women left the table and spoke in subdued voices at the other end of the restaurant. When they returned Helen tapped Merida on the shoulder and said something in her ear. Merida shot a cold look at Clarissa, then leaned to Francois, whose eyes narrowed as he listened. He then turned to Simon. Simon left his seat and went behind the bar, steering Salvador into the kitchen. A few moments later, the two men reappeared and stood behind the bar with hard expressions on their faces. They were all in this together. If Clarissa thought she had any chance of getting away she would have left, escaped, bolted up the cliff.

15

SUNSET ON THE HILL

It was Merida who made the announcement.

'Before we have dessert, let's go watch the sunset.'

There were approving nods from Vera and Carol as they stood. Francois and Simon got up. Fred and Margaret remained seated. As did Richard.

'I've seen plenty of sunsets,' he said, slurring his speech.

'Not like the ones you get here,' Vera said. 'Come on, up you get.'

She took his arm and gave it a tug. She didn't let go of his shirt. He was about to yank away his arm when she tightened her grip. Their eyes met. Drunken irritation gave way to uncertainty as he reached for his backpack and got to his feet, puzzled by the behaviour. Fred was puzzled too.

'Leave him alone.'

Vera turned on him, her top lip curling.

'When I need your advice, I'll ask for it, you stupid little man.'

'How dare you speak to me like that!'

'Leave it, Fred,' said Margaret. She caught Clarissa's eye. She was by no means a slow-witted woman and she seemed to have cottoned on to the danger. She stood, nudging her husband to do the same.

With everyone standing there was no choice but to follow suit. She reached down for her bag. She had no idea where all this was leading but once she was with the others heading out the door she caught up with Richard and tried not to leave his side. He was inebriated and swayed as he walked, his backpack no doubt adding to his lack of balance. She was about to thread her arm through the crook in his elbow but she was ousted by Carol, who pushed her aside with a quick thrust. Clarissa stumbled and almost fell.

She was indignant at first, but soon saw that Carol's imposition could prove fortunate. Vera and Carol were steering Richard towards the hill. Helen and Merida had taken the lead. She glanced back. Francois, Simon and Salvador were yet to leave the restaurant. Simon's gaze bore into her but she ignored it. Fred and Margaret were right behind her.

Nothing good would come of this night. With the exception of the Spices, they were all colluding together. Any one of them might have killed Anna and then sent Alvaro to deal with the body. For whatever reason, Alvaro was then despatched. Perhaps he had got cold feet and threatened to confess. If they could kill an investigative journalist and one of their own people, they were more than capable of killing two ageing sleuths.

Her mind rocketed back to when she stood at the bus station in Puerto del Rosario, eyeing off the tour party one by one. It had never occurred to her, not then, not on the journey south, not at that first lunch in Cofete and not during the tour of Villa Winter that these people – Francois, Simon, Vera, Carol and Helen – all knew each other, and knew Salvador and Merida as well. There had been almost no indication of any sort of affiliation or friendship or familiarity. She had been thoroughly duped.

Would there be any way to extricate herself from this awful mess? She clung to hope. It was all she had. That, and her wiles.

She slowed her pace. When Fred and Margaret came level with her, she said, 'Don't react. Whatever you do, don't turn around and don't point. Now listen. There's a car parked beside the first ruin on a track to the south of the hill heading to the beach. The keys are in the ignition. When the coast is clear, take the car and get out of here. No questions. Just do it.'

'What about you two? We can't leave you here.'

'There's no choice. They're not going to let us out of their sight.'

'What's going on?'

'Not now. Keep walking but slow your pace. Stop at the base of the hill. Pretend to tie a shoelace. Wait until Francois and the others are no longer watching and then make a run for it.'

'What if they see us?'

'You just have to risk it. Be careful. Stay alert. They're not interested in you. Not yet. But you could be next so get the hell out of here.'

She could see from their terrified faces they believed her. She hoped they had the wit to make the getaway. It wouldn't be easy.

She walked on ahead of them, filled with trepidation. She needed courage, not fear, and sharp thinking. Pity she lacked a weapon. Although they were thoroughly outnumbered. She would have needed a gun.

When she reached the base of the hill Merida was waiting for her, a malevolent smirk on her face. What kind of nurse was she? A cruel one. Not one she would trust with any sort of ailment.

As if on cue, a dart of pain shot through her hip. She'd been doing her best to ignore the discomfort. She only had four painkillers left and if she and Richard managed to stay alive, they were in for a long night.

Merida ushered her on. The hill lacked height but it was a steep ascent. After the ordeal of the last two days, her legs complained with every step. At about halfway, her hip wouldn't stop throbbing. She'd been sitting for too long and now the muscles were contracting. She needed those painkillers but with Merida following close behind there was no way she could take them.

The hilltop had been levelled with a stone circle in its centre. Her body was relieved to stand on flat land but her mind was anything but. The view was tremendous but it was impossible to enjoy it. The striking crimson hues streaking across the western sky over the deep indigo ocean was a magnificent sight to behold and under other circumstances she would have felt exhilarated. Instead, she was filled with dread.

She went over to where Vera and Carol were standing arm-in-arm with Richard. They were perched at the very edge of the hilltop. The hill fell away sharply to the land below, the descent much further on the western side as the land sloped down towards the beach.

'You don't have to go through with this,' Clarissa said when she was near enough to be heard.

'Go through with what?' Richard said as though she was talking to him. She saw straight away he was going to be even more of a liability than ever. 'What's going on?'

'That's what we were about to ask you,' Vera said.

Merida grabbed Clarissa's arm and yanked her forwards.

When they were all aligned facing the sunset she said, 'We thought maybe you knew nothing. But when Salvador went back to the villa, we knew you were lying.'

'The jacket and the pail,' Richard said despondently. Why did he have to open his mouth? The fool. Clarissa needed to get close to him, prevent him from revealing anything more. But with Vera and Carol holding on to each arm, there was not a chance. She couldn't even gain his attention. He was too busy looking down at his feet. Merida ignored his remark. She wasn't interested in Richard. Instead, she pinned Clarissa with her gaze, her face, much to close for comfort.

'You didn't spend the night asleep in those fireside chairs. We knew that all along. It was when Salvador discovered one of the nails in the lid of the chest had been hammered in bent that we knew you'd been snooping.'

'I told you I should have straightened that nail,' Richard blurted before Clarissa had a chance to come up with an alternative explanation or an outright denial. Fear gave way to fury at the stupidity of the man. If it hadn't been for Vera and Carol, Clarissa had half a mind to shove him down the hill herself. Had he learned nothing from all those years spent writing crime?

'It's always the small details that get you found out,' she said, playing for time. 'Quite impressive, really, that Salvador spotted it.'

'He's an exacting man.'

'Let go of me,' Richard complained.

'No chance.'

'I told you we should have walked back to Cofete yesterday,' Richard said, his voice filled with reproach. After a long pause, he said, addressing the others, 'I never wanted to stay overnight in Villa Winter. It was all her idea.

I tried to persuade her, but she wouldn't have it. And she wouldn't leave things alone, snooping around. It was Clarissa who wanted to prise open that chest. Not me. It's her you should be hurling off this hill. I'm innocent in all this.'

Vera slapped him hard around the face. 'Will you shut up!'

He lurched backwards, trying to bring a hand to his cheek, but neither woman was about to let go of her grip.

'I reckon one big push from behind should do it,' Carol said. 'Which one goes first? Merida, do you have a preference?'

'We should wait for Salvador. See what he wants to do.'

As they stood watching the sunset fade away, Clarissa recalled the altercation they'd overheard in the restaurant earlier. Jacket and pail, Salvador had said. Pail? No, he'd said nail. They should have waited longer to see if he'd divulged anything more. Then, they might have managed to get away from Cofete, make it up the cliff road before they were detected. As it was, Salvador's intimate knowledge of the nails in that lid meant he had been the one to nail it shut. Was he the murderer? Probably. What about Alvaro? Did Salvador kill him too? And what of that nonsense about the supposed killer lurking in Cofete? It was a deception, part of their twisted game, nothing more.

'So that was what the search of the village was about,' she said. 'And all that talk about Steve and Dave. It was you all along. All of you.'

No one answered. Richard had taken to whimpering. He complained he needed to visit the bathroom. Carol exploded with laughter. Clarissa couldn't bring herself to look at him. He was truly entirely pathetic.

The sound of a car engine greeted her ears. She looked

behind her with alarm. Surely Fred would not be so stupid as to set off now, with everyone so close.

Richard's whimpering grew louder. Vera went and stood behind him.

'You scared of heights, Richard?'

'Not particularly.'

'I've had enough of this.'

She pulled back her hands, palms flat, ready to push him over the edge. Neither Carol nor Merida appeared likely to interfere. Vera took a step back. She was about to rush forwards when they heard a man's voice yell, 'Stop!'

Heads turned. It was Simon.

'Not like this. Come on.'

She would have preferred being shoved off the edge of this cone-shaped hill than have to face whatever new fate was in store. They could easily have survived the tumble, albeit with a broken bone or two.

They walked down the hill in single file, Carol leading the way and Merida bringing up the rear. Clarissa took care where she placed her feet, her hip complaining with every step. She dreaded what faced them at the bottom. Fred and Margaret bound and gagged or worse, murdered.

But it was not Alvaro's car in the car park. There, parked pointing in the direction of Villa Winter with the engine running was the tour bus.

'I thought the bus had broken down,' she said as they approached. 'Starting motor, Francois said. He had trouble starting it at the lighthouse.'

'You people will believe anything.'

'He pulled out the coil wire,' said Merida.

How did she know that? She wasn't there.

The more this pack of hounds revealed, the worse things looked. The entire Villa Winter tour was some kind of ruse.

She was too tired and too concerned for her own safety to figure out why.

They were herded into the bus.

'Where are those two porkers,' Vera said, referring to the Spices.

'They went back to their shack.'

'Shouldn't we get them as well?'

'Leave them where they are. We'll deal with them later.'

Clarissa shuddered to think what would become of the Spices if they didn't use Alvaro's car to get away. She sneaked a look in the direction of the restaurant and the south side of the village but they were nowhere to be seen.

The drive back to Villa Winter felt like a death march. Francois drove up to the courtyard entrance at the rear. Merida slid open the side door and ferried the captives into the house with the help of the other women. All three women had battery operated torches. The men stayed by the bus. Clarissa glanced behind her as they were entering the stairwell and saw Francois and Salvador unloading the boot. It was too dark to see what they were removing.

'What are you doing with us?' Richard said.

No one answered him. For a moment Clarissa anticipated they would be taken down to the bunkers, but they were shoved up the stairs in single file, Carol leading the way. Vera pushed Richard ahead of her. Clarissa followed and Merida brought up the rear. Ten treads in, Richard lost his footing on some loose concrete and looked about to topple backwards. Clarissa braced. Carol reacted quickly, grabbing his arm and yanking him forwards behind her.

Carol led them into the tower and on into the attic of the north wing. Merida raised her torch. Backlit, they were shoved out onto the balcony.

'Salvador said to put them in there,' Vera said, gesturing at the small door.

'Out here will do,' Carol said. 'We can lock the whole wing.'

'You're kidding me. They could climb out over the balcony.'

'This decrepit pair?'

'I guess, but even so.'

'Vera's right,' said Merida. 'We shouldn't take any chances.'

She steered Richard to the little door.

'Get in there.'

'I won't fit.'

'You'll fit.'

He hesitated. She grabbed him by the hair and pulled him down to his knees then kicked him hard. Instantly compliant, he crawled through the doorway, cowering, his backpack not making for an easy entry. Clarissa needed no persuading and followed, entering the all-too-familiar space. The door slammed shut and they were plunged into darkness. The sound of the key turning in the lock seemed final.

They sat on the rough concrete floor to either side of the door. Footsteps faded. When they could hear no voices or movement of any kind, Richard groaned loudly.

'Did you see what she did?'

Clarissa hissed, 'Keep your voice down. We don't know if anyone has been put on guard duty.'

'You think someone is still out there?' he whispered, leaning towards her and exhaling his foul, alcoholic breath.

'I'm sure of it,' she said, recoiling.

'My head hurts.'

'I'm not surprised after all you sloshed.'

'You saw her yank my hair.'

'Yes, Richard,' she said, thinking there was much worse to come.

It was hard to know how to sit. Searing darts shot through her hip. The pain was excoriating. When did she last have painkillers? Before they went for the beach walk. She needed to take the penultimate two but Richard would hear the blister pack and then, no doubt, ask for the remaining two. She couldn't risk it. She bent her knees and leaned forward and a corner of the letter tucked in her bra dug into her flesh.

'Can you read German?' she whispered.

'Not since high school. I suppose I might have a rudimentary grasp. Why do you ask?'

'Just wondered.'

The letter could stay where it was. It would burn with her if the incinerator was where they were doomed to end up. That thought sent a shiver down her spine. For how long would they be forced to wait before their fate was revealed?

For a long while, neither spoke. She checked the time. It was only eight o'clock. She was alert with fear and pain. Richard breathed heavily. His breath reeked of booze. He moaned now and then that his back was playing up. That if he didn't stand up straight and walk about, before long he wouldn't be able to move at all. But he couldn't stand up and walk about. The ceiling was too low. He began fidgeting. Then he rummaged about in his backpack and his fanny pack and when he didn't find what he was looking for he let out a soft cry of dismay.

'Whatever's the matter?'

'I could have sworn I packed the painkillers.'

She said nothing. She toyed with the idea of giving him the last two tablets but that would mean coming clean that

The Ghost of Villa Winter

she had stolen them in the first place. Unless she pretended they were hers. Perhaps she should? Perhaps later, she would.

Richard gave up his fidgeting and his moaning and settled down, his breathing soft and rhythmic. She used the quiet to go back over the last two days. The tour had been a contrivance, that was obvious, and Clarissa, Richard and the Spices were innocent bystanders caught up in the unfolding of dark events planned for that weekend. If only they had managed to unlock the attic-room door when Helen had her medical emergency and leave with the tour bus. Or if Richard's sensitivity to the dust had not caused them to stay at Villa Winter overnight. At least then they would have known nothing about Anna. But something told her none of that would have made an iota of difference. One way or another, they were not bystanders, they were victims. Even if they had made it back to Cofete, they would have faced the same danger. Helen's faked medical emergency, the tour bus that had not really broken down, everything had been a set up. Why go to all that trouble? And for what purpose?

She stood up carefully, raising her hands to feel for the rafters. Standing, she stepped from side to side. It made a difference to the discomfort. Helped her to think. What were they up to downstairs? Why the delay? Why not come up and kill them and get it over with? Then again, any delay gave hope. When she checked the time again half an hour had slipped by. All was quiet. Too quiet. She sat back down beside the door and kept still, her hearing acute.

After what felt like an age, she thought she heard a floorboard groan under a footstep not too far away. She held her breath. A door creaked on its hinges. Someone had come out onto the balcony. Clarissa called out, 'Is that you, Carol?' She doubted it was. No one replied and a lengthy silence followed. No footsteps to indicate the guard's departure. She waited. Before long, there was a commotion in the distance far below. Someone yelled up the stairwell. Sounded like Salvador. A man's voice, much closer, yelled back. It was Simon. Clarissa seized the opportunity.

'Will you stop that right this second, Richard!' she yelled.

'I didn't do anything.'

'Yes, you did and you damn well know it. Pervert.'

'I am no such thing!'

'That's what they all say until they show their true colours. I said stop it. Get off of me!'

'I'm nowhere near you.'

'Then what is that I can feel inching up my leg?'

She emitted a piercing scream. The next instant the key rattled in the lock and the little door opened. Clarissa was ready with her phone and shone it into Simon's face, blinding him. He shielded his eyes.

'Switch that damn thing off.'

She obliged and as she feigned fumbling with the device, she set her phone on record and set it down on the floor out of Simon's line of sight, the microphone pointing in the direction of the door. In the darkness, he would never know.

'What is going on in here?' he said, shining his own phone torch around.

'That's what I'd like to know.' She gave Simon a withering look. 'You, a prison counsellor, what are you doing messed up with people like that?' she said, diving straight into her interrogation.

He pulled back, disarmed by her remark.

'You have no idea what you're talking about.'

The Ghost of Villa Winter

She had to think fast. She decided on the direct approach.

'It was you, was it not, who killed Alvaro.'

He scowled.

'Don't be ridiculous. It was Salvador. He was furious with Alvaro. Everyone assumed he was straight. But he wasn't. Not entirely. At least, he was willing to have sex with his fellow inmates. It was unconscionable. When Salvador found out he lost it.' He paused. Clarissa noted the gay emblem on his shirt. Strange. 'I was trying to help Alvaro,' he said. 'He was a client.'

'A client?' Richard said. Clarissa wanted to kick him but he was out of reach.

'I would say a psychopath,' she said, hoping to keep Simon on track. 'Having not only killed that poor woman but dismembered and incinerated her.'

'No, well, yes, maybe. He was a murderer, true. But he didn't kill that woman and he wasn't in prison for murder.'

It was a lot to take in.

'If he didn't kill Anna, who did?'

'How do you know her name?'

'It was Salvador, wasn't it?'

'She wouldn't stop snooping.'

She supposed that was confirmation enough. She persisted with her main line of inquiry.

'And Alvaro killed the priest.'

'That was not meant to happen. Things got out of hand. Alvaro always took things too far.'

'Greedy.'

'Not greedy. We had no idea about the charity money. The priest knew too much.'

'And he was going to expose you.'

There was a pause. Clarissa wasn't sure how to fill it.

Then Simon did what perpetrators do to captives when they believe the end is near. They spill all.

'Alvaro told Juan to take the money to make it look like theft.'

'And he hid it in that cave,' Richard said.

'Then Trevor comes along and ruins your plans.'

'Things would have been alright if Juan had timed the tides.'

'He got swept out on the currents.' Richard again, determined to have a three-way exchange. She dearly wished he would shut up.

'How did you know about Trevor and the backpack?' she said, hoping he didn't have a connection with Claire and Paco.

Simon laughed derisively.

'Trevor is a stupid man. Helen was on the beach that day when he went around trying to find the owner.'

'And Trevor doesn't know any of this?'

'Of course not.'

'And you are well-placed to make sure you'll be one of the first to know if he does.'

She knew in an instant the moment she divulged to Trevor what she now knew she would be putting him in mortal danger. Assuming she got out of this current situation alive. Her mind rushed back to the ordeal he had put himself through fearing someone would turn up for the backpack at any moment. And all along his fears were valid.

She realised she had an answer to why they were in this predicament. Simon had known all along she was trying to get Trevor freed. That Villa Winter tour leaflet she had been given in the café that day, that had been planted on her on purpose. She strained to recall the woman who had given it to her and if she'd resembled Vera or Carol in any way.

The Ghost of Villa Winter

Two birds and one stone, isn't that what they say? Both her and Anna disposed of in the one weekend. She should have heeded the alignment of Pluto, Saturn and Mars, the planetary propensity for violence and death. Instead, she'd allowed herself to be swayed by a Venus-Mercury-Neptune connection, failing to acknowledge the deception and illusion that always came with Neptune. Damn astrology. It was too unreliable.

Salvador yelled out again and Simon pulled his head out of the doorway.

'Enough talk.' He looked at Richard. 'And you, settle down and leave her alone.' He turned to Clarissa. 'What's he on, Parkinson's meds?'

They heard the key turn in the lock and footsteps fade as Simon headed downstairs.

'What was all that about?'

'Don't worry, Richard. At least one crime is now solved. Alvaro killed the priest. Sounds like Salvador killed Anna and probably Alvaro as well. I'd call that a result.'

'But we are trapped. And about to be murdered, most likely.'

'I don't think so. Switch on your phone torch, please.'

She fished about in her canvas bag and produced the key she'd pocketed last time they were locked in the attic.

'Where did you find that?'

'It's the key to the other attic door.'

'The one that wouldn't open?'

'Given how hard it was, I thought perhaps the key fitted a different lock.'

'You never said.' He sounded hurt and betrayed. She ignored him.

'I'm hoping it'll work.'

'Hopefully they didn't leave the other one in the lock.'

Ever the voice of optimism.

Her theory proved right. One turn and the door opened.

Richard shone his torchlight around.

'Give me that, please.'

He obliged. She urged him to crawl through the doorway first. She followed. Once through, she used the phone torch to re-insert the key and lock the door. Then she stood and pointed the way, shielding the bulk of the glare with her hand and only allowing enough light to guide their way.

'Hurry, we don't have much time.'

He was close behind her. She directed the light and steadied Richard as he stepped over the threshold and entered the attic room. Then she guided him through to the tower.

'Where are they?' he said.

'That's what we are about to find out.'

'Why don't we just run off.'

'Not before I've found the second bunker.'

'What second bunker?'

'The one Salvador so emphatically stated doesn't exist.'

The one Gustav Winter was so keen she discovered, Clarissa thought but didn't say.

She took a tentative look down the stairwell. There was no light coming up from below and no light in the courtyard. Even so, there was no telling if anyone had been posted on guard duty. It was a chance they would have to take.

'Careful on the stairs.'

'I'm always careful.'

'You've had a lot to drink, Richard, and we don't want you falling.'

'I'm as steady as a rock.'

The Ghost of Villa Winter

For once, he was, and she thought he might have sobered up.

At the bottom of the stairs she hesitated, before taking another risk and entering the living room. The hessian basket hung from its hook by the door. Three steps and she foraged for the magazine, eager to discover who had written that article. When her fingers touched the glossy paper, she thought she could smell perfume. No, not perfume, incense. It was very faint and seemed to be coming from the direction of the fireplace. She didn't dare investigate. She stuffed the magazine in her bag, fished about in her pocket for the blister pack of painkillers and downed two in a single gulp of spit and left the room, making sure to ease the door shut behind her.

She then led a very anxious Richard through the courtyard and on outside. Freedom, and she wanted to bolt for the cliff, but not yet. She needed to assess the goings on below. Locate the second bunker. Although if there was any indication that one of those the conspirators was being sent upstairs on guard duty, they were in deep trouble. The locked door would buy them some time but how much was impossible to know. There were few hiding places around the villa. And they'd never get away if they didn't have a decent lead. Neither of them was fit and able enough to outrun any of the others. They were thoughts that caused Clarissa's heart to hammer in her chest.

With Richard close on her heels, she rounded the north wall and headed down to the front of the villa where the kitchen door exited below the tower. Somewhere there was access to the second bunker. She carried on down. She heard Richard muttering under his breath. She hissed for him to shut up. He was an absolute encumbrance.

There was no telling how much time they had, but she guessed not much.

There was no door, none that she could see, no entrance of any kind, but soon they could hear voices echoing, and the smell of incense was stronger. A deep droning voice seemed to be incanting some ritual. Salvador. There was a chorus of Oms. Simon had been called downstairs to participate in some kind of ritual. They were preparing for something. It was then Clarissa smelt smoke and when she looked up, she thought she saw smoke rising out of the chimney. They had lit the incinerator. There could be no doubt of their fate, although she assumed Alvaro's body would go first. It was a reasonable assumption but there was no time to waste. She hurried Richard back up the length of the north wall. From there, they would be exposed, especially as they passed the courtyard entrance. There was no choice but to risk it.

'Keep up, Richard, there's no time to lose.'

'My back is killing me.'

'Ditch the water bottle.'

'I'm not ditching the water bottle.'

'Then stop complaining. Or would you rather be dead?'

She could have handed him the last two painkillers, but she stubbornly resisted the impulse. She couldn't abide his pathetic attitude. He should thank his lucky stars she didn't simply march off without him and leave him to his own devices. That, she knew, would mean certain death.

She headed along the rear of the villa, pausing when she reached the courtyard entrance.

She took a deep breath and inched her way forward, careful to keep her body out of sight as she peered in. There was no sign of anyone but it was impossible to tell. The courtyard sat in gloom, the loggia in total darkness.

She pressed her back to the wall and took a few slow breaths in an effort to quell her racing heart. If she'd been religious, she would have crossed herself or said a prayer. Instead, she darted past as fast and as quietly as she could. On the other side she waited for Richard to do the same, crossing her fingers that he wouldn't trip or kick a stone or groan or do anything else he was capable of. When he made it past, she looked heavenward and said Thank you.

A few more metres and they'd reached the end of the villa wall. From then on, was open country. She hurried along the track keen to put as much distance between them and the villa as fast as possible. When the track headed down past the villa to Cofete, she grabbed Richard's wrist and set off cross-country, keeping close to the cliff, aiming to make a slow but steady ascent until they met with the cliff path somewhere between the villa and the village.

The going was tough the ground stony and littered with euphorbias. It was dark, but a crescent moon had graced them with its presence and they would have to make do with what light it had to offer, which wasn't much. Dodging rocks and low bushes made the going slow. Neither one of them could risk a fall and the painkillers she'd downed in the living room hadn't kicked in. She kept pressing forwards, resisting the temptation to run. She resisted looking back, too, although the pull was great. Behind her, she could sense the villa, the weight of all it represented as though the very rocks with which it had been built were impregnated with some evil force, a force able to reach outwards, reach as far as Cofete and beyond, an evil force still able to destroy her. When she did turn, the villa stood, a black mass in the darkness.

The further they went the more urgent she felt. It didn't

matter how far they got, the others had a vehicle and they were younger and fitter and they didn't have injuries.

She could only hope the ritual was dragging on. That re-locking the door would buy them enough time. At least the realisation that they had escaped would take a fraction longer, and they were dealing in fractions, or so she thought.

Richard puffed and lumbered behind her, weighed down by that ludicrously heavy backpack. He was more of an impediment than ever but she had to try to save him. As much as she might have liked to abandon him, she couldn't. It would make her as evil as the others. There was no point in offering him the painkillers either. They'd be on the other side of the cliff before they worked.

It seemed to be taking forever to find the cliff path. They picked their way across a small gorge and then another soon after. She counted five gorges before they reached what she thought was to be a sixth but it turned out to be the path. The cliff towered above them, a dark giant, the way up its forbidding face lit dimly by the moon. The path represented freedom and with her feet placed firmly on the grit, she had a premature sense that they had already escaped, before she glanced to the north and made out Villa Winter and the realisation hit her that they were not that far away. Worse, tackling the perilous ascent at their age put them at a greater risk of being re-captured should the others realise they were missing and catch sight of them. She couldn't afford to think like that. It was paralysing.

'It's uphill all the way from here, Richard,' she said grimly. 'Are you ready?'

'Can I just drink some water.'

'Go ahead. I will too.'

She took the opportunity to take a long hard look back the way they had come. She thought only about a kilometre separated them from the villa. They'd been walking for about fifteen minutes. Even so, any time now, she imagined the ritual would have come to an end and someone would be going back to the attic to check on them.

She screwed the lid back on her water bottle and dropped it into her canvas bag. It would have been better not to have to carry anything. Richard really should discard most of the contents of his, she thought, but she said nothing as he deposited his giant-sized water bottle in the main pouch of his backpack and did up the zip.

The path looked as though it headed straight up the cliff. Clarissa led the way. At first the ascent was moderate, but soon they were both breathing heavily. It was when the zigzags began that Clarissa knew they were in for a big climb. Still, she had Fred to thank for alerting her to the path, their only escape, and she supposed she had to be thankful the moon was up enough to light their way but not enough to make them visible to onlookers. Also, there was not a breath of wind. And the night was cool and not unpleasant. In all, they were near perfect conditions. She wished the same could be said for the path, which was narrow and pitted and gritty and strewn with rocks. One wrong footfall and she would careen to her death. She kept to the cliff side of the path, holding on to the cliff face for reassurance as much as balance, leaning that way and avoiding looking at the edge.

On and on they trudged. When they reached a zigzag the cliff face disappeared and for a few terrifying paces there was no support, no reassurance. Instead, they were forced to traverse the adverse camber on the slippery grit.

The zigzags followed a bulge in the cliff and on the lower portion of the path the gradient was not too onerous. Although her thighs had other ideas and she had to force one foot in front of the other. She dared not look back at Richard.

The going got tougher the higher they went. She knew the upper portion of the path would be the hardest since the cliff steepened near the top. She tried to comfort herself with the thought that the locals had chosen the safest and best route, but it didn't make the going any easier. The only salvation was the painkillers which finally began to work and, much to her relief, she found the climbing motion didn't impact her hip.

By the time they were about halfway, it was Richard who posed the biggest issue.

'I'm not sure I can do this,' he kept saying, and she kept ignoring him.

When they reached a wider portion of the path she stopped and turned and said, 'Why not take off the backpack? It will make things so much easier.'

'I am not taking off my backpack.'

'Well at least lose the water bottle.'

'And die of thirst?'

She gave up. He was insufferable.

The going grew hairy after the fourth switchback and as they neared the steepest section of the ascent, the sense of exposure intensified. She didn't want to take another break but Richard begged her and begged her. She kept lumbering on until she reached a section of path she considered safer, and leaned her back against the cliff.

'What is it this time?' she said, catching her breath.

His reply was unexpected.

'I wanted to thank you.'

'For what?'

'I've made up my mind, Clarissa. I'm going to leave her.'

It took her a moment to realise who he was referring to.

The Ghost of Villa Winter

Is that what he had been thinking about all this time? His wife? Although she had to credit him with courage. Hopefully not Dutch courage. Hopefully, he wouldn't change his mind. It was a bold move, for him. Life changing, and it would release him into a grand new future of freedom and creativity, of that she was sure. He would grow wings and soar in no time, regain his standing, rediscover or discover for the first time what he was really made of.

'That's fantastic, Richard. Congratulations. I am really proud of you.'

'You are?'

'Truly.'

She wouldn't normally have gushed praise like it and she wondered if she didn't sound a touch patronising. She hoped not. She wanted to affirm his decision, reinforce the wisdom of it. When they reached safety, maybe on the descent to Morro Jable, she would discuss with him his plans for the future.

'Trish will kill me, of course.'

'She won't. She can't. Stand your ground. You're doing the right thing. Now, we better get on.'

At the final zigzag, she had to brace herself before she tackled the adverse camber. It was better not to think, better to shrink the awareness down to a narrow slit. As she inched her way around the bend, losing the cliff face on her right and then a few steps further rediscovering it on her left, she could see the end of the path up ahead. The moonlight was fading, the moon setting, and they would need to use their phone torches before much longer. Only, she didn't want to light up this portion of the path. From what she could already see, the drop was precipitous. There was no longer the bulge to soften the descent. Instead, there was this dizzying fall.

She pressed on. She tried to forget about the narrowness of the path, tried forget about the height and focus only on the strip of ground beneath her feet. She wasn't prone to acrophobia but in her exhausted and fearful state, that void beside her made her palms sweat.

She wanted to tell Richard not to look down. She wanted to tell him to keep himself pressed against the cliff face and take it easy; the path was nowhere near as steep as before but it wasn't only narrow, it was curvy and boulder strewn. She wanted to tell him they were nearly there and all that lay ahead of them was a much easier descent down into a valley and they would be in Morro Jable before they knew it. She wanted to tell him all of that but he had started complaining again that his back was killing him and he could hardly see and he would have to stop and have a big long rest at any moment as he was fit to drop. And, he said, he was parched. Then he said he was gasping. He was dehydrated, that was certain.

They were almost there. Clarissa estimated another fifteen or twenty paces and they would be at the top. She was about to tell him that when he said, 'I'm going to have to swing off my backpack soon and take some water, if you don't mind.'

She didn't answer. Her foot landed on a small rock and slid sideways towards the cliff edge. She leaned in to the cliff to steady herself and quickly regained her balance. Her heart pounded in her chest and her palms were wetter than ever. She pressed on, taking each footstep with care.

Richard was right behind her. She told him to be careful but she didn't turn. She wanted to warn him to be especially careful, that the path was getting even narrower, but she wasn't feeling that steady herself. She made out a boulder protruding from the rockface up ahead. The path went around it, sloping downwards with an adverse camber as it did.

Four paces and she reached the boulder. There was nothing for it but to pick her way by. Her legs trembled with each footstep. She gripped the handles of her canvas bag with one hand, the other raised, reaching out for the cliff face and not quite touching it. Balance was critical and she wasn't sure she had much balance in her. One step, two steps, three steps more. It was easily the most terrifying moment of her life.

Once she'd rounded the boulder she said, 'Richard, there's a...'

'You keep going. I'll catch you up.'

At that moment when he announced he was stopping, the moon disappeared and the night went black.

How on earth would he see? How on earth would he navigate by the boulder?

'Richard, we're only a few...'

The next she heard was the skid of gravel, a few skittering pebbles and a man's fading cry.

For a few moments, she froze where she stood, trembling. There was nothing to be done. Richard was gone. No one could survive an unbroken fall like that.

A whisker of wind brushed her face, reminding her of where she was. She had to rouse herself to keep moving. Seven more paces and she reached the crest.

The horror of his misstep implanted itself into her mind. She stood back from the cliff looking out into the night and waited for the trembling to stop. A few squares of chocolate helped. Then she began the slow and steady descent into the valley, the way now lit by her phone torch.

16

LUNCH WITH CLAIRE

'You're looking remarkably well, considering.'

Claire eyed her aunt appraisingly beneath her shock of copper hair, taking in the worn expression, the absence of her aunt's usual *joie de vivre*. Claire was decked in loose trousers and a contrasting blouse. She was, as ever, striking to behold. In her company, Clarissa always felt maternal and proud. But she knew straight away this lunch would not entail their usual convivial exchanges. Already she felt under observation, and she prepared herself to field the inevitable interrogation.

Almost two days had passed since Clarissa had made it back to Morro Jable, two days in which to process the events and deal with her guilt, especially over the painkillers. Would they have helped? Two days and a gamut of emotions that refused to go away. It wasn't possible to explain the build-up to Richard's death to anyone, least of all her niece. As for the rest, she'd already told her story to the police three, no four times. Now Claire wanted the blow-by-blow. She wasn't getting it.

'It was an ordeal,' was all she said and she turned her

The Ghost of Villa Winter

face to the window.

They had claimed a table with a view. The wind had picked up and white caps appeared on the open ocean beyond the bay. Closer to shore the water remained calm, the bare rock of the headland sheltering Las Playitas.

Claire waited, expectantly. Clarissa's mind emptied. They sat in silence. Eventually, Claire relaxed in her seat, giving in. The waiter arrived with menus and they spent some time choosing what to eat. Clarissa chose fish fillets.

When the waiter returned to take their order, Claire said, 'Why not have fish of the day?'

'The fillets will be fine.' She wasn't going to admit she couldn't face the memory of Richard and his fish meal in Cofete, the way he had picked through the bones. He had irritated her then but now she found his finicky manner endearing.

Over a crisp white wine, Claire gave updates of her house and garden, Paco's upcoming photographic exhibition and her work with the local women of Tiscamanita. 'My Spanish has improved no end since I started engaging the locals in my history project. The photos they bring, the stories they tell. It's marvellous.' Her enthusiasm for Fuerteventura was boundless. Clarissa wished she could share in it. Ever since she had taken on Trevor's case her experience of the island had been a touch tarnished, but nothing could trump what had happened last weekend. She had come to believe the island was a magnet for darkness. Surely not. Surely not somewhere so exhilarating, somewhere as majestic and timeless as here. Bad things don't happen in paradise, do they? They do. Sadly.

The meal came, and as Claire picked up her knife and fork, she said, 'And how's your hip?'

'Much better, thanks to the physiotherapist.'

Although it was still giving her some discomfort. Claire had insisted she see a health professional the moment she divulged the pain. For once, she had taken her niece's advice and booked an appointment for the previous afternoon. One session, and the chap had freed up tight muscles and explained how she could avoid a similar situation in the future. Although the pain was returning and she knew she needed to visit a doctor for a proper diagnosis.

The meal was delicious, the fish sweet and tender, the salad filled with flavour. Her mind drifted back to the fare in Cofete, to her decision to remember the food as the singular highlight of the weekend, memories tarnished by her knowledge of the chef, her suspicion that out of all of them he was most likely both Anna and Alvaro's killer. It was his meat mallet, after all, that Francois had paraded about, even though he denied it. And he had been all too quick to suggest storing the body in his cool room.

As the waiter took away their plates, Claire said, 'I almost forgot. I brought the dictionary.'

She gave her aunt another inquiring look as she placed the book on the table.

'Are you going to tell me?'

'Just a letter I found.'

'At Villa Winter?'

Clarissa nodded.

'I wish you'd open up more. It would do you good.'

Claire's phone sprang to life and gave Clarissa a reprieve. What ought to have been a pleasant lunch was proving more arduous than she'd anticipated. She wished Claire would stop probing her. She didn't care to relive any of it, least of all those moments trudging up the cliff, and the horror she felt when Richard fell.

The lonely trek down to Morro Jable had proven almost

as nerve-wracking as the climb, the pitch blackness of the night, the path that zigzagged for a stretch down a steep-sided flank, forcing her to go back on herself. If it hadn't been for the block of chocolate and the protein bars, she feared she might not have had the energy to make it after the climb. Then, when she neared the end of the long and narrow valley, she was forced to pass a large farm compound, setting off the dogs which barked incessantly, and she had no idea if they were chained up or free. No light went on. No one came out to see who was there. No doubt the occupants presumed she was a rabbit. Things quietened once she hit the dirt road which was mostly flat and she could at least hope for a passing vehicle, although hopefully not a zebra-striped bus. No one came. Her anxiety grew and grew the closer she got to civilisation. She was certain the others would set up a search, but she made it to Morro Jable where a night-worker took pity on her and drove her to the police station.

She'd only told Claire that final portion of what had happened on the phone and it was obvious she was holding back. As it was, her mind kept presenting her with unwanted flashback stills of the highlights of her weekend. A weekend she would much rather forget.

When Claire put down her phone, Clarissa said, 'If you'll excuse me.'

She rose from the table and headed in the direction of the facilities. As she cornered the wall at the rear of the premises where more diners were seated, her gaze landed on the table for two tucked beside the bar. There, enjoying what appeared to be a lavish seafood platter, were Steve and Dave. Without a moment's hesitation she went over, arranging her face into what she hoped was an endearing smile.

'Fancy seeing you two here.'

The lads both looked up at once, recognition appearing in their eyes. Steve laughed to mask his awkwardness.

'Fancy meeting *you* here.'

It was her turn to laugh.

'Small island.'

'I'm not sure I caught your name.'

'Clarissa.'

'Steve and Dave.'

'You missed quite an adventure,' she said, scrambling for a lead in.

'We heard about that author,' Steve said. 'You were friendly with him, right? Sorry for your loss.'

'We heard the police arrested the entire tour bus, with the exception of you and Richard and that red-headed guy – Fred, wasn't it? – and his wife.'

'They arrested Salvador and Merida, too,' she said. 'The whole lot of them.'

Two pairs of eyes studied her face.

'Not sure what they'll all be charged with,' said Dave.

'Murder,' Clarissa said.

'I'm not so sure,' said Steve. 'Last I heard they were all being questioned over the death of that Alvaro guy. An ex-con, wasn't he? Can't imagine the cops will care too much he's gone.'

It was true. So far, the police were not that interested in Alvaro's murder. They were calling it a disappearance. And there was no evidence of murder, thanks to the disappearance of the meat mallet. She'd given her statement to the police twice in Morro Jable and twice again in Puerto del Rosario. No one seemed to believe her story. And as for the body in the chest, no journalist by the name of Anna Trower had been reported missing. Last anyone knew she was on holiday in a remote area of Madagascar. Clarissa found it hard to convince the officers that she had seen the body with her own eyes as there was no evidence it had ever existed. She was treated by all and sundry as a dotty old English lady losing her marbles. When she described the scene with the incinerator, one officer muttered something about conspiracy theories and laughed. The photo of Anna on her phone meant nothing to them. She didn't look that dead, one officer had said. And it was true, she didn't. She looked asleep, thanks to Richard making Clarissa close her eyes. When she'd told the police about Alvaro's murder and they'd told her they couldn't find a trace of him, she knew why no one had come looking for her and Richard when they'd made their escape from the attic. Salvador and his crew had been too busy disposing of Alvaro in the incinerator. No doubt their turn awaited. In those police interviews, she'd held back revealing her secret recording of Simon's confession after getting nowhere explaining the truth. A smart move, she had thought at the time. She needed to consult her lawyer, get him to take a copy before letting the police have access to her phone. For all she knew they might accidentally delete the recording and she had no idea how to transfer it onto another device for safekeeping. Her lawyer would know what was best. The fact remained she had solid evidence Trevor was innocent, or so she thought. Her mind was like a washing machine with all these thoughts sloshing around with the smalls. None of this she felt comfortable divulging to Claire, let alone the lads.

She wished them a pleasant holiday and went to the bar and collected a dessert menu while she gathered herself together. On her way back she paused by the lads' table again.

'Sorry to interrupt you once more, but something has me puzzled,' she said.

Both men froze and she knew in an instant they were holding back just as much as she was.

Steve set down his fork after spearing a prawn. 'Go on.'

'What made you two leave Cofete that day?'

Dave gave Steve a cautionary look. Steve told him not to worry. 'Salvador and a wad of cash,' he said to Clarissa with a note of triumph.

'I don't follow.'

'He told us to set up a fake car crash to block the road on Sunday morning. Too easy, we thought, considering the amount he gave us.'

'Not really a crime,' Dave added. 'He even provided the vehicles. Or the keys to them. They were parked in Morro Jable.'

'And you didn't think to ask why?'

'We were not about to question a thousand Euros.'

'But we did wonder, didn't we?'

'We did. And we came to the conclusion it was none of our business.'

'Surely the police will want to question you?'

'Only if they find out,' Dave said. Was there menace in his tone or was it her imagination?

Steve laughed to lighten the mood.

'We're leaving on the next flight. Bound for Australia. Not sure the local cops will bother with us.'

'I expect you're right. Well, your secret is safe with me.'

She decided there was probably nothing to be gained from letting the police know what they did. The recording would be enough to nail the perpetrators. As cocky as they were, she rather liked the lads. They had what some would call bottle. Gumption. Spirit. And aside from allowing themselves to be drawn into Salvador's web, she found them harmless. She almost felt sorry for them. After all, they were the ones the others had set up to be the fall guys. No doubt Salvador and his crew were busy pointing the finger right then. She wondered if she should let them know they were being framed. No, she would come across as paranoid. Besides, they would soon be gone from here. She thanked them for filling her in and wished them a safe flight home.

She popped into the Ladies on her way back to her table. She had to rearrange her face again on her approach. She knew she hadn't done a good job when Claire said, 'What is it? You were ages.'

'I just noticed someone and stopped for a chat.'

Claire clutched the edge of the table with both hands, her eyes fiery under her shock of copper hair.

'Are you going to tell me what's going on?'

Clarissa gave her a pleading look.

'Nothing's going on. My mind is a scramble, that's all.'

'I'm sure it is.' She let go of the table and sat back and gave Clarissa a thin smile as if to convey her disappointment in Clarissa for refusing to divulge to her own kin what was playing on her mind. 'You need a long rest,' she added with a note of sympathy.

A long rest was the last thing she needed. She wasn't an invalid.

'Why don't you come to us for a few days?'

'I'm heading back home soon.'

'There's no need.'

'A break from this island is what I need. Thanks, all the same.'

The look of sadness on Claire's face was hard to stomach.

. . .

Back in her apartment, she placed the German-English dictionary on the highly polished table in the main living room and went and poured herself a glass of spring water, cold from the fridge. With pen and paper to hand, she opened the letter she'd found tucked behind a drawer in the living room of Villa Winter. Anticipation stirred. Maybe, just maybe the letter would yield a clue about the villa, or even something that would explain the motives of that murdering cult. She hoped to find a reference to the second bunker, or to some occult ritual the Nazi visitors engaged in.

The sun beamed into the room, brightening the already bright and cheery yellow walls. She read over what she could already glean of the letter. The addressee was not named. The author was a woman, Cynthia. She gave no surname. Clarissa set about translating the sentences word-by-word using the dictionary and then an online translation site to assist with meaning. It took her two sentences to realise it was a love letter. A love letter filled with longing and missing and expectation. So lovely to see you. When I remember our last meal together my heart quickens. That sort of thing. No mention of Villa Winter or the Nazis or secret plots or any such thing. The translating was a laborious task and when she was about half way she almost gave up. She was so disappointed by the end of it she felt like tearing up the letter. Why go to all the trouble of hiding that letter behind a drawer if all it contained was romantic drivel that applied to no one in particular that could be identified? She recalled the other letter she found, the one in Alvaro's car written in the 1980s, and she dismissed it right away as most likely another red herring. Besides, she was running out of time and she needed to compose herself. Her appointment with the lawyer was at three.

17

SOME FRUSTRATING NEWS

She left the apartment early, allowing plenty of time for the walk, finding herself needing to be out in the fresh air, not cooped up in her apartment with all those walls boxing in her flashbacks and recollections. Making her angst even worse, Richard Parry's death was filling the newspapers in Fuerteventura, in the Canary Islands, in Spain and even back in Britain. His bereaved wife and his publisher appeared to be making a meal of his sudden and tragic demise. They were quick off the mark. Taken in his prime, they said. He had so many more books left in him. Little did *they* know. Clarissa suspected the pair were whipping up interest to increase book sales. And why not? Publishing was a tough industry. But it increased the attention on her and she knew it was only a matter of time before the press would be beating down her door wanting her account of the weekend. So far, she'd ignored all phone calls from unknown numbers. But someone somewhere would find her and then she'd have no peace at all for a while.

The painkillers were only the tip of her guilt. She had known all along that doom was following her that weekend.

She had seen it in the planets. An alignment of Saturn and Pluto and Mars impacting not only her own horoscope but those of many others besides. Although, she wasn't one to go about predicting death and that weekend the alignment had been impacting the whole world anyway. You can't live your life using astrology to determine your every movement. Still, the planetary alignment lingered in her thoughts. Would she have sniffed out more cosmic harbingers if she'd applied herself? Was it her responsibility? No. But she was the one who led him up the cliff path. She was the one who didn't offer him his own painkillers when he needed them most. The karmic ramifications were enormous. Then again, he chose to get drunk and he chose to be reckless and he chose to be stubborn. He wasn't a child and she wasn't his mother. She needed to divest herself of all her agonising. In the final analysis it wasn't her karma. It was his.

She crossed the road at the pedestrian crossing opposite the plaza. Children played on the play equipment. Parents watched. City dwellers sat on seats beneath the spreading trees. Cafés dotted around the plaza's perimeter were abuzz. A thin stream of cars headed up the hill towards the outskirts of the little city. Clarissa headed downhill towards the old quarter surrounding the port.

Grand, colonial-style buildings lined the city streets. Before long she was crossing the plaza at the rear of the old church which had pride of place surrounded by municipal buildings and banks. A normal sunny afternoon, the streets cooled by the light ocean breeze, and she remembered why she had grown so fond of Puerto del Rosario. It was unpretentious and scarcely bothered to cater for the cruise ships putting in for the day, other than providing historically interesting streetscapes peppered with sculptures. She could live here, she knew, and her life would benefit from

The Ghost of Villa Winter

the proximity of her niece. But then there were all her friends back home. Her life, in fact. Still, it was an interesting thought and a nice distraction.

A short stretch of plaza past some government offices and she found the front doors of the church were open. A handful of tourists in shorts and T-shirts were milling about on the steps outside. She made a right at the next corner and headed down Calle Primero de Mayo, a bustling street closed off to traffic and given over to pedestrians with lots of seating and outdoor dining. The street took her down to a pretty beach nestled in its own little bay and sheltered by a long harbour wall. Sunbathers peppered the sand and there were many heads bobbing in the water. On the far side of the beach to the north, a cruise ship was anchored. Beyond, the cranes of the little cargo port.

She turned up a narrow side street and entered a modern building. She'd arrived at the lawyer's five minutes early and waited in reception on the first floor. In her bag was her phone with the recording she'd made of Simon's divulgences. Recalling what he'd said filled her with optimism that at last Trevor was on the road to freedom. It wasn't until after she was ushered through to Mr Pérez's office and he'd listened to her recording that her optimism gave way to frustration.

'Mr Pérez, surely it will be enough to set him free?'

She'd always found it incongruous that the matter of Trevor's freedom was discussed in this swanky office in the wealthy business district of town. Air conditioned, stylishly furnished and hushed, in marked contrast to the busyness out in the street below, let alone the prison cell where Trevor languished. Mr Pérez pressed his fingertips together in a gesture meant to convey both his superior knowledge and wisdom, and his willingness to give the matter the time of day. His leather swivel chair was pushed back and he had one leg crossed ankle-to-knee over the other. He was being casual, masculine, patronising perhaps, but Clarissa was untroubled by it. She observed a small square of vivid purple paper stuck to the sole of his shoe.

'The problem is Alvaro. He cannot be cross-examined since he is dead. We only have Simon's word for Alvaro's involvement in the death of the priest, possibly corroborated by Helen if she cooperates. But why would she? And Simon himself wasn't there at the church. He only has Alvaro's account of what happened that day. That is what the other side will argue. The testimony amounts to hearsay. And besides,' he said, pointing at her phone on his desk, 'it's an unlawful recording. We can't use this in court.'

Clarissa began to lose hope of ever securing Trevor's freedom. Surely the recording cast enough doubt to re-open the case?

Mr Pérez called through to his secretary who appeared a moment later. He handed her Clarissa's phone and told her to put the recording onto four memory sticks. The woman nodded and left the room.

'But Simon is under arrest,' Clarissa said. 'They all are, the entire sect.'

'Not for long. The police cannot pinpoint the killer. There's no evidence and none of them are going to confess or implicate any of the others.'

She sat back in her seat, deflated. Beneath her breath she said, 'They get away with murder and Trevor remains in prison.'

Mr Pérez looked at her sympathetically. 'I wish I could give you better news, but you have provided little evidence. Of course, we have your own testimony, which should count for something. Pity it cannot be corroborated by Richard.'

That last remark stung. Mr Pérez needed a lesson in compassion.

'What about Fred Spice?' she said.

'The Spices are back in England, but if the police do take the matter seriously, they'll get the local police there to conduct an interview.'

She sighed. 'They didn't see anything anyway. Nothing useful. Although they did witness me and Richard being herded up the hill by the others. I told Fred and Margaret to use Alvaro's car to get away from the village, which they did, I understand.'

'Inspector García says the police have been unable to locate that car. They say either your friends in Cofete were quick to locate it first and dispose of it, or there was no car.'

'Are you accusing me of lying?'

'Of course not. I am just relating what I was told.'

She refrained from explaining how she thought the entire weekend had been planned in order to kill her. She would only get the same response she got from the first police officer she told in Morro Jable. Derision. There were too many conspiracy theories associated with Villa Winter. They didn't need another one. The humiliation had been hard to bear.

There was a soft knock and his secretary reappeared with Clarissa's phone and the memory sticks. She put them all down on the desk and left the room without uttering a word.

'Try not to be too despondent,' Mr Pérez said, uncrossing his legs and making to stand. 'You've had a rough weekend. Let's see how things unfold.'

He handed her two memory sticks. She thanked him for his time. He shook her hand and gave her a reassuring smile.

Out on the pavement she considered her options. The police station? Or straight back to her apartment. But that would be defeatist. Walking at a brisk pace, she headed back the way she'd come. When she got to the church, she turned right down a side street, pushing through the police station's heavy glass entrance door on the next corner and approaching the main desk before she had a chance to change her mind.

It took another ten minutes before the officer dealing with her case appeared and took her through to an interview room. Inspector García had conducted the fourth interview, the second after she had returned to Puerto del Rosario. He was a patient, understanding man who she thought enjoyed the culinary benefits of a loving wife and the comforts of a large family at home. He gave off that kind of vibe. She was lucky to find him on shift.

Another officer joined them. After a brief explanation, the policemen listened to the recording on her phone. Clarissa studied their faces, looking for reactions of surprise, outrage, horror, confusion, anything to indicate they were taking her seriously. Instead, neither officer displayed any emotion whatsoever. It was as though they were listening to the weather report of a little-known town in deepest Russia. The moment the recording came to an end she reached and pulled the phone over to her side of the desk. She thought twice about giving them a memory stick. They would most likely lose it or bin it, judging by the disbelieving expressions growing on their faces.

'Well?' she said dredging up hope.

The younger officer spoke. He was thick set and clean cut, a rookie type fresh out of training school. 'This is Simon Slava?' His voice was nasal and heavily accented.

'I told you it was.'

The Ghost of Villa Winter

The men looked doubtful, she supposed in part because Simon was presumably a well-known and highly respected psychologist, social worker and counsellor. Perhaps he wrote prisoner reports and appeared in court as an expert witness. She had no idea, but judging by the reaction of the officers seated in front of her, who appeared to find his confession inconceivable, he must have established an impeccable reputation.

'Why would he confess?' Inspector García said.

'He told us because he assumed we were about to die.'

It was obvious. Isn't that what villains did, confess their previous crimes to the next victim just before they wield the knife? She waited expectantly but neither officer spoke. Then she said, 'My lawyer has a copy of the recording and he's considering the options. Will you re-open the Trevor Moore case?'

The junior officer suppressed a laugh. Inspector García gave her a sympathetic look. It was the same look Mr Pérez had given her and she found it patronising.

'On the strength of this?' he said.

'That is what I meant.'

'We still have no evidence, and we cannot use this in court. You recorded Simon without his knowledge.'

She emitted a forceful sigh to show her displeasure, not that it would make one iota of difference.

'Mrs Wilkinson,' Inspector García went on. 'Alvaro is missing presumed dead. There is no evidence he committed any crime. But we will re-interview Helen. If she admits to being on the beach in Puertito de los Molinos that day Trevor found the rucksack, then maybe we have something. At least it will validate Simon's confession.'

In a flash, Clarissa saw another possibility. 'My niece and her husband were in the village that day. Maybe one of them saw her.' Suddenly, identifying Helen seemed her only hope. At the very least it would stop these officers treating her as though she was a silly old crone. 'Can I have a photo of Helen to show them?'

'Ask them to come in to the station.'

After a brief handshake and a polite thank you, she left the interview room and rushed back to her apartment. She needed as much evidence as she could muster and that evidence was thin on the ground. After calling Claire and begging her and Paco to visit the police station at once, she realised her only other hope was to get Steve and Dave to own up to the road block, implicating Salvador in some kind of conspiracy. That would throw a lot of suspicion on the matter. Why didn't that occur to her before? She knew why. Because she'd been convinced the recording would clinch things.

She had no idea what flight the lads were getting on. There was nothing for it but to take a taxi to the airport. She flew around the apartment as she readied herself for yet another excursion that day, and then she hurried down to the street, taking care on the apartment block's polished tiled stairs.

There was a taxi rank a block up from her apartment. The plaza opposite was filling with families passing a pleasant late afternoon, and she had to dodge many pedestrians on the pavement who seemed to appear from nowhere and block her path. She knew it was just stress causing her to react but when she got to the taxi rank, she was breathless and her heart was pounding. She felt like a character in a film, racing against time to tell her newly beloved beau destined for some faraway place that she would marry him after all and please would he stay. She regained her composure during the short ride to the airport,

The Ghost of Villa Winter

but soon lost it again once she'd paid the driver and was out on the concourse rushing to the departure area hoping to intercept the lads before they checked in.

She bolted up the stairs and then stood and eyed all the tourists queuing. There was not a Steve or a Dave to be seen. She wandered up and down scanning every queue. She was about to give up when she spied the pair seated in a small café on the other side of a long and thick queue of especially weary-looking travellers. She rushed over and as she neared the lads' table, Steve looked over at her in amazement.

'What are you doing here?' he said as she attempted to recover her breath.

She launched into her request without any preface, clutching the back of the vacant chair at their table as the others in the café area eyed her with interest.

'Will you please, please tell the police what you told me about the road block. You won't get into trouble. Well, only for a traffic offence. I'll pay whatever fine they give you. But my friend's freedom is at stake and these people are going to get away with murder, three murders in fact, if you don't tell them what you did.'

'Three murders!'

'Bloody hell!'

They both appeared genuinely shocked. She went on, hoping to reinforce the urgency, the vital importance of their confession.

'And my friend now in prison in Lanzarote was wrongly found guilty of one of those murders. You have to help.' She paused, wondering if she should mention his profession, hoping it would endear him to them. Although reactions could go either way. She took a risk. 'He's a writer.'

'A writer, is he? Maybe he'll put us in one of his books.'

They both sniggered. She was taken aback until she saw they were taking her seriously. Then Steve mouthed something to Dave who shrugged and nodded.

'When are you due to take off?'

'Flight's delayed. We've got another couple of hours.'

She thought fast. That was not long enough to get there and back from Puerto del Rosario.

'What if I get the police to come to the airport. Save you missing your flight. Will you own up?'

'Sure.'

She telephoned the police station and managed to persuade the duty officer in her intermediate Spanish of the urgency of the matter. He put her through to Inspector García who told her an officer would be sent immediately. She didn't hold out much hope of that occurring before take-off but was pleasantly surprised when fifteen minutes later both García and his sidekick entered the Departures foyer and ambled over.

'YES, I SAW HER,' Claire said. 'She stood out from the others as she was so thin. Legs like spindles. We passed her on the way back to our car.'

Clarissa put down her phone. She could scarcely believe her ears. All along, Helen had been on the beach, just as Simon had said. She'd seen Trevor trying to locate the backpack's owner. Clarissa's mind burst with the revelation. She was another step closer to quashing Trevor's conviction. It wouldn't amount to much in court but at least the police might start to take Simon's confession seriously. With a bit of luck, they would launch an inquiry, go on the hunt for evidence.

She went and sat down on the sofa. Her eyes drifted

around the room. A heavy wall unit took up much of one wall. The other furniture matched its dark wood. French doors led through to the entrance hall. She could hear a woman's voice outside the apartment, echoing in the stairwell. Soon, a door clunked shut and all went quiet. As she sat in the stillness, tuning in to the sounds of the street down below, and the distant bonks and clunks coming from the other apartments, fatigue consumed her. It had been a busy day. She was anxious to learn the outcome of Steve and Dave's interview with the police but she thought it wise to leave that alone. If the police didn't find the roadblock enough of an indication that foul play was at hand, nothing would, and Clarissa would be stripped of all her faith in the island's justice system. She would call Inspector García in the morning.

It was the police who phoned her, just as she was about to climb into bed for an early night, Inspector García thanking her for her pro-activeness and her powers of persuasion. They would be re-interviewing everyone involved in the case in the morning and sending a forensics team down to Cofete to do a thorough sweep of the village and Villa Winter.

'Make sure they access the second bunker.'

'What second bunker?'

'There's a bunker below the bunker. I have no idea how you access it but that's where I overheard that strange ritual. It's in my statement. Pedro Fumero will know how to get down there. He's the grandson of some of those who worked there.'

'I'll make sure they do. You're not leaving the island any time soon? I'll be wanting to question you again, I'm sure.'

'I'm extending my stay.'

'Good.' There was a pause. Then he said rather quickly, 'Sorry to doubt you, Mrs Wilkinson.' And he rang off.

Despite her fatigue, sleep wouldn't come. She tossed and turned and then got up and made a cup of tea and took it with her to the second living room beside her bedroom and leaned against the windowsill in the dark. All was quiet in the apartment block but there were still a few teenagers milling about in the plaza below. Lights were on in most of the apartments across the street. The eateries were closing. She sipped her tea and soaked in the easy-going atmosphere, imagining all those people in their apartments going about their lives, families, children, grandparents. Just normal life. She felt far removed from anything normal. Part of her was still in that attic room with its low ceiling and tiny door. Another part of her was walking up the cliff.

She drained her cup and wandered back to the kitchen. Tomorrow was another day. She wished she could visit Trevor, but knowing Simon could soon be released from police custody, if he wasn't already, she couldn't risk it. Once he discovered she had visited the prison, he would assume she had divulged the news of the priest's real killer and that could put Trevor in danger. The only way she could secure Trevor's safety was by staying away. Besides, there was one more thing she could try that she thought the police wouldn't think of as they had enough to occupy them with the Cofete investigation.

The following day, Clarissa caught the bus to Casillas del Ángel. Trevor had told her of the two old men whom he'd seen outside the church both times he visited the village. They sounded like stereotypical retired farmers hanging around in the centre of town to while away the hours away from their wives. She hoped she would find them there. If not, she would wait, and she would come every day until she found them.

The bus pulled up in the centre of the village. She alighted and crossed the main road at the pedestrian crossing. As she headed down the narrow side street she felt as though she was walking in Trevor's footsteps. As though she had somehow invoked all she had gone through in Cofete in order to gain her wish to free the beleaguered author. Absurd. She could see the church up ahead, a corner of it. About fifty metres and she crossed another street and entered the plaza.

Here was everything she loved about the inland island villages. Casillas del Ángel was tucked below an imposing mountain and comprised a sprawl of farmhouses fanning out from a central hub, all renovated and tarted up for the modern world with the exception of the occasional rundown house or ruin. A sense of timelessness pervaded the plaza which she found restorative. The old church sat in a swathe of concrete paving edged with a low whitewashed wall. Young trees lined the perimeter. Seating was spaced along more paving that stretched to the low building facing the church. It was a school. She noticed a statue of a kneeling man on a giant boulder decorating the near corner of the plaza. The mountains in all their barren splendour could be seen above the rooflines all around.

The grand façade of the church was composed of black basalt, in marked contrast to the whitewash of the rest of its walls. Within a rounded arch was a carved wooden door. Above the arch two large bells sat in the bell tower. This was the church where the priest was found murdered. This was the church where the gay men from the prison in Tefía in the 1950s and 60s came every Sunday for mass. It was that knowledge which had brought Trevor back here for a second time and helped to seal his fate.

On the other side of the church, standing in the shade of a palm tree and camouflaged in their pale brown clothing that matched the colour of the trunk, were the two old men she had hoped to find.

The men observed her cautiously from beneath their hats as she approached. She greeted them with an engaging smile. The shorter of the pair shifted awkwardly.

'Beautiful day,' she said, hoping to put them at their ease.

Neither of them spoke nor returned her smile.

'I was hoping to find you here.'

'You were?'

'My friend was telling me about you.'

'She was?'

Her comments weren't working. They both looked at her expectantly. There was nothing for it but to come straight out and ask them. In her canvas bag was the photo of Alvaro she'd taken of the framed photo in the restaurant in Cofete. The one of him with the grin and the surfboard. On her way to the bus stop in Puerto del Rosario she'd taken her phone to a photo shop and had the image printed. She dipped a hand in her canvas bag, extracted the photo and showed it to the two men.

'Have you ever seen this man before?'

Both men stared hard at the photo. A light of recognition appeared on their faces.

'It's him.' The older of the two men stabbed the photo again and again. 'We saw him enter the church that day the priest was killed.'

Relief rippled through her. She could scarcely believe her ears.

'Are you sure?'

'Unmistakable. No one has an underbite like that. He looks like a freak.'

'He was in a big hurry, too. Left the church door wide open.'

'When I went and closed the door, I found blood splatters on the doorstep.'

'It rained later that day, too. You remember, Carlos.'

'Washed the blood spatters right away.'

'There was no sign of any blood the next day.'

'And what about this man?' She held out the photo of Trevor she carried with her just about everywhere.

The men shook their heads. 'Not on that day. We saw him on a different day. We told the police already.'

'Did you tell the police about this man?' she said, holding up the photo of Alvaro.

'We gave them a description but they weren't interested. He could have been anyone, they said. Without his name, there was nothing they could do.'

Besides, she thought, they had already made up their minds Trevor was guilty.

'Will you testify in court that you saw this man?'

'Testify?'

She held out the photo of Alvaro one more time.

'This is the man who killed the priest.'

The men exchanged glances.

'We thought it was him. We were pretty sure it wasn't that Englishman. Didn't I tell you, Carlos. I said, that Englishman is no killer.'

'Will you tell the police what you just told me? Will you testify in court?' she asked again.

The men shrugged.

'Happy to.'

Clarissa wanted to kiss them. Instead, took down the men's names and contact details and caught the next bus back to town. When the bus pulled up in the town centre, she headed straight down to the police station. She felt like a regular. She also felt humoured by the staff, although their goodwill would run out eventually. Or soon. For now, she still had their patience. And luck was on her side. Inspector García entered the foyer as she approached the main desk.

'We meet again,' he said and led her through to the interview room.

Once they were seated, he said with a triumphant ring to his voice, 'We are going to interview Fred Spice. He did drive Alvaro's car back to Morro Jable.'

'I know he did. Well, I assumed he did.'

'We've found the car. Turned up on a ferry bound for Gran Canaria.'

'Thank goodness!'

'Looks like we have a case after all.'

'I have some fresh evidence, too.'

'More?' he said, humouring her. 'Do tell.'

'I hope this will satisfy you.'

She handed them a copy of the names of addresses of the new witnesses and related what they had told her. 'Blood spatters, no less. Although that cannot be confirmed. But we have a positive identification from two eye witnesses.'

Inspector García leaned back in his seat.

'You've done our job for us, Mrs Wilkinson.'

She wanted to correct him, tell him she was not a Mrs, but it was a minor irritation.

They were interrupted by another officer entering the

room. He whispered in García's ear and left. A smile spread across García's face. 'It appears your story has more corroboration. That journalist you mentioned, Anna Trower, has been reported missing.'

'She has? I'm relieved. I was beginning to question my own sanity.'

'I always believed you, Mrs Wilkinson,' he said, making to stand. 'As I explained, we needed corroborating evidence.'

He showed her out of the station and she headed back to her apartment. The day had grown hot. The streets baked in the midday sun. There wasn't much shade. She bought a bread roll from the bakery downstairs and made herself a sandwich with local goat's cheese and salami, washed down with a celebratory cold beer.

After lunch, she telephoned Mr Pérez with the news. When she asked him if he thought there was now enough evidence to get Trevor freed, he said, 'But Alvaro might have arrived at the church to find the priest already dead, murdered by Trevor. The other side will say that.'

Exasperation rose. Whose side was this lawyer on? Where was his vim? She needed an optimist, not a defeatist. She had half a mind to find another lawyer.

'But these men saw Alvaro leave the church in a panicked rush. One even recalls blood spatters. And they never saw Trevor that day. Besides, Simon's testimony has been corroborated by eyewitnesses who saw Helen on the beach that day Trevor found the backpack, and the Australian lads have confessed to the road block. Also, Alvaro's car has been found. Surely, all of that will help us?'

There was a brief pause.

'Without a doubt.'

'Thank goodness!'

She hung up. She had done all she could for Trevor. It was now in the hands of the authorities.

She slept soundly that night for the first time since she had taken a misstep on the beach and hurt her hip. She awoke early, refreshed. At last, she could start to put the recent past behind her and with Trevor's release finally on the cards, she could relax and maybe even begin to enjoy her time on the island again. She was done with gathering evidence, done with trying to puzzle things out. From now on, she would focus on the present and the future. Although her inquisitive mind had other ideas.

Over breakfast, it occurred to her that misstep on the beach happened on the same day she had been given the leaflet advertising the Villa Winter tour. She should have paid closer attention to the warning. She had let down her guard. She hadn't even noticed who was in the café that day or on the beach. She most likely encountered Vera and Carol, two nondescript middle-aged women she would never have paid any attention.

Thinking of the leaflet reminded her of the magazine she had filched from the living room in Villa Winter. She had put it in her suitcase when she got back to the apartment, intending on taking it back with her to England. She went and fetched it, keen to read the whole article.

She turned to the first page to discover the article had in fact been written by Anna Trower. As Richard had explained, the tattoos were a form of branding associated with a little-known quasi-religious cult with small groups of adherents spread throughout Europe. The final page of the article, one she had failed to photograph, described a group based in Fuerteventura. It was rumoured the cult were Holocaust deniers with affiliations to Neo-Nazi far-right extremists. But Trower said that was untrue. Unlike traditional Neo-Nazis' White Supremacism, this particular cult was multicultural, its ethos embracing racial diversity while condemning gender diversity, and thus appealing to homophobes. They were highly secretive and their methods were suspect. There had been speculation over a number of apparent suicides of gay men attributed to the cult in France and Germany. The group in Fuerteventura had come to the attention of a local church when they tried to hand out offensive leaflets at a charity event. There was a photo of the church. It was the one in Casillas del Ángel.

Trower must have infiltrated the group. Hence all the detail in her piece. And the priest must have quizzed someone in the group about their leaflets. That was all it had taken to get both of them killed. A cult of murderers.

But you wouldn't know it to look at them, Trower wrote. And that was the scary part. They mingled in society, as ordinary as you or I. Clarissa's thoughts rushed back to Simon's shirt and the rainbow emblem. Was that just a trick to confuse, all part of the weekend's role play, or was it a trophy? No homophobe would wear a gay pride shirt, surely?

Thinking of Carol and Vera and Helen, Clarissa concurred with Anna Trower, the cult attracted ordinary folk, ordinary folk with deviant views and murderous hearts. She made a mental note to give the magazine to Inspector García to help add context to their investigations. She was left wondering what the ghost of Gustav Winter had made of it all. He was plainly not impressed. Ghosts don't haunt without good reason. It seemed to her he'd wanted to preserve the purity of the past, as dark as that was likely to be. He certainly seemed to have wanted her help in driving that group of ne'er-do-wells away. He'd have had no chance. That cult didn't have an ounce of supernatural sensibility between them. So, he'd seized on Clarissa. She was no Nazi sympathiser but she did hope his ghost would now lay to rest.

The island suddenly felt too small. She toyed with booking a flight back to England but she knew that was out of the question while the investigations were continuing. Besides, what was there to go back to? Her big old house that was sorely in need of renovating. Her friends, who kept her in funerals and little else. At least here she had family, and Claire and Paco were really very nice people. Her Spanish had improved immensely. And there was so much to do here, so many possibilities. Would she stay? The owners of the flat she was renting were keen to sell and had asked if she might be interested. It was in the perfect location and the apartment block was about to gain an elevator. The apartment itself had two large bedrooms, two living rooms and two bathrooms. It was ample for her and going for an excellent price.

As she weighed up her life and thought over the events of the last few days, her desire to visit Trevor with the news outweighed the risks. Another outing was in order. It was visiting day at the prison. She telephoned ahead to let them know she was coming and set off straight away.

The walk to the bus station took ten minutes. As she crossed the concourse, for a brief moment she pictured the zebra-striped bus pulling up and the tour party mingling, all as innocent as you please. Standing there that day observing the motley assortment of passengers as the calima had rolled in, it was as though nature had thrown dust in her eyes. Her perception of human character had been weak at best that day, even as she'd thought she was being shrewd. And harsh.

She headed through the grand station building to the

parking bays at the back to find the bus to Corralejo almost full and about to leave. She sat in the first available seat, three back from the driver. She settled in, confident she was not about to endure another hair-raising ride hurtling along a cliff road. Relaxed, she gazed out the window and, once they were out of the city, she enjoyed the mountains and volcanoes they passed. Half an hour and a short walk from the bus stop later, and she bought at ticket at the ferry terminal. She had made the trip so many times she felt like a commuter. Passengers were already boarding the ferry. The seats in the middle at the front were best. She loved to watch the water as the ferry rolled gently on the ocean swell. Another half an hour and she disembarked and headed up to the bus stop which was further away but not far. She didn't have long to wait. The bus took a route through the main tourist enclaves and she didn't take much interest. In Arrecife she had to change buses again to get to Tahiche and the prison.

It was a long journey from Puerto del Rosario to the prison and she recalled when Richard had offered her a lift and her stomach lurched. But the fact remained it was possible to make the journey by public transport and she was grateful for that.

She alighted the bus. The final leg of her journey comprised a long walk to the prison's main entrance and on the way, she mulled over how Salvador and Merida had somehow met Simon and Francois, and then Helen and Vera and Merida. Had they all met online? The dark web, maybe. Did the cult have a database of members?

Clarissa had never cared much for prisons. She'd managed to time all the legs of the journey perfectly to take full advantage of what little time she had with no hanging about. Seeing Trevor walk out into the visitors' area and shuffle over to the table she had chosen, one as far away from the prison officers as it was possible to be, her heart reached out to him as it always did. He looked forlorn and downtrodden. He was thin and his hair unkempt. His mental health seemed to have deteriorated since the last time she'd seen him but there wasn't time to ask about that. Instead, as soon as he was seated, she filled him in on the events of the weekend. He listened politely, although judging by his lacklustre responses to the various twists and turns, he wasn't that engaged. After all, to him, nothing she had been through could compare to his own incarceration. If anything, it sounded like a grand adventure in the retelling. She cut the story short and showed him the photo of Alvaro.

'Him!' he said, stabbing at the image. 'He was the bane of my life. He only got released last week.'

'What was he in for?'

'Smashed someone over the head with a surfboard on Cofete beach. And there was a right dust-up when the police arrived. He's psycho.'

Her thoughts hurtled back to the fragment of surfboard Richard had found on their beach walk. And the button she'd picked up.

When she mentioned Simon, a look of revulsion appeared in his face.

'Simon Slava? What about him?'

'He was part of the cult.'

'Why am I not surprised.'

'He was your counsellor, right?'

'Yeah, the slimy creep. Funnily enough, I told Simon that Alvaro had been having sex with guys in here. You should have seen his face. I have never seen someone so suave and self-assured look so rattled the next instant. It was hilarious.'

The Ghost of Villa Winter

And Simon had been more than happy to tittle-tattle. So much for trying to help Alvaro, as he'd said in his confession. He'd gone right ahead and told Salvador the salacious news. And now she understood why Salvador had killed Alvaro. Not over any incompetency when it came to disposing of Anna, but because he'd had homosexual encounters while serving time.

She carried on with her story, now she had Trevor's full attention. After a while, his expression changed. He looked worried.

'What is it?' she asked.

'Simon spent a lot of time in our last session asking about you. I couldn't understand it. He wanted to know who you were and where you stayed in Fuerteventura and why you were so bent on having me freed. I didn't tell him a thing, but I guess you were not hard to trace.'

'You have nothing to feel guilty about.'

Aware of their limited time, she went on. When she told him about the escape and the journey up the cliff, he hung his head and sighed.

'You put yourself at risk because of me. And now Richard Parry is dead, also because of me.'

She reached for his hand.

'You mustn't blame yourself. These people are evil and you are a victim, too. You must remind yourself of that.' She quickly recounted all the evidence she'd gathered. 'At least now you have a future.' She reached for his hand and gave it a firm squeeze. 'There's no guarantee of your freedom and no time frame. You know how these things work. But there are witnesses and enough evidence, I hope, to get you out of here.'

'You've done so much for me. How will I ever repay you?'

'You can repay me by writing. Keep on writing. Write the memoir, tell your story.'

'When I get out, I will.'

Their time together was all too short and she made the laborious journey back to Puerto del Rosario.

On her way from the bus stop to the ferry terminal in Playa Blanca, she found she was in no hurry to catch a ferry. There was plenty of time. She had all afternoon and she might as well enjoy a bit of Lanzarote for a change. She called into a café with an al fresco seating area. The place was crowded and she took the only remaining table and ordered a coffee. Then, she pulled out of her canvas bag the letter with the 1980s date stamp.

She'd forgotten about the letter tucked in her capris until she was putting them in the washing machine the day before. Her heart had missed a beat when she realised what she had almost done. She'd brought the letter with her to read on the bus but forgotten about it, again. That secret pocket was a little too obscure, even for her. Either that, or she was going senile.

She opened the pages and started reading, hoping it was not another love letter. It wasn't. It was addressed to Alvaro, but a much younger Alvaro than the one recently incinerated. He had had an English father by the name of Edwin Banks, and it was this father who wrote to his son begging forgiveness. For what? Clarissa wondered. The letter didn't say. Sounded like Alvaro had had a troubled childhood. Clarissa shrugged inwardly. So did half the planet.

When she looked up a woman of about her age was staring at her. They exchanged a smile. The woman hovered and Clarissa realised she had nowhere else to sit.

'May I join you?'

'By all means.'

The Ghost of Villa Winter

She gestured at the vacant chair as she slipped the letter in her canvas bag.

A waiter came with Clarissa's coffee. As the woman reached for the menu, Clarissa caught her eye, held out her hand and said rather formally, 'Clarissa Wilkinson.'

The woman was slightly taken aback, evidently not used to being spoken to by strangers. 'Edna Banks,' she said with some hesitation, taking Clarissa's hand. Clarissa saw in her manner that she had much she wanted to hide.

'Banks?' she said, hoping to break the ice. 'That's odd. This letter is addressed to a Banks.'

Edna laughed. 'Common name.'

Clarissa put the letter down on the table beside her cup. The coincidence got them chatting. Clarissa spent the next hour waiting for her ferry deep in conversation with a retired policewoman whose career highlight was nailing a notorious London gang.

'And what brings you to Lanzarote?'

'Even criminals take holidays. Some make it permanent.'

'Revenge, then.'

'Something like that. To settle a score.'

They exchanged contact details and Clarissa said next time she was visiting the island she would get in touch. For a whole hour, she had not thought about her own recent history once. It came as a blessed relief.

The woman left and Clarissa thought she should too. As she slid her hand in her canvas bag to check the letter was safely buried inside, her fingertips touched something small and metallic feeling, her fingers curling around the two remaining painkillers, Richard's painkillers, the painkillers that may, that would have saved his life.

Dear reader,

We hope you enjoyed reading *The Ghost of Villa Winter*. Please take a moment to leave a review, even if it's a short one. Your opinion is important to us.

Discover more books by Isobel Blackthorn at https://www.nextchapter.pub/authors/isobel-blackthorn-mystery-thriller-author

Want to know when one of our books is free or discounted? Join the newsletter at http://eepurl.com/bqqB3H

Best regards,

Isobel Blackthorn and the Next Chapter Team

You might also like:
A Perfect Square by Isobel Blackthorn

To read the first chapter for free, please head to:
https://www.nextchapter.pub/books/a-perfect-square

ABOUT THE AUTHOR

Isobel Blackthorn is an award-winning author of unique and engaging fiction. She writes mysteries, dark psychological thrillers, and historical fiction. The third book in her Canary Islands Mysteries Series *A Prison in the Sun* won the Finalist Award in the Readers' Favorite Book Awards 2020.

Isobel's writing appears in journals and on websites around the world, including *The Esoteric Quarterly, New Dawn Magazine, Paranoia, Mused Literary Review, Trip Fiction, Backhand Stories, Fictive Dream* and *On Line Opinion*.

Isobel's interests are many and varied. She has a long-standing association with the Canary Islands, having lived in Lanzarote in the late 1980s. A humanitarian and campaigner for social justice, in 1999 Isobel founded the internationally acclaimed Ghana Link, uniting two high schools, one a relatively privileged state school located in the heart of England, the other a materially impoverished school in a remote part of the Upper Volta region of Ghana, West Africa.

Isobel has a background in Western Esotericism. She holds 1st Class Honours in Social Studies, and a PhD from the University of Western Sydney for her ground-breaking research on the works of Alice A. Bailey. After working as a teacher, market trader and PA to a literary agent, she arrived at writing in her forties, and her stories are as diverse and intriguing as her life has been. British by birth, Isobel has lived in England, Australia, Spain and the Canary Islands. She currently resides in rural Victoria.

ALSO BY ISOBEL BLACKTHORN

Other Books set in the Canary Islands

The Drago Tree

A Matter of Latitude

Clarissa's Warning

A Prison in the Sun

Dark Fiction

The Cabin Sessions

The Legacy of Old Gran Parks

Twerk

Other Fiction

Nine Months of Summer

A Perfect Square: An esoteric mystery

Esoteric Works

The Unlikely Occultist: A biographical novel of Alice A. Bailey

Alice A. Bailey: Life & Legacy

Also by Isobel Blackthorn

All Because of You: Fifteen tales of sacrifice and hope

Voltaire's Garden: A memoir of Cobargo

CPSIA information can be obtained
at www.ICGtesting.com
Printed in the USA
LVHW051155260121
677454LV00011B/400/J

9 781034 280903